SWITCH

ADRIANA LOCKE

Copyright © 2017 by Adriana Locke

All rights reserved.

No part of this book may be reproduced in any form or by any electronic or mechanical means, including information storage and retrieval systems, without written permission from the author, except for the use of brief quotations in a book review.

Cover Art:
Kari March, Kari March Designs

Editing:
Lisa Christmas, Adept Edits

BOOKS BY ADRIANA LOCKE

Carmichael Family Series

Flirt

Fling

Fluke

Flaunt

Flame

Landry Family Series

Sway

Swing

Switch

Swear

Swink

Sweet

Gibson Boys Series

Crank

Craft

Cross

Crave

Crazy

The Mason Family Series

Restraint

The Relationship Pact

Reputation

Reckless

Reputation

Relentless

Resolution

The Exception Series

The Exception

The Perception

Dogwood Lane Series

Tumble

Tangle

Trouble

Standalone Novels

Sacrifice

Wherever It Leads

Written in the Scars

Lucky Number Eleven

Like You Love Me

The Sweet Spot

More Than I Could

Standalone Novellas

Battle of the Sexes

608 Alpha Avenue

907 For Keeps Way

Sign up to receive an email for all new releases at www.adrianalocke.com.

To everyone that loves, even when it's hard.

And to Mandi Beck. My peer, Pres, and, most of all, the easiest friend a girl could ask for.

ONE

GRAHAM

I'M NOT USED TO THIS. Hell, I'm really not even *okay* with this.

The stillness before the sun comes up is *my time*. I get more accomplished in that precious window than I do all day long. Why? No one else is up and around to bother me.

That is until my brother Ford came back to town.

Glancing across my desk, he's leaned against the wall with a paper cup in his hand. His sandy, military-cut hair has started to grow over the last couple of weeks since he was released from the Marines with more medals than an Olympian. He knows his morning visits annoy me, but like our other siblings, a part of him finds frustrating me amusing. Assholes. Still, as he meanders his way towards my desk, I can't *really* be mad. At my oldest brother Barrett? Possible. At my youngest brother Lincoln? Often. But Ford? It's hard to do.

"Do you show up here *just* to throw off my day?" I try, and fail, to hide my grin.

"What can I say?" he laughs. "The military doesn't approve of staying in bed. After all those years in the service, old habits are hard to break." He takes a sip from his cup and sits in the black leather chair across from me. "I need to find a new routine. I've had one imposed on me for so many years, it's a little odd not having someone threatening to have my ass before dawn."

"I can assure you I'll be tossing you out on your ass if you keep showing up here before the day starts. It throws me off schedule." Glancing at my watch, I scowl. "And so does being late."

Ford raises his brows. "Your new secretary starts today, doesn't she?"

"She's supposed to. Mallory Sims. Remember her?"

"Sort of. Did I go to high school with her?" He scratches his head. "Damn, that feels like a long time ago."

"Because it was," I laugh. "She's a friend of Sienna's."

At the mention of one of our twin sisters, the youngest of us all, Ford looks worried. I get it. It also worries the fuck out of me to know I've stooped this low. And low it is. But I didn't have a choice.

My former Executive Assistant, Linda, up and quit on me a few weeks ago. She was everything you could want—efficient, orderly, experienced. She worked for my father before I took over for him and knew this business inside and out. When she left, I realized she was irreplaceable.

I've gone through so many temps in her vacancy, hired people from ads placed in newspapers, and even tried promoting one woman from another department and none of them worked. Not one of them meshed with my style or filled the role as I needed them to.

One weekend night, after missing a family lunch because you couldn't see the top of my desk for papers, contracts, and files, Sienna called. She'd run into a girl we used to know. In the midst of conversation, my sister realized she had experience as an administrative assistant, needed a job, and grabbed her resume for me.

It looked good. Her references checked out. She had experience as not just a secretary, but as an Executive Assistant. I also remembered her from before and was fairly certain she wasn't a psychopath. So I forwent the standard interview and just hired her. What did I really stand to lose?

"Can I just ask what on Earth made you think that was a good idea?" Ford asks. "I mean, I love Sienna and Camilla, but their friends aren't exactly . . . employable."

"Desperation is the name of the game."

My brother stands. Although he's a couple of years younger than me, he's a few inches taller. "It must be."

"Tell me about it," I groan. "But there is a method to the madness."

"Let's hope. If not, I'm calling Dad and letting him know you've lost your mind and we need to vote you off the board."

"I vaguely remember Mallory. She must've been a freshman or sophomore my senior year. I had Latin Club with her," I say, picking up a pen.

"You and Latin Club. I just . . . I can't."

"Fuck you," I say, throwing the pen at his head. Because Ford has reflexes similar to Lincoln's, it misses and clinks against the wall. "You better be glad one of us takes things seriously. Can you imagine our family being reliant on Barrett? Or, worse, Lincoln? We'd be investing in baseball and Skittles."

Ford picks up the projectile. "Speaking of Lincoln, how weird is it to see him so pussy-whipped?"

"It's one of the oddest things I've ever seen happen with my own eyes. He went from total man whore to monogamy at the flip of a switch."

"Danielle must have some good pussy," Ford chuckles.

"That or a magic wand."

"Yeah, but I get it. I think he made the right decision. Seeing some of the shit I've seen overseas really puts things in perspective for you. Often the things we think are important aren't." Ford's gaze hits the floor. "But," he recovers, pasting on a smile, "Lincoln doesn't have to worry about money. We have you."

"If only I had an assistant."

"What time was she supposed to be here?"

Glancing at the clock, my irritation grows. "Six minutes ago. She's supposed to start at eight."

"That's what you get for choosing employees out of Sienna's circle."

My hand flies through my hair as every worst case scenario plays out before my eyes.

Looking at Ford, I know his main concern: Landry Security. I can't blame him. This is his dream, much like managing Landry Holdings is mine, and he can't get to work until I do mine. I get it, that's why it drives me insane that Mallory isn't here and I'm not working at full capacity.

Sighing, I shrug. "Her resume was infallible. The references she listed all checked out—sang her praises to be exact. They all said she has unlimited potential and would be an asset, even knowing it's Landry Holdings we're talking about. I can't believe she's late. Who does that? On their first day, no less?"

My brother tosses the pen on my desk. "If you need help with Landry Security, let me know." I can tell he's antsy and is trying to play it cool and that frustrates me. He shouldn't be worrying about this. He should have faith in me, and my lack of a fucking assistant is shaking that.

"I'll be fine," I reassure him. "I have a plan. Even though things here have been a little more unsettled than I'd like with Linda's departure, I have been moving forward. Landry Security is happening."

Ford's hand rests on the doorknob and he looks at me. His brow is furrowed, reminiscent of our mother's when she's trying to decide how to broach a subject with us.

There's no way he knows how much this has affected me. Losing sleep. Popping antacids like a motherfucker. All because I. Don't. Fail.

"I'll help you however," he reiterates carefully.

"I know. And I do appreciate that—"

"But you're too fucking anal retentive to let anyone else get involved at this stage," he grins.

"I prefer the term 'professional.'"

"I bet you do," he laughs. "I know you have control issues and all, but consider trusting someone else to help out. You don't have to do it all yourself."

"This is my legacy. You have your hero medals. Barrett has his public service. Lincoln has batting titles and Golden Gloves. I have *this*."

"No one wants to usurp you," he insists. "We just want to help." When I just look at him with no response, he sighs. "Fine. But cut the new girl some slack. If you look at her like that when she walks in, she'll probably march right back out."

"What? I don't give off the empathetic boss look?"

"Uh, no. You give off the asshole dictator look."

"Good. At least she'll know what she's in for," I wink. "Now get out of here so I can figure out what to do when I fire Mallory Sims on her first day at the office."

He chuckles. "I'll call this afternoon and see if anyone has sent you to the psychiatric ward."

"Make sure the walls have extra padding. If it's an added expense, charge it to Barrett."

"Will do." With a shake of his head, he disappears out the door. The silence I love so much descends around me, the only sound coming from the coffee maker in the corner. The city below the third-story windows encompassing two walls of my office is just beginning to awaken. I love to watch everything sort of turn on for the day. Being awake and working before that happens makes me feel like I'm a step ahead of the game. That no one got anything over on me while I was sleeping.

Sleeping, like my new employee probably is when she should be here.

I fire off an email to Human Resources, letting them know I plan on not hiring Ms. Sims after all, and print out their response to hand to the almost-employee if she ever shows up.

Slipping off my suit jacket, I hang it on the hook behind the door. Rolling my sleeves up to my forearms, I'm mentally going over the list of applicants to replace Mallory when a loud clamor booms from the entryway into the suite.

As I round the corner and peer into the reception area, I spy a woman bent down. The floor is spattered with miscellaneous items. Bobby pins, sheets of paper, a water bottle, and a paperback are being scooped up and shoved into a large bag.

Irritated at another disruption to my day, I lean against the doorframe. A million thoughts roll through my mind, most of them along the lines that as CEO of Landry Holdings, I should not be dealing with this hassle. As my temples begin to throb, I fold my arms over my chest.

She stuffs the last sheet of paper into the bag and stands. Her eyes flick to mine and she stills. I think I do too.

Her skin is pale and creamy, a soft framework for the deep chestnut hair hanging to her waist. A dress the color of moss in the summer showcases toned arms and a long, lean line from her shoulders to her calves. A thin rope belt cinches her trim waist, one that I can imagine digging my fingers into.

I clear my throat. "Can I help you?"

With something besides getting out of that dress?

"I think you probably can," she says, then blushes a pretty shade of pink. "I'm sorry, I didn't mean it like that. What I mean is . . ."

She's flustered. It's adorable and sexy at the same time. I should say something, interject, help her out, but I don't. I like this entirely too much.

"I'll stop talking now." She flashes me a pretty smile, one that catches my attention in ways it shouldn't at eight sixteen a.m. Taking a step towards me, the toe of her shoe catches on the water bottle she didn't pick up and she comes barreling my way.

Before I know what's happening, I reach out and catch her under a spray of loose leaf paper.

"Oomph!" she heaves as she lands in my arms and I'm surrounded by a sweet, floral scent.

I should let her go. I should back away, direct her to the front desk to get directions to wherever she's going, and retreat to my office. Regardless of how sexy her breasts feel pressed against me or the way her ass pops as my fingers lace together at the dip at the bottom of her spine, I have things to do today. Important things. Lots of them. Even if I can't pinpoint one at the moment.

Large, nearly golden eyes peer up at me. They're crystal clear, almost like I can see all the way to the depths of her soul. They're incredible tones of the purest gold and I can't look away.

The feel of her body against mine sparks something inside me—a carnal, visceral reaction that's led by feeling rather than intellect. "Are you okay?" I ask, trying desperately to use the brainpower I'm known for in most circles and not the cock I'm known for in others.

"I think so." She pulls her gaze away from mine. A connection is actually snapped between us and I'm almost certain she feels it too because her features fall. "I'm just running late . . ."

Hell. Fucking. No.

I'm afraid to ask the next question. If the answer is what I think it is, I'm going to kill my little sister.

TWO
MALLORY

BREATHE, MALLORY, BREATHE.

It only takes a fraction of a second to realize why that's a horrible idea. As the sweet, rich scent of sandalwood couples with the feel of his fingertips pressing into my back, I know it's flight or fight. Cut off all oxygen or pull away from his arms. Suffocate or step away while I can, because if I keep breathing him in, I'll be a puddle at his feet in two seconds flat. I'm a logical woman. There's no way I'm stepping out of his embrace.

Don't breathe, Mal. Don't. Breathe.

Focusing on the feel of his hand against me, the way his arms hold me up like he's some kind of savior, the morning events spin wildly in my mind.

The failed alarm. Spilling tea down my new dress. One of my favorite heels snapping as I nearly fell backwards when Graham Landry's picture loaded on my laptop screen.

This seemed like a great idea. The opportunity to work at Landry Holdings glittered like a gift from above laid beautifully in my lap. I need this job. I'd been praying to find something since I left Columbia and left every hope and dream I'd ever had behind. When

I ran into Sienna Landry, a friend from high school at yoga class, we started talking. We weren't the best of friends, hanging out only here and there back then, but she was always so sweet and kind. When she mentioned this job, it seemed like kismet. That is, until I pulled up the website this morning.

Whatever I expected Graham to be, he's not. At least physically. That's why I can't look him in the face as his fingers tense against my dress, and all I can do is imagine him touching me elsewhere.

My cheeks heat at my errant thoughts. As I witness the greens of his eyes mix with a color I can only describe as sapphire, I know I need to say something. But when I open my mouth, nothing comes out, and I suddenly feel the oxygen deprivation hitting me full force.

He leans closer. This doesn't help, nor does my panic that he'll get stuck in the syrup on the sleeve of my dress.

"Breathe," he whispers. The cool mintiness of his breath is a stark contradiction to the fire radiating off him in every other way. Still, his words force into my brain and I drag in a quick lungful of air. "There you go." His voice is as warm and smooth as his cologne, and somehow, it seems to break the spell over me. A giggle slips past my lips before I can stop it. It's my go-to reaction, especially when I've had too much to drink, and I'm definitely a little buzzed.

Graham shakes his head, his hand subtly pressing me closer to him, a move I pretend was intentional.

I clear my throat in an attempt to swallow my nerves. "This isn't exactly a good first impression, huh?"

"Depends how you look at it," he mumbles under his breath and releases me far too quickly. Straightening his navy blue tie, he takes a purposeful step away. While the heat continues to roll off him, it seems now it's for a different reason. "You do realize you're seventeen minutes late."

"I do," I gulp. "I had an accident this morning . . ." *And once I saw your picture, I had to do what any reasonable female would do: find my prettiest panties and matching bra.*

His eyes darken as if he can read my mind. I stand before him, his smolder making me wonder how in the hell I'm going to work alongside him every day.

Maybe I can work on top of him. Or under him. Or . . .

"I assume you're Mallory," he says, clearing his throat.

"Yes." I extend a hand, not sure if that's necessary since we were basically hugging a few seconds ago. "You must be Mr. Landry?"

He takes my palm in his, the size of his twice the size of mine, and shakes it gently. "I didn't recognize you. You've . . . changed."

"So have you."

The corners of his lips drift up, pulling mine along with them. The exchange causes my heart to flutter, and I nervously tuck a strand of hair behind my ear.

As quickly as it came, the softness in his eyes vanishes. It's replaced with a resolution—but to what, I don't know. "First things first, I'm going to need you in your seat, ready to go, at eight on the dot."

"Of course," I reply. Suddenly, I'm transported back to Latin club and he's standing at my desk, asking me if I have a partner for our end-of-year project. My hands shake now, just as they did then.

"Second, please, call me Graham."

"Okay."

He takes a deep breath, running his fingers through his rich, chestnut-colored hair. "I know we knew each other once upon a time and you are friends with my sisters, but that won't factor in to your performance here. If that will be any issue at all, we need to discuss it now."

"Graham," I say, throwing my shoulders back and ignoring how hot he looks with his furrowed brows, "as the CEO of Landry Holdings, I'm certain you did your due diligence before hiring me. If not, you got lucky because you have my word that I will blow your expectations out of the water."

His brows pull tighter, his freshly-shaven jaw working back and forth like he doesn't quite know what to do with me. As his tongue darts across his bottom lip, leaving a trail of wetness behind, I gulp.

I know exactly what you should do with me.

He cuts the distance between us in half. As he looms overhead, my brain scatters, once again feeling like he just read my thoughts. It's unnerving. So much so, in fact, that I'm ready to apologize. Before I can, he speaks.

"Get situated at your desk, and I'll alert Human Resources to your arrival."

After a lingering look that keeps me in place, he vanishes through the solid wood door and I can finally breathe again.

***

Graham

A CATASTROPHE. THAT'S WHAT THIS fucking day is.

The clock flips to noon, reminding me how much time I've wasted today. I'm usually heading out for a quick bite to eat in between meetings and calls, having already put in a full day's work for most people. Today? Nothing. I've got nothing except a serious case of blue balls and a migraine to boot.

Linda was in her mid-fifties. On Friday, she would get here an hour early, send me a weekly recap mid-day, and forward me a finalized schedule for the following week before she left. She crocheted me a blanket last winter.

That's the assistant I want. Sharp. Efficient. *Not hot.*

I don't know which way to go to stop the bleeding first. There's so much to catch up on—weeks' worth of business, the security company to iron out, a stack of files higher than I've ever allowed to accumulate. But here I sit, a file open, untouched. Twenty-six calls to return on my desk phone alone and today was the day it was all supposed to get done. That was the plan and all I can do is sit here with half my attention aimed towards the door.

I'm not sure if Linda ever laughed when my door was closed in the nearly ten years she worked for me. Mallory has five times today.

I'm also not certain if Linda ever smelled like lavender or wore a dress that was soft to the touch.

"Stop it," I groan to myself, trying to wipe the image of her full lips out of my mind. "You're acting like Lincoln. Damn it."

As if on cue, my phone rings and his name glows on the screen. "Hello?" I sigh.

"You sound pissier than normal," Lincoln snickers.

"I was just thinking about you."

"That's what they all say," he jokes. "Seriously, though—what's up?"

"You, my little brother, were wrong."

"Uh, about what?"

"Mallory Sims."

"Sienna's friend?"

"I like to think of her, for the next few hours, anyway, as my new executive assistant."

"What was I wrong about? I don't even know her."

I whistle through my teeth. "I expected more from you, Linc. You have a reputation in this family and I counted on that. You failed me."

"What the fuck are you talking about, G?"

"She's hot." I let that sink in a second. "If you weren't all in love with Danielle, I probably wouldn't even let you in my office ever again."

"Maybe I need to drop by today," he jokes. "I'm not sure what you're pissed about. If I needed a secretary, I'd get a hot one. Before Danielle, I mean. I would've before Danielle."

Rolling my eyes, I lean back in my chair. "Of course you would've because you're an animal."

"*Was.* I was an animal." He pauses. "I was an animal, wasn't I? God. At least I have the memories," he sighs.

"Good for you. Go relive those while I try to figure out how to manage this."

"Need tips? I have some awesome tricks from all that animalistic behavior and I'm willing to share. Hell, someone should be able to use them these days."

"No, Linc."

"Oh! Barrett told me one the other day about grapes—"

"Lincoln. Stop." I tap my pen against the glass on top of my desk and wait for his laughing to subside. "I'm being serious here. How am I supposed to work with a girl that looks like she should be . . ."

"Wrapped around your cock?" he offers.

"Not helping."

Lincoln bursts out laughing again. "Sorry. I think this shit is funny as hell."

"You would," I mutter.

He finishes his amusement and clears his throat. "So, what are you going to do? Can you just ignore it? Or do you have to let her go because you can't control yourself?" He pauses. "That's it! I knew it! There's a kinky animal buried in those stuck-up suits of yours trying to claw its way out, isn't there?"

"Lincoln . . ."

He cackles. "You need me for advice. This has to be one of the best days of my life. I knew you'd need me sooner or later."

"There is nothing about this situation that warrants your advice. Come to think of it, there's nothing about life that would make me need your two cents."

"Take a piece of ice and put it—"

"I swear to God, if you don't stop, I'm sending Ford over to kick your ass."

"You'll send Ford because you can't do it," he teases.

"I'll send Ford because some of us have a fucking job to tend to, asshole."

We both chuckle and I feel the tension ease just a bit. Rising from my desk, I look at the back of my closed office door.

She's out there, just a few yards from me. Human Resources says she's catching on, even deferring lunch today so she can learn more. I like that. That's a good sign. My hard cock is not.

"Did you know she was hot before you hired her?" Lincoln asks. "If so, that's very un-Graham-like."

"No. In my defense," I say over his objection, "I knew her in high school. She wasn't hot. She was super smart."

"So she was a nerd like you?"

"Anyway," I sigh, continuing on, "I felt like I knew her. Her references were stellar. It never crossed my mind that *this* would be my issue."

I keep thinking I'll wake up, she'll walk in, and this will have been a dream. A wet one, nearly, but a dream nonetheless. But until that happens, I need a fucking plan and all I can come up with is ordering uniforms. Ugly, puke green, with a collar up the neck. No skin. At all. And maybe a muzzle because, as confusing as it is, her voice and smile fuck with me as much as her body.

Lincoln chuckles. "I still don't see how this is a problem. Think of her as . . . office décor. She'll just give you something to look forward to in the morning. How interesting can . . . whatever it is you do all day . . . be? This is a godsend, G. Embrace it."

"I want to embrace it. That's the fucking problem. I can't have temptation staring at me all damn day."

"You can if you're strong enough to say no. I mean, I've never been particularly good at that, but I'm sure it's on your geek gene somewhere."

"Out of all our siblings, you are my least favorite."

"I can live with that," he laughs. "I gotta go though. I have a meeting in a few. I'll call you tonight."

"Call while it still qualifies as night and not morning, okay?"

"I'll try."

The line goes dead and I realize I'm still standing behind my desk, looking at the door.

THREE
MALLORY

THE WATER IS HOT, NEARLY scalding, lapping against my chest. The air in the bathroom is steamy, fogging up the mirrors as I relax in a blissful, lavender-scented bath. All thoughts of the day—the insane tempo of Landry Holdings, the exhilaration of a first day, my sexy-as-hell boss that I can barely look at with a straight face—begin to melt into the water.

Filling my body with the lovely mist, I feel Graham's hand on my — "Excuse me."

"Oh!" I yelp, jumping in my office chair and bumping my knee on the underside of the desk. "I didn't see you standing there."

"Because your eyes were closed," Graham points out. My cheeks flush as I wonder how long he stood there and watched me. It's a full minute before I realize he's awaiting an explanation. It's another minute before it's obvious he will either get one or he'll keep standing there.

"I was visualizing," I say, hoping we can now move on. "Visualizing what?"

Getting ready to visualize you naked, but you ruined that. "I was doing a quick relaxation technique. Walking through what I plan on doing when I get home to relax from the stress of the day."

His sun-kissed skin pulls together along the ridge of his forehead. He looks at me like I'm crazy. I return the favor as a buzzing noise quietly sounds from my desktop phone, alerting me it's five o'clock. The light at the top dims. How efficient.

"Was today stressful for you?" he asks.

"Kind of." I rub my knee from the ding to the desk and stand. "It was my first day. Aren't they always stressful?"

"I haven't had a first day in a long time," he grins.

"That's probably true," I admit. "Trust me, they stink."

"'Stink'? Are we back in high school?"

"Would you rather me say 'suck'?"

I don't mean it to come out so sassy, so much like an innuendo. I guess that's just what happens when a man stands before you in a suit and looks so good, you aren't sure he could look better stripped down.

His shoulders are wide, filling out the top of his jacket, his trim waist fitted with a brown leather belt. Everything fits him so perfectly, I'm sure it's custom-made. So many men get worn by the suit. Graham Landry definitely wears his.

"I think we need to change the subject," he says, clearing his throat. "How do you feel about your day?"

"Good. Gina, the girl from HR, trained me most of the day. There's really not a lot here that's different from any other administrative assistant job I've had. Just new systems, but they're pretty easy to figure out."

"Besides being late, I thought you did a good job. Gina said you caught on fast."

He leans against the door, one foot over the other. I force myself not to let my gaze drop down the lines of his body and instead focus on the lines of his face. Not that it's any easier, but more politically correct and it'll be good to have a clear image for when I visualize it between my legs when I get home.

"I just drafted an email, defining what I'm going to need you to take on in order to make this an effective working relationship. I know it's past five, but if you can peruse it before you leave today and send me a response, that would be helpful."

"Sure."

He flashes me a half smile, one that he appears to have to force himself to give, and disappears inside his office again.

The breath comes out heavier than I anticipate as I plop back down in my chair. Waking up my desktop, I wait for my email to open. As referenced, there is one new message in my inbox.

To: Mallory Sims, Administrative Assistant
From: Graham Landry, CEO
Re: Requirements

Please note the bulleted items below. They are non-negotiable.

• Be on time. You must be at your seat, ready to go, by eight a.m., Monday through Friday.
• Keep your desk neat. Organization is key.
• I will email you a list of daily priorities by eight a.m. each morning. Ensure those tasks are completed before you leave (in addition to what may arise during the day).
• My family are the only people allowed in my office without an announcement. Additionally, they're the only people I may be interrupted for during a meeting.
• Please familiarize yourself with the packet of information I left for you under your car keys (which I picked up from the floor and placed on the corner of your desk.)

A simple response to this would be appreciated.
Graham

Is he for real?

Glancing across the desk, there is a set of papers under my keys and I have no idea when he put them there. I've been here all day. Turning back to the list, I look it over once more. Before I can hit reply, my inbox dings again. The body of the message is empty; only the "Re:" field has text.

> To: Mallory Sims, Administrative Assistant
> From: Graham Landry, CEO
> Re: Amend previous email to include: Keep eyes open at desk.

I'm not sure he's kidding.

> To: Graham Landry, CEO
> From: Mallory Sims, Administrative Assistant
> Re: Requirements
> That all seems reasonable. I will see you tomorrow. On time.

"HEY, KITTY." I GREET MY kitten with a nuzzle behind her grey ears. "What happened in your world today?"

She stretches, the little bell on her collar jingling. The sun has nearly set and my apartment is soaking up the final few rays coming through the window. I flip on some lights and glance around on my way to the kitchen. It's coming together. The walls still need a fresh coat of paint, but I just don't have time to dedicate to that. Still, it looks a ton better than it did when I moved in here a few months ago. The couple before me had a more modern approach to decorating. Everything was white and black and straight lines. It was absurdly boring. The pottery pieces I've collected over my entire life help add some color and make it feel more like my own space, something I've never really had.

Eric's face zips through my mind and I feel my heart pitter just a little. I miss him. Of course I do. I didn't leave him because I didn't love him. I left him because he basically told me he planned on leaving me eventually.

"*You did what?*" *he hissed.*

"*I dropped out of school,*" *I told him.* "*Nursing isn't for me, Eric. It sounded like a good career path initially—good money, good job market. But I hate it. Loathe it. I'd rather stick a pencil in my eye and gouge my eyeballs out than do some of those things. I just thought I could love it, and you thought it would be good for me.*"

"*It is good for you,*" *he laughed angrily.* "*Mal, what do you think you're going to do with your life? Huh? Making coffee in some businessman's office is not a career path.*"

"*I don't just make coffee! I'm the Executive Assistant to the CEO. I've worked there for four years and have been promoted twice. I'm the highest paid administrative personnel in the building and I managed that while I was going to school for the last year. They say I'm a natural and I love it, Eric. It's what I was born to do. Business is—*"

"*Mal, sweetie, business isn't for you. It's for . . . other people.*" *He took off his jacket and looked at me.* "*Your boss probably likes having a young piece of ass in the office. Why wouldn't he?*" *he sighed as red-hot tears blurred my eyes.* "*This is going to sound blunt, but you need to hear it. Your boss is blowing smoke up your ass to get you to spread your legs. And if you think I'm going to work my ass off to take care of you forever, you're crazy.*"

My heart broke, his words strangled me. "*I don't,*" I cried. "*Why would you say that to me?*"

He looked at me with pity in his eyes. "*Do you think I don't realize what you did? You hitched a ride up here with me so you don't end up like your parents. You thought I was your Golden Ticket.*"

"Eric," I said through a smattering of tears. "I came because I love you."

"I love you too. But . . ." The look he gave me, more than pity, of indifference, slayed me. "You don't really think you and I are going to last, right? I mean, we have fun. Sex is great. But we're not, you know, marriage types."

Leaving him was the hardest thing I've ever done because it wasn't just leaving him. It was leaving my life there, everything I knew as an adult, everything that was comfortable. Yet, being on my own, while scary as all get out, has been liberating. Making choices from dinner to my job are all mine. I'm actually creating my life and figuring out what works for me. For the first time in my life, I feel like I might be strong enough to do it. There's nothing in the fridge when I look inside, which is fine considering I'm not really hungry. As I try to determine whether a visit to the yoga studio or a bath is in order, the phone rings.

"Hello?" I say after I find it at the bottom of my purse, directly under the water bottle that caused all the commotion earlier today.

"Hey, you!" Joy chirps. "I got the job."

"That's fabulous! When do you start?"

"Next week. We need to celebrate."

I cringe as I sink at one of the mismatched chairs at the kitchen table. Joy's description of celebration doesn't mesh with the description of my wallet. Her parents are friends of the Landry's, meaning they have money. Lots of it. They could probably wallpaper their house with it if they wanted to.

"I'm going to be working a lot this week," I say, figuring it's the truth. "I'm not sure I'm going to have time to go out or shopping or whatever you have in mind."

"Sienna and I are going shopping tomorrow after work. You're invited, of course, but if you can't, I understand, you working girl, you," she giggles. "I need a completely updated look. Professional, but with a twist, you know, because there's no reason to look stuffy."

"Of course not," I chuckle.

"Sienna said she might be going back to Los Angeles soon. I don't think she planned on staying home so long, but she really missed her family." Joy giggles.

"I'd miss them too," I say, fanning my face. "Can you even imagine them all together in one room? I've only seen them in groups of two. I think my ovaries might explode."

She bursts out laughing. "Graham isn't how you remembered him, huh?"

I stand, the blue-and-white checkered cushion sticking to my legs. "I could kill you for not warning me," I huff. "I had an hour—an hour!—to wrap my brain around the fact that he looks nothing like he did at eighteen. Not that it was helpful. I needed a friendly sit down from my *best friend*," I emphasize, "and an explanation of what I was getting into."

Joy's voice bounces through the line, her amusement in this situation annoying me. I march through the house and into the bathroom and begin filling up the tub.

"I didn't realize you didn't know. I guess I didn't think much about it. I mean, I talk to you practically every day. I forget you weren't here."

"Paybacks are a bitch," I warn her.

"I was going to warn you. I swear. I just didn't realize you actually accepted the position and were starting today."

"Because you don't listen," I sigh. "You don't, Joy."

"I do too! I'm just . . . busy. I have so many balls up in the air right now . . ."

She continues on in some tirade about how hard her life is now that her parents have started to wean her off financially. They want her to get a job. She thinks they're being unreasonable. It's a little hard to hear when you've had a job, sometimes two, since you were fifteen.

"Mal?"

"Oh, yeah, sorry," I say, stripping out of my dress. "I'm here."

"Who's not listening now?"

"I'm getting in the bath," I say, turning the water off. After dumping in a handful of bath salts, I test the temperature with my toe. Perfect. After sinking in the tub, I rest my head against a towel. "There. What were you saying?"

"I was just asking how your day went. That's all."

"It went well, I think. It's nothing too complicated and nothing I haven't done before. They're paying me really well too."

She pauses. "That's it?"

"Yeah. I mean, what are you wanting me to say?"

"Damn it, Mal! You know I've fantasized about the Landry boys since we were ten. The closest I've ever gotten to one is a quick kiss with Ford behind his mother's car in sixth grade. I used to beg Camilla to have me stay the night just so I could try to see her brothers."

"You've always been a little hoochie," I laugh, my thighs pressing together as Graham's chiseled face floats into my mind.

"So?"

We both laugh as the water soothes my tense muscles. I close my eyes and sigh. "Graham is outrageously good-looking."

"You aren't complaining, are you?"

"No, no, of course not," I say hurriedly. "It's just really hard to concentrate when he's on the other side of the wall all day. I have to call in his office and alert him of calls or appointments, and his voice comes through the line, and I literally have to talk myself out of not taking a bathroom break and getting myself off. I just hope this works out . . ."

"I'm going to pretend I don't hear that *thing* in your voice."

"What thing?" I ask defensively.

"That bit of uncertainty. Just stop it. Everything will be fine."

It's easy for her to say. Her bills are paid regardless if she works or not. It's not that simple for me. I only got into the private school that she, Camilla, and Sienna went to because I worked my butt off in middle school, filled out the paperwork for a scholarship, and practiced for a week straight for the entrance interview. We couldn't afford it. And, frankly, my parents didn't think a good education was really that important. I'd finish high school and go get a job at the factory or be a cashier at the hardware store and be happy. If I mentioned pursuing something different, they rolled their eyes and told me to be realistic. I wanted more.

Through pure determination on my part and maybe a toss of luck from up above, the administrators of the school let me in with a scholarship. It was the best day of my life.

Now I sit in this mediocre apartment and look around. The porcelain in the tub is cracking and the corner of the mirror above the sink is broken, and I fight off the unsteadiness that wobbles in my gut.

"Will it be okay?" I ask. "I feel so out of touch."

"Out of touch with what?"

"With . . . me. I don't know who I am or what I want or what's even possible for me anymore, Joy. I'm having a midlife crisis," I pout.

"You can't have a midlife crisis at your age," she scoffs.

"You totally can. I think it's called a quarter-life crisis, actually."

"Stop sounding all doom and gloom."

"I don't," I toss back. "I'm just emotionally drained from today. Cut me some slack."

She sighs. "I'm glad you came back here."

Her reference to me not moving to North Dakota with my parents is thinly veiled. She knows I don't have a terrific relationship with them and had I followed them north to the oil fields where my father is now working, I'd be miserable. But coming to Savannah, the place I call home even without my parents, was a risk.

"Me too," I whisper. "I just hope this doesn't end up on the list of 'Mal's bad decisions.'"

"It won't. Things will work themselves out. They always do. Look at me, having a job and all. Who'd've thunk it?"

"True," I giggle. "But I certainly don't know what I'm doing right now," I sigh. "But what choice did I have? Stay in nursing with a guy that made it clear he doesn't see a future with me or suck it up and move on? This whole thing isn't what I wanted or thought would happen, and I'm not sure where to go from here."

"You've started that by taking the job with Graham. I think you're doing great," Joy says softly.

"If only I can stop thinking about him in a purely unprofessional way," I giggle.

"If you figure out how to do that, share the knowledge. I've battled that almost my whole life!"

I sink further into the water. "You know what I really want?"

"Besides Landry naked?"

I roll my eyes. "I want to feel . . . like the me I used to know. I want to feel alive. I want to wake up and smile. I want to accomplish things, to feel powerful. I want to have things to look forward to, have goals, find someone that wants to laugh with me, go hiking, or get ice cream. That sounds stupid, doesn't it?"

"No, no, it doesn't," she says.

Swirling the water around the tub, I think about what I just said. It's the first time I've been able to really verbalize how I feel. I miss feeling like the girl with the drive to get into private school. I don't know her anymore; I sacrificed her for a relationship in which I was little more than a plot device.

"You know," I say, sitting up, the water splashing onto the floor, "Now that I think of it, I can't remember a time when I was with Eric that I was truly happy. I just kept thinking that I would be happy, things just needed to line up the right way."

"That sounds stupid."

"I know." My shoulders slump. "I kept thinking if I do this or do that or this happens that we would be happy."

"Then why did you stay with him, Mal?"

I shrug. "We had fun together. Especially at the beginning, we saw movies and played euchre and had great sex," I laugh. "It always felt like something was on the horizon. It just never materialized. Before I knew it, years had gone by and I felt like I didn't even realize who I was."

"I had no idea."

"Me either," I sigh. "I knew I felt sort of depressed and blah, but I didn't realize why until he told me he didn't see a future together. That sent a spark of reality through me. I thought, 'How did I, Mallory Sims, get here?' I don't remember him holding me or asking me how my day was," I say, the words coming faster as all of it hits me, "or caressing me. He didn't ask my opinion or tell me he was proud of me or encourage me to do anything."

"Love makes you do funny things."

"I guess."

She doesn't even try to conceal her frustration. "The moral of this sad, depressing story is fuck Eric."

"Fuck Eric," I whisper.

"On that note, I need to go. I have a packet to read tonight before I go in tomorrow. It looks lame as hell, but I'll give it a quick skim. Otherwise, I'll regret it tomorrow."

"Go get 'em, tiger," I tease. "I'll talk to you later."

"Bye!"

I toss my phone on a pile of towels and let my face dip beneath the water. Holding my breath, I'm reminded of the last time I couldn't breathe.

Damn it, Graham.

FOUR
GRAHAM

REACHING OVERHEAD, I ADJUST THE desk lamp so it shines directly on the schedule in front of me. I should've had this done before I left the office this evening. I never leave without having the next day laid out. Even since everything has been in flux, I've stayed decently together. Today, however, was a bomb that shook everything more than the day Linda left. Leaning back and placing the pencil in my hand in the center of the notebook, I consider Mallory. I should be mulling over her performance and not the way her ass felt against my hand. I need to be thinking about how she will fit in the Landry system, not how her chest fit snugly against mine. It would make sense to predict how she'll benefit the family brand, not how she somehow makes the entire office seem a little brighter.

I'm. So. Fucked.

Leaping to my feet, the chair flying backwards and rattling the bookshelf behind me, I let the frustration I've felt creeping up get the best of me.

The house is dark as I make my way down the hall from my office to the living room. The door to each room lining the hallway is open, pressed firmly against the wall, just like I like it.

Flipping on the light in the living room, I sink into the brown leather sofa. I hit a button on the remote and the electric fireplace kicks on. The flames flicker beneath the mantle, sending shadows over the painting attached to the rockwork of the chimney.

This is my favorite place in the world. When I bought this house shortly after taking over Landry Holdings from my father, I knew this would be my escape from the business world and I also knew how important it was to have that. Dad had the home my mother created; I had to create my own.

The dark hardwood floors, warm golden walls, and pieces of tobacco-colored furniture. Here, tucked away in the living room, where I feel like I can drop all the hats—and sometimes, masks—that I wear daily. There's nothing to juggle as I put my feet up on the leather ottoman and breathe. Well, nothing except that distraction that nibbles at my brain. The tumbler of whiskey earlier didn't quell it. The three-point-one miles I ran with Ford didn't either. Walking in the door to my home didn't offer me the sense of peace I feel every night when I return from a day's work. I'm as off as I have been all day.

Maybe that's the problem. She bamboozled me.

Mallory, Mallory, Mallory, what am I going to do with you?

My chuckle breaks the silence. I know exactly what I want to do with her, to her, for her—everything I can't. Everything I won't.

A chirping sound rings from the kitchen counter and I pad through the house, my bare feet slapping against the wood, until I find it. "Hello?" I ask, glancing at the clock. "It's one a.m., Barrett. Aren't you supposed to be getting your beauty sleep?"

"I find it insulting you would suggest I need beauty sleep."

"Noted." I take out a new glass and pour another finger of whiskey.

"So, what's happening?"

"Did you talk to Linc today?"

The sound to his voice, a dose of amusement laced with annoyance, piques my curiosity. "Yeah, he called me earlier today."

"That's it?" he barks.

"Yeah. I'm not sure what you're getting at."

"The little shit is making me look bad!" he jokes. "I mean, I'm the oldest brother. I'm the fucking Governor, for heaven's sake. And he has to go and get engaged and set a fucking date before I can even pop the question?"

My glass hits the marble counter with a thud. "There is so much about that last bit that I'm going to need explained," I say, running a hand through my hair. "Lincoln got engaged?"

"Apparently. And they're getting married at the Farm. And soon. I don't remember the date, but it's in the next few weeks."

"You must've misheard," I suggest, hitting the speakerphone button and setting the phone on the counter. "He couldn't have scheduled the date. Engaged? Maybe. I think we all expected it. But set a date without talking to me? There's so much to plan, to protect. It's Lincoln, but he's reasonable. He wouldn't do that."

"He did it, G."

"Then who the hell is putting it together? Who is making sure his interests are protected? Tell me he signed a fucking prenup," I groan.

Barrett sighs. "I don't know. He just calls today and asks if I can be in town for it. It'll be a pain in the fucking ass, but of course I'll be there. I'm just pissed he couldn't have waited awhile."

"Glad to know I'm the last to know."

Irritation sweeps through my body as I stand in the middle of my kitchen, looking at my phone like it'll be forthright with answers.

"I had no idea he didn't even tell you," Barrett says, his voice now tempered.

"Well, he didn't."

"I was just calling to bitch about him making me look bad. Now I feel bad for telling you."

Peeling off the black t-shirt I slipped on to run with Ford, I wad it in a ball. "Logically speaking, what did you expect, Barrett? You've been with Alison a while. You're moving her with you to Atlanta.

Her kid calls our mom 'Grandma' now. Were we all supposed to chill out and wait until you finally grew the balls to ask her to marry you?"

He doesn't answer, just sighs deeply into the line.

"Why haven't you?" I ask. "Is something going on that I don't know about?"

"No," he says quickly. "It's nothing like that. I just . . . I keep thinking she's going to walk out. She hates so much of this life I live, and although Hux is taking it like a champ, she's in constant worry mode over it. I get it. I respect it. But I'm afraid if I really take that next step, it'll jinx it."

"Barrett, do you think a ring on her finger will change anything? It's just a symbol of something you already have. She needs that."

I bite back the bile in my throat, the bitterness creeping quicker than it has in a long, long time.

I remember her face, the long black locks splayed across my pillow. The sound of her voice as we debated philosophy into the wee hours of the morning.

"All people need to be loved, Graham." She gazed into my eyes, the first rays of morning light streaking across her face. "I need you to love me. I need you to show me you do, to quell that thirst in my soul."

"What do you want from me, Vanessa?"

"I want you to put me first, above everything else. Like I do you."

"Is this about me having to go home this weekend?" I brush a strand of hair out of her face. "I have to. I told my father I'd be there late Friday night."

"How can you love me and leave me here? I need you too, you know. You always leave me when they call."

"They're my family. That company will be mine. What am I supposed to do?"

"Stay with me," she breathes, planting kisses up my chest. "Need me like I need you."

I thought I did need her. Maybe she convinced me that I did, but I fell for it hook, line, and sinker.

"How did you get so smart about relationships?" Barrett charges, pulling me back to the present. "You holding out on us?"

"Nah," I say, downing the whiskey. The burn pushes the bitterness down with its fire. "Not me."

"Why not you? Don't you want to settle down, G? I know you have your tail on the side, but aren't you getting tired of that shit?"

Of course I want to settle down. The logical part of me knows if I never find a woman and fall in love again, I'll miss out on a huge part of life itself. Family is the most important thing in the world to me, and there's nothing more I'd like than to have my own. But the other part of me, the part that remembers what all of that feels like when you realize it's all smoke and mirrors, is just as strong. Maybe stronger.

"When the time is right," I tell him. "But I don't have the time or energy to give to someone right now."

That's true. I barely have enough time in my day to do what I need to do to keep everything going. But that's only half the story.

He doesn't need the other half.

FIVE
MALLORY

"PLEASE, PLEASE, PLEASE," I PRAY as the elevator inches north. "I can't be late!"

My black heel taps against the tile, my hand clenching around my bag, as I watch each number slowly light up. Kicking myself for not getting gas last night and waiting until today, I'm at the door before the buzzer goes off. As soon as the right floor dings, after what feels like an eternity, I dash out.

The landing forms an "H," with offices lining each long hallway. Pivoting to the right, I turn left and dash, more carefully than yesterday but not any slower, down the hall to the double glass doors that open into what is now my office. They close softly behind me.

My heart is thrashing beneath a wine-colored blouse that nicely showcases my boobs. I feel good in it, but not as good as I feel with Graham's eyes on me.

I tiptoe across the room and slip into my seat. Glancing at the clock, I have four minutes to spare. As my bag hits the floor, the large wooden doors to Graham's office swing open. I sigh, but not from victory—I whimper from pure delight.

His hair, combed to the side with a spike at the front, is a little darker than usual. My fingers itch to touch it, to see if it's still wet from the shower. He's a perfectly put-together image of power and sex appeal in a navy blue suit, crisp beige shirt, and a tie that incorporates both colors in a diamond pattern. Then his cologne hits me and I think I'm going to faint away.

Slipping off the black wire-rimmed glasses from his face, his brows arch in a hurry. "I didn't hear you come in."

"Four minutes early," I point out with a smug smile. Despite six outfit changes, having to stop for gas, and a mini-traffic jam, I made it on time. He doesn't even attempt to hide the fact that he checks his watch.

"Good to see."

"Yesterday was an anomaly," I say, leveling up to my desk. "Everyone gets one bad day sometimes, right?"

He doesn't answer, just watches me with a neutral face as I pull out a few odds and ends from my bag. "What's that?" he asks.

"This is a stress ball," I point out, tucking it in my desk drawer.

"I think a happy face on a ball staring at me all day would give me stress." He crooks his neck as he peers at the light purple device I place on my desktop. "What about that?"

"This," I say, holding it in the air, "has essential oil inside. I can roll it on my wrists, the back of my neck, wherever . . ."

His eyes flip to mine. His chest rises and falls heavily. "Can you keep that out of sight?"

"Sure," I say, blushing.

The glass doors swing open, distracting us both. A younger, lighter, more athletic version of Graham walks in wearing sweatpants and a long sleeved shirt. He has a huge grin on his face. "Mallory Sims," he singsongs, extending a large, calloused hand.

"Lincoln?" Although I haven't seen him in years, except on television, I'm fairly certain I'm right. Those genes aren't found in that combo just anywhere. He stands by Graham and the two of them together, side-by-side, makes my head spin. And panties melt away.

Good God. Don't let him visit much.

"I guess my reputation proceeds me," he winks. "Can I call you Mal?"

"You are not nicknaming my assistant," Graham huffs.

Lincoln's shoulder hits Graham's, knocking him sideways a step. Graham mutters something, which causes his younger brother to chuckle.

"Lighten up, G." He turns to me. "What do you think of my brother here? Did he treat you right on your first day?"

"She's my employee, Linc," Graham says just loud enough for me to think he didn't want me to.

Lincoln ignores him, watching me with a wide smile. "I know he's not charming right off the bat and kind of a nerd with that suit and— when did you start wearing glasses?" he asks, looking at his brother.

"Mallory? Remember how I told you my family are the only ones that can come in without advanced notice?" Graham asks.

"Yes."

"If you see this guy in here again, call security." Lincoln and I laugh as Graham just shakes his head.

"It's nice to see you again," Lincoln offers. "You know, I just moved back to town. My girl, Dani, doesn't really have any friends here. I think the two of you might hit it off."

I look at my boss. His body language—crossed arms, pressed lips— tell me everything I need to know. His eyes are trained on me, his gaze burning into mine. His eyes darken as my heartbeat picks up and I imagine him doing just what I want him to do. Lift me up, pull up my dress, and discover that, today, I'm wearing no panties.

He cocks his head slightly to the side. It's as if he's issuing me some warning not to go there. Little does he know, I've gone there. Multiple times. *All the way* a few times as I got ready for bed last night and once before I got here today. What's a girl to do when he looks like that?

"Oh, who cares what Graham has to say? He's all bark, no bite," Lincoln promises, bringing me out of my daze. "Well, except that time in St. Petersburg . . ." He glances at Graham. "That's probably not a story to tell in front of your new employee, huh?"

"Why are you here this morning?" Graham asks, pulling his gaze to Lincoln.

"If I remember correctly, the sign out front—you know, the large one in big, black letters?—says LANDRY on it."

"So does your mailbox," Graham grumbles.

"Look," he sighs, "Barrett told me he told you the news last night. I know you're pissed, but—"

"Can we talk about this in my office?" Graham asks, exasperated.

"I thought this was your office?" Lincoln retorts, the smile on his face making it obvious he's doing it just to rile his brother up.

"You two are hysterical," I say, not able to wipe the grin off my face.

Lincoln walks in front of my desk and leans against the corner. "You were right, G. I should've remembered her."

"You didn't?" I say, my mouth dropping in faux shock. "How could you forget me? Don't you remember the time you were chasing your sisters and I with a worm at the Farm and I fell and had to get stitches in my chin?"

"That was you? Wow, Mallory," he whistles between his teeth. "I remember you as a little girl with braces. You're . . . beautiful."

"Thank you," I offer, blushing at his compliment.

"Didn't I hear you got engaged yesterday?" Graham interrupts, his arms crossed over his chest. His watch sparkles in the light as he almost glares at Lincoln. "And are getting married in a few weeks?"

"Congratulations," I say, watching Lincoln's ass as he lifts off my desk. He turns to me and gives me a dazzling smile.

"Thank you. I'm pretty jacked about it, to be honest. I gotta go get tuxes and all that shit and I don't even hate it."

"Because it means you get her," I volunteer.

"Yeah." He looks at the floor, his cheeks a touch flushed. "She really fucked up everything in my life," he beams. "I'm going to be a daddy. I mean, I'm going to be responsible for another human, and while I'm not sure that's a good idea, it's happening and I'm looking forward to it. It's crazy how fast shit changes."

His entire face is lit up by his admission and I wonder who the lucky girl is. Not just because she wrapped up this handsome guy, but because he's obviously head-over-heels for her. My heart tugs in admiration and jealousy because I've never had someone look at me like that. Ever. Maybe I pretended Eric did, but seeing it like this makes it apparent I haven't.

"Let's finish this in my office," Graham says, disappearing inside the doors.

"Nice to see you again, Mal." Lincoln gives me a peace sign and joins his brother, closing the door behind them.

I look around the room. I'm not sure if it was this boring from the get-go or if I was so busy yesterday that I didn't notice. Or if Las Vegas would seem dull after the Landry's left. I imagine the latter is the case.

They bring such an air of excitement to a room. When they walk in, everything seems to come to life. I can't explain it, but damn it if I can't feel it.

I wonder what they're discussing on the other side of the door, if Graham is more like Lincoln when he isn't in the role of CEO. I've imagined what Graham's laugh sounds like and what kind of music he listens to. He's so hard to predict. I wouldn't know where to even start. I doubt I'll ever know that much about him. It wasn't on his stupid bullet-point list, but I can read between the lines.

His daily email, the list he promised he'd have for me to do each morning, is glowing in my inbox. Instead of attacking it first, I dig inside my bag. After a few seconds, a framed picture of me and Joy is on one corner of my desk, a shot from us hiking at Sandpiper Trail that always makes me smile. A white, freesia-scented candle sets next to my computer. "There," I say out loud, clicking on Graham's email. "Now I can get to work."

I'M PORING OVER A SET of files Graham left for me while I was gone for lunch, lost to the numbers and notes, when I hear him clear his throat. Jumping at the sound, I see him standing in the doorway, watching me.

"You scared me," I gasp.

He's been running his hands through his hair, his tie slightly askew, and I know better than to look him in the eye. If there's one thing about my new employer I know already, and there might *just* be the one thing, it's that he can read my mind. I'm sure of it.

"How's that coming along?" he asks.

"Good. I'm almost finished. I did find a few errors though in the coding, which I know wasn't what I was supposed to be doing," I say, quickly, "but I couldn't help but note them. That's what the green flags are on the side."

His lips twist in amusement. "That's interesting. I did that last night." He seems to get lost in his thoughts for a second. "How many did you find?"

"Three? Want to see?"

He comes up behind me as I open the folder. My fingers stumble as I flip through the papers in search of the green flags. His cologne, subtle from the wear of the day, floats around me, teasing me. I gulp and try not to flinch as he reaches over my shoulder, his suit jacket brushing against me, as he points at the first flag.

"I was off by .002?" His breath is hot against my ear, sending an array of goosebumps across my flesh.

"Yes," I say as evenly as I can as I flip to the next flag. "On this one, it was .003. Not much, but still incorrect."

"I'm impressed." He doesn't move, doesn't change position, just rests his palm flat against my desktop. Hovering over me, he completely dominates the space. There's nothing I can say, nothing I can think, that's not in his control. He knows this. His breathing is completely even, his tone completely cool. "How long did this take you?"

"An hour or so."

"Can I ask you something, Mallory?"

"You're the boss."

"Do you like working here?"

"So far, yes, I do."

"Do you think you'll like working here in the future?"

I'm not sure what he's getting at. It seems to be a loaded question, or a question that he's using to lead me to another one, but I can't think straight with him leaning over me like this. All I can think about is if I move, I'll brush his arm. If I tilt my head back, my face will be inches from his. If I turn around, I'd be in his personal space.

"Is that a no?" he asks, his voice husky.

"Oh, no," I stammer. "I mean, it's not a no. I think I'll like working here for a long time. I hope so, anyway."

After a pause, he pushes off and stands. I'm afraid to look back. My eyes stay trained on a small indentation above the door ahead of me like it's the most interesting thing in the world. He sighs, but I don't think I'm supposed to hear it.

"Good job with the file." He comes around the front of my desk, his glasses in his hand. "I'm happy to have you on board. I don't think I've said that."

"You haven't," I say, testing his reaction with a grin. His lip quivers, but he doesn't quite return it. "But it's nice to hear."

"How about this," he says with a flurry, "With the circumstances what they were, we didn't have time for an actual interview. What if we have an informal interview tomorrow. A working lunch, maybe?"

I grin nervously. "That might be a good idea."

"Why is that?"

"I'll admit, I've never worked somewhere before where I felt so . . ." His gaze deepens, a shadow crossing his face.

"So what, Mallory?"

I look away and plead with my cheeks not to heat. There are so many ways I feel about this position, about working for Graham Landry, and none of them I want to say out loud.

He won't let me go without answering. There's no use in trying.

"I don't know how to take you, exactly. I accepted the job because, quite frankly, I needed one pretty desperately, and I know your family. But the Graham I remember and the one standing in front of me..."

The movement he makes towards me is nothing more than a flinch, a probably unconscious motion as my words trail off. Still, my breath catches in my throat and the heat in my cheeks rises a few notches.

"You aren't the Mallory I remember, either." He whips in a deep inhale and blows it out slowly. "I don't want this to be awkward."

"It shouldn't be. There's no reason for it to be," I lie, omitting the fact that it's so difficult because I can't stop imagining him naked. "Maybe we just didn't have that getting-to-know-you phase. You know, as the people we are now."

"Maybe." He slips his glasses back on his face, his features softening. "Block off an hour and a half for my lunch tomorrow. Get with Gina in the morning and let her know your substitute for lunch will need to stay longer than usual."

"Yes, sir."

He almost smiles. Almost.

SIX
MALLORY

I SEE MY REPLACEMENT STANDING on the other side of the glass wall, talking to another employee. Her name is Raza and she's super sweet, but today, I'm not looking forward to seeing her.

"I should've worn the black dress," I chastise myself, looking down at what I did choose. The eggshell blue shift took entirely too long to pick out and almost made me late. I accessorized it with a couple of gold bangles and nude heels and took extra care to curl my long locks into beachy curls. It's cute and fine for a day at work. Because, as I keep reminding myself, this is not a date. It's a lunch interview, a part of my work day. A routine thing that happens between two people that work together.

Only most people don't work with a man that looks like a Greek god that sounds like a Southern gentleman.

He's avoided me all morning. Or maybe this is just a normal day at work—I don't know. I haven't been here long enough to establish a true normal routine. I suspect, however, there's nothing normal about Graham Landry.

He's been polite, yet firm, when I've called back to transfer calls or alert him of a visitor. All of his communication with me has come via email. I haven't seen him since I arrived and that has me more on edge.

Raza bounces through the door, her usual cheery self. "How are you, Mallory?"

"Good." I stand shakily and put my purse in the locking drawer at the bottom of my desk. "I'm not sure how long I'll be. An hour and a half, maybe. Did Gina tell you?"

"She did. Do you have some sort of appointment?"

"Yeah." I twist my lips. "I have a working lunch with Mr. Landry."

Raza's eyes light up like a schoolgirl's. "I'm jealous," she whispers conspiratorially. "But I'm not sure I could be in a closed room with him for that long without a restraining order at the end."

My attempt at a smile is broken and a little wobbly because I'm not sure how this is going to work either. With a slight wave, I grab a notebook and a pen and take the handful of steps to the large, heavy wooden doors and knock.

"Come in." His response is immediate and bold, not at all like the tepid Graham I've dealt with all day.

The door swings open too easily, denying me that last sweet second to get my wits about me. Before I'm ready, he's in sight.

His desk is wide and heavy-looking, made of dark wood with antiqued accents. In most offices, this piece of furniture would be the focal point. In this one, it's the man behind it. There's nothing that could possibly outshine him.

He's wearing a black suit and tie and is leaning back in an oversized black leather chair. Light pours in his office from the glass walls that probably allow you a fantastic view of Savannah, if you were so inclined— meaning if you weren't a female and Graham wasn't present. Because when he's here, nothing else matters.

"Close the door behind you," he instructs.

Once the clasp latches, I turn to face him again. This time, I don't let our eyes meet. I need just a second to compose myself.

Just a work appointment, Mal. Just like with Mr. Beenmeyer.

Glancing up at Graham just in time to witness him unfold himself out of his chair, I find myself laughing out loud.

Mr. Beenmeyer didn't look like he was packing double-digits.

"Something funny?" Graham asks, smoothing down his tie.

"No. Not at all."

He casts me a puzzled look. "Would you like to order lunch in?"

"Oh, um, I went ahead and ordered lunch for you at Hillary's House. It was in the notes—that you order from there every day when you don't have an appointment. And since this isn't really an appointment..."

"What about you?"

"I ordered for myself and prepaid it on my credit card," I tell him, omitting that I was a little shell-shocked at the prices and opted to order the cheapest thing on the menu.

"I had them charge yours to your account like normal. Everything should be delivered shortly. I know they're late, but you'll have to take that up with them."

"And with whom should I take up the fact that you paid for your lunch today?"

"What?"

"Mallory," he sighs, "when I ask you to have lunch with me, please don't disrespect me by buying your own."

Biting my lip, I nod as quickly as I can. "That's not what I meant by it." He just nods, his annoyance down a few notches but not gone altogether. "Go ahead and take a seat."

We get situated across from one another. I study his face while he moves things around his desk. If I look closely enough, I can see the Graham I remember. The dimple in his left cheek is barely noticeable, but I'd venture to guess it's still heavenly when he smiles a real smile, something I don't think I've seen from him.

As he types furiously on his keyboard, I wonder what makes Graham Landry happy. What makes him loosen that tie around his neck. What it would take to lose this façade that has to be some sort of veneer because how can someone as beautiful, successful, and wealthy seem so . . . joyless? As I start to consider what he might do after work, he folds his hands together on top of his desk and looks at me. "I just sent you an email about a new venture Landry Holdings is taking on. It's called Landry Security and my brother Ford will be at the helm. He'll be in soon for a strategy session that I'll ask you to sit in on. We want to get this up and running as soon as possible, and since I've been short-handed in here for much longer than I care to admit, I'm behind. Also something I hate to admit."

"Things happen," I shrug. "You have to be able to roll with the punches."

"I don't roll with the punches," he chuckles. "I like all my ducks in a row. On a chain, if possible."

"How's that working out for you?"

He falls back in his chair, seemingly surprised by my question. I do what he does to me—I wait him out. Just when I think he's going to wait all day if it takes that for me to speak next, he shocks me and answers.

"It works for me. I know my style isn't for everyone, Mallory. I like to have a plan for the back-up plan. It's how I keep all the balls I juggle daily in the air."

"What if one falls?"

"They don't," he replies, a brusqueness to his tone that ripples across the desk and chills me. "Failure is not an option, especially when it comes to anything for my family, and this business is a family business."

The passion he feels for his family and work is palpable, something I've never seen in anyone firsthand. It's another dimension to this man that I suspect has a lot of layers. "They're lucky to have you running things for them."

"That works both ways." Before I can press him on this, he changes the subject. "What should I know about you?"

I inhale a deep breath. "I think my resume pretty much said it all. I just moved back to town. Nursing school wasn't for me."

"Do you mind if I ask why?"

"Have you ever had to inject something into someone?"

His face blanches. "No."

"Yeah, not my thing. I also felt like I was going to get everything everyone had that came in. I just couldn't imagine living every day with a box of bleach wipes in my purse, you know?"

"I'm one hundred percent sure I couldn't work in the medical field. It's too unpredictable."

I wince. "Yeah, I can't imagine you in a room full of people going every which way, coughing all over each other, liquids squirting everywhere."

"That's a disgusting image you present there, Ms. Sims," he chuckles.

He rests one ankle on the opposite knee and strokes his chin, watching me intently. "I'll admit, I was surprised you were interested in the medical field to begin with. You always seemed so . . ."

"So what?"

He shrugs, weighing his words. "You were so studious before, so serious. Focused. Your Latin was impeccable. I remember you telling me you wanted to be an attorney and I couldn't imagine you in front of a jury. Then we had a disagreement over our paper and I could exactly see you in front of a judge, winning your case," he admits. "Law is a far cry from nursing. What made you change your mind?"

My spirits tumble as memories I haven't thought about in a long time roll through my memory. When life was simple and hope seemed free. Before my senior year came and I was put in my place by my parents and made the best decision I could under the circumstances.

"I actually moved to Columbia with Eric Johnson."

"Do I know him?"

"Probably not," I say, not wanting to dwell on Eric, even if he did know him.

Graham leans forward and narrows his eyes. "What does moving to Columbia have to do with you not going to law school?"

"It just didn't work out. I was nineteen when we moved. I had to get adjusted there and I needed to work to save money to go. Part of that went to helping Eric get his degree and then, when it was my turn, I chose nursing. It seemed like a fast degree that would pay well."

"Do you plan on going back now?"

My shoulders rise and fall. "I'll be honest, I'm not sure what I plan on doing. So many things have changed for me and I'm not really sure where I sit these days. I've worked as an Administrative Assistant for years now. Even when I was going to nursing school, I worked at Beenmeyer Company. It's all I really know and can do well."

I look away because I feel like he's trying to read me again. I'm afraid that this time, he'll realize what a mess I am. That's not something Graham will appreciate in all his organizational bliss.

"Eric Johnson," he says finally. "Is he still in the picture?"

"No. I told him I wanted to drop out of nursing school, we had a fight, and I ended up leaving him."

Something passes through his eyes. "I'm sure you don't want to talk about that. I apologize for pressing you."

"It's fine," I concede, finding my footing. "You didn't press me. It's still so raw for me to discuss." *Especially with you.* "So, what happened in your life?"

"I went to the University of Georgia and got a Master's in business. Pretty predictable, right?"

I grin. "Yes. But there has to be something more. No one gets through high school and college with no crazy tales."

A knock comes to the door and Graham sags back in his chair. He holds up a finger to tell me to wait a second.

I sit quietly and listen to him converse with Raza, her giggle drifting through the room. I can't help but roll my eyes.

"Let's eat over here," he says over the rustle of a plastic bag.

I stand and follow him to a circular table near a window. As he places the containers at our seats, I take a moment to admire his office.

It's a large corner office with bright white paint, dark wood, and a loveseat against the back wall. A glass table is in front of it with what appears to be a handful of magazines of some sort and a small figurine that I can't make out. A tree stands in the corner in a beautiful terracotta pot. Everything is clean, organized, smart . . . and slightly uptight. Just like Graham.

"Ready?" he asks. When I look at him, he raises a brow. "Like what you see?"

"It's gorgeous."

"I'm glad you approve." His lips twist and I know he knows I wasn't just referring to the abstract painting on the far wall. "I had your credit card reimbursed for your lunch."

"I—" My objection is silenced by a look from Graham. "Thank you," I gulp.

"That pained you, didn't it?"

"What?" I say, opening the container in front of me.

"To just say thank you."

"Kind of," I laugh. "I'm just not used to someone doing something for me without expecting something in return. I've learned it's easier just to do everything yourself."

He cuts his sandwich in two pieces and lays half of his alongside my side salad. My mouth opens to object, but closes as his quirked brow silences me.

"First of all," he says, "you're right—it is easier to do things yourself. I understand that. It's hard for me to trust anyone."

"Is that why you went through so many assistants before me?" He raises a brow.

"Sienna told me," I say. "She also might've said you're a little difficult to get along with, but if I give you time, I'd like you."

"Did she?"

"She did," I shrug. "Lincoln too, now that I think of it," I admit. "I'm hoping they're right."

"So you don't like me now?" The way he says it, a slight tease to his tone, is enough to send my hormones into a frenzy.

"I didn't say that," I blush.

He considers this as he takes a bite of his Rueben. I twirl my fork around in my salad, trying to focus on the colors of the tomato and lettuce and not on the way his eyes are beginning to turn a slight shade of blue.

"I'm not sure I like you either," he says, not looking at me. "But I'm not sure I want to."

"And why not?"

"Because . . ." He dabs a linen napkin on his lips. "I think that would give you an unfair advantage over me."

My cheeks flush the color of the tomato on my plate. I'm not sure what that means, but his gaze tells me it's a compliment. "I'll be late," I assure him. "That'll help."

He laughs, the realest laugh I've heard from him. It's wonderful. "That would definitely help. I can't handle being late."

"Or disorganization," I add.

"Or being unprepared." He grins. "I guess I have a lot of issues, don't I?"

"That's what it sounds like," I tease. "I just hate it when people don't wave at me when I let them pull out in front of me. It's so rude. I did you a favor and now you're going to be snotty? It's really hard for me not to ram them with my car."

"So you have anger management issues then?" he teases. "That's really, really good to know."

"No. I have a hard time managing assholish behavior."

"Remind me to keep you away from Barrett," he winks.

"So you have no assholish behavior?" I ask, popping a chunk of lettuce in my mouth. "None at all?"

"No. I don't think so."

"Interesting . . ." I take a sip of my water. "Okay, then. Name me three words that describe you."

He takes a bite of his sandwich. The wheels turn as his head cocks to the side. "Careful. Purposeful. Confident."

"Those are boring," I sigh dramatically.

"Maybe I'm boring," he winks. "What about you? Three words."

"Dependable," I say, tilting my head to look at him out of the corner of my eye.

"Nice one," he says, rolling his eyes.

"Searching."

"For what?"

I pop a tomato in my mouth. "A missing piece."

"To what? A puzzle? A mystery?"

"Me. I've never felt like me. Is that odd?"

"Absolutely," he grins.

"I look back on my life so far and wish I would've done something I wanted to do. There was always someone telling me I couldn't or shouldn't, and I believed them. It's my fault," I sigh. "But what if I'd tried? What if I'd tried business or law or had taken a cooking class? Who knows where I'd be now."

He leans back in his chair. "I have the opposite problem. I'm afraid to stop moving because I might stall. The one time I tried it, I . . ." He clears his throat. "You have one more."

I want to dig deeper on that, to see what he means, but I know it's futile. He's not going to talk anymore about it. "One more. Okay, I'm going with *adventurous*."

He chokes on his food, excusing himself and disappearing through a door next to the sofa that I hadn't seen. When he returns a few minutes later, his eyes have a twinkle to them.

"Are you all right?" I ask, trying not to smile at the look on his face. He shakes his head, this time refusing to look at me. "I'm fine." He returns to his seat and takes a long drink of water. After the cap is slowly screwed back on, his eyes find mine. "I'll admit something to you."

"Shoot."

"You confuse the hell out of me."

A giggle topples from my lips. "Really? In what way?"

His eyes narrow as he chooses his words. "In every way. On one hand, you're incredibly efficient, finding my mistakes yesterday in the file. You thought ahead to order lunch today. You've really impressed Gina, and Lincoln loved you—but don't take that to mean anything. You're a beautiful woman. That's kind of a shoo-in with my little brother."

"Gee, thanks," I say, trying to deflect from the fact that I'm just replaying "beautiful woman" over and over again.

He laughs again, the sound a melody better than I expected. It's warm and soothing, but has a gruffness to it that reminds me of a five o'clock shadow—just scratchy enough to lend a little rogue that ups the sex appeal by a hundredfold. "It was a compliment," he says, leaning forward. "On the other hand, I have no idea how you maintain your efficiency. You struggle to get here on time every day. Your desk is a mess. I have no idea how you keep track of anything."

"Steel trap," I say, patting my temple. "And I take slight offense to you calling me a mess."

"I didn't."

"No, you did," I laugh.

"I said your desk is a mess."

"My desk is a creative climate," I suggest. "It's been proven that the smartest people in the world work in an atmosphere other people would call disorderly."

"Or a mess," he winks.

"I refuse to accept that term," I shrug playfully.

"Can you accept to straighten it up? It's driving me crazy. I want to stop there every night on my way home and just reorganize it for you."

"Don't you dare!" I giggle.

He reclines back, the sun illuminating his face. The lines around his eyes are smooth, his jaw slack and unclenched for maybe the first time since I started. He almost seems like a different person altogether.

"It is my office," he suggests. "I would venture to say there's not a lot you could do about it."

"What if I got up and went to your desk and moved things around? How would you feel?"

His eyes hood, his bottom lip working back and forth in between his teeth. I sit across from him, my hands in my lap, held hostage by his gaze.

His lip pops free and I exhale sharply. "I'd feel a lot of ways," he whispers. "None of which I really want to feel."

"Why not?" I ask softly.

We both know we aren't just talking about a moved stapler or a mishmash of files. As that really sets in, the air around us gets heavier. Hotter. *Hazardous.*

"Those things always lead to dangerous situations," he says, his eyes trained on me.

I shift in my seat, the throb between my legs growing stronger by the second. "People do it every day and survive."

"They may survive, but don't things get messy?"

"Only if they do it right."

His chair flies backwards and he's to his feet and next to me before I know what's happening. He doesn't ask that I stand, but he doesn't have to. It's implied and my body reacts accordingly to his silent command.

We stand face-to-face, our breathing ragged. Our chests heave with the anticipation, the possibility, of what might come next.

"You are, quite possibly, the most dangerous of them all," he says, his voice rough.

"Why is that?" I breathe.

"There's no plan for you."

"But you've already penciled me in, haven't you, Graham?" I ask, finding the courage to play this little game with him. Being strictly professional is incredibly hard, and this is way too easy.

I can flirt with the best of them in a bar or on a college campus. But here, with him, it's a game all its own. A level I had no idea I'd ever be a contender in. Maybe I'm not, but I'm going to play the hell out of it while

I'm here . . . even though if I keep it up, I might not be here for long. "What do you want, Mallory?"

"I want to do all the things you ask of me and do them better than you ever expected they could be done."

A rumble emits from his throat as his eyes darken. My knees go weak and I grab the table with my left hand to ensure I don't fall.

He licks his lips and flips his gaze to my mouth. I think I whimper as I lift my chin, waiting to see what he does next. My entire body is on fire for this man, my heart thumping so hard I'm sure he can hear it.

He moves so my back is pressed against the table, our food long forgotten. His hands are on either side of me, caging me in. Our eyes locked together, he leans in, a slow smirk spreading across his gorgeous face.

"Excuse me, Mr. Landry. Ford is here to see you," Raza chirps through the line.

We exhale simultaneously, a giggle escaping with mine. There's nothing funny about this, but the energy has to come out in some way.

"Mr. Landry?" she asks again.

"I'll be right out. Thank you, Raza."

"Oh, you're so welcome, sir." The line clicks off and Graham marches across the room and punches a button. The light on top indicates he's not to be disturbed.

I busy myself with cleaning up our lunch, and before he's at my side again, I have everything bundled up.

"Thanks for lunch," I say like nothing just happened.

"Mallory . . ." He runs his hand through his hair, leaving one lock sticking up. Knowing what that will look like if we walk out together, I reach up, hesitating for a split second, before smoothing it out.

His hair is silky against my fingers. He jumps when I touch him at first, but doesn't back away. "What are you doing?"

"Nothing went on in here. I refuse for it to look like something did. That's the way rumors get spread, Mr. Landry."

"Mallory, I..."

I get a final look at his face, reach up and straighten his tie as his eyes go wide, then turn towards the door. "I'll send Ford in."

"Mallory!"

"Yeah?" I turn to the side. He's standing by the table, his hands in his pockets looking frazzled. When he doesn't respond, I place my hand on the knob. "I'll have that file back to you before I leave today. Thanks again for lunch."

I walk out before I can change my mind.

SEVEN
GRAHAM

"DON'T LOOK AT ME LIKE that," Ford says, counting out a final ten push-ups and then hopping to his feet no worse for the wear. "Your ass could be down here doing these with me."

"Absolutely I could." I take a sip of tea from my seat on the porch swing. "But I'm not."

The air is crisp, a wind blowing across the lawn of the Farm. Our family's getaway is an escape from the hustle and bustle of life, where we all come to congregate and get fresh air and have big scale family dinners. We all have a space here, a bedroom that we use when we need a spot to land. Granted, I don't ever use mine, but the others do. Ford is staying here until he finds a place of his own.

"I'm thinking about hiring Barrett's trainer, Achilles," Ford says, stretching his arms overhead. "I'm having a hard time getting a hard enough workout in on my own."

"Paying someone to kick your ass. I've never understood that," I joke. "Seems like you could just run another mile or lift another set and do it without shelling out money."

"It takes effort to look like this," my brother says, flexing his biceps.

"Do you forget you basically look like me? Just less good-looking?"

"You wish," Ford laughs. "You should see how your assistant looks at me."

I glare at him and he only laughs harder. "How are things going with Mallory?"

I let my mind go to the one moment that I keep replaying. Her looking up, her eyes filled with every ounce of lust I was feeling, along with a dose of uncertainty. The way her lips parted in anticipation, how her chest rose and fell as she tried to stay calm. The smell of lavender is as fresh as it was as I breathed her in for the first time.

"That good, huh?" Ford chuckles.

"She's smart. Doing a good job." I rise from the swing and lean against the rail.

"Nice vanilla answer. I love your evasiveness. You're turning into Barrett."

I roll my eyes.

"I chatted with her a bit before I left your office today," he informs me. "I like her."

My head snaps to his. "What do you mean?"

My brother's laugh comes immediately. "Just like I thought."

"Just like you thought what?"

"It's only natural. She's a nice girl. She's seems smart. She's gorgeous as hell."

I take a quick sip of tea to keep him from looking at me too closely. "I'm not following along."

"Only because you're still chasing her tail, which is exactly my point."

"Whoa," I say, standing up straight. "I think you're ahead of yourself."

He climbs the stairs to the porch and leans against the rail on the other side, grinning at me. "I haven't been around much these last few years. I only know what our siblings tell me, mostly meaning Camilla, plus what Mom and Dad volunteer. But none of them have ever mentioned you with a woman. Not seriously."

"This is not news."

"But why, Graham? It's like everyone in the family is moving on, starting their own thing. Lincoln is having a kid. Barrett will eventually grow a pair and do the same. I'm not averse to the idea myself. But you? Don't you want a family of your own some day?"

"Sure."

I leave him standing on the porch as I head into the house. I don't close the door behind me because I know he'll follow. Sure enough, when I get into the kitchen and turn around, he's standing in the doorway.

"I'm not pressing you," Ford says. "To be honest, I couldn't give a shit about what you do with your life as long as you keep working because that benefits my bottom line."

"Fuck off," I chuckle.

"But I do think you work too much. I think you take shit too seriously. I think one day you'll look back on your life and wish you'd lived a little more." With a simple shrug, he turns and starts down the hallway. "I'm jumping in the shower. If you leave before I get out, lock the door." His footsteps fall against the steps, his weight causing the floor joists above me to creak as he makes his way to the bedroom at the end of the hallway upstairs.

I hate when he does this. He says something semi-insightful and then leaves you to think about it. I don't want to think about it.

The kitchen is quiet, the only sound coming from the birds outside.

This is why everyone loves it here. It's almost its own world.

I venture out onto the back porch, Ford's words echoing in my head. He's wrong—I am happy. I live my life exactly how I want it. I designed it this way.

I had to.

A myriad of imagery races through my mind. I can see her tears rolling down her tanned cheeks, feel my stomach twist in what I'm sure is some kind of death knell. I see my father's disapproving face and my mother's look of sympathy, and I know I can never do that again.

The last time I went off plan, I nearly lost everything. Anxiety sets in, my head filling with what-ifs—questions I'll never have answers to. Maybe answers I don't even want because it won't make any difference. Things are what they are. There is no changing that. I go through my well-practiced routine of reminding myself I'll never lose control like that again in order to gain some relief.

My phone buzzes and I pull it out, happy for the distraction. I see a familiar number, a woman I meet sometimes for a bite to eat and then a quick fuck. It's routine between us, neither of us wanting more than a release. I return her message with a quick text that I'm busy tonight, even though I'm not. I'm just not feeling it.

Even as I type that out, I know it's a lie. I am feeling it, just not with her. As my brain begins to parade images of Mallory Sims through my memory, my lips part into a smile.

"What is it about you, Mallory?" I ask out loud, my voice carrying off in the wind. Unfortunately for me, the wind doesn't answer.

As my brothers have attested, there's no denying her beauty. She's fucking beautiful with her sexy lips, bright eyes, curvy body. Her brains make her a step ahead of the other women I see occasionally, because brains and beauty in one package? That's heaven, a combination that just does it for me. But I've seen it before. Once, to be sure. Or so I thought. And that's precisely why I'm not about to do it again.

As hard as it is, figuratively and literally, to work with her every day, I have to make it happen. She's the best thing to happen to my office since Linda. The fact that she opens up parts of me that haven't been touched since Vanessa is the scary part.

I let the sun shine down on my face, warming me. As my eyes shut, it's Mallory's giggle I hear and the heat of her breath I imagine on my skin. Instead of going back in the house like I should, stopping this stupid little fantasy before it gets out of hand, or worse, routine, I stand on the porch and relish the feeling for a few more minutes.

The fact that I'm not just imagining her beneath me, losing myself inside her, but thinking about her smile, the way she tells a story—that's a problem. It's the scariest part of all.

***

Mallory

MY BRIGHT RED TOENAILS WIGGLE in front of me. "This close, Joy. This. Close." I bring my hands to my feet and stretch on the purple yoga mat under me.

"You were this close to half of the dreams I've had in my life," she laughs from her Downward Facing Dog. "I used to practice writing 'Joy Landry' in my notebooks. I wasn't even sure which one I wanted. Come to think of it, I don't think I really cared."

I struggle to keep the smile off my face, but when I look at Joy and our eyes meet, we both start giggling. "Graham, Joy. Oh. My. God."

"What are you going to do about it?" she asks. "You work for him. It's not like you met him at some charity ball or something."

"I've been thinking about that," I say, touching my toes. "I'm just going to go with the flow. See what happens. I mean, let's be real. Nothing is *really* going to happen. It's Graham Landry and me."

"Shut up. Don't talk about yourself like that."

I roll my eyes. "You know what I mean. He can have whomever he wants. Even if I get lucky and somehow get lucky," I grin, "that's all it will be."

"Will you be okay with that?" she asks skeptically.

"I hope . . ." I say, grimacing as the muscles in my legs start to burn, "I'm more than okay with it." Standing, I look at her. "I'm taking risks, remember? I've never been able to just flirt and be spontaneous and have fun. If Graham plays back with me, then he does.

I'm more than happy to be on the receiving end of that. If he stops or gets weird about it, I'll stop. It's pretty simple."

She smiles and goes back to her stretching. I go back to my endless thoughts.

I'm not sure it is as simple as I just made it out to be. I explained it like it's a purely physical attraction, and it is, for the most part. But I can't deny I enjoyed talking to him yesterday. Our banter was fun, easy, and having him interested in what I had to say, even if he was humoring me, was the most fun I've had with a man in a long time. Maybe ever. That's sad, but it's also true.

The bells chime on the door of the yoga studio where I work parttime in the evenings. It's closed, the last class wrapping just a few minutes ago. Sienna introduced me to yoga in high school when it was the trendy thing to do. She does it off and on, but I was hooked immediately and haven't stopped. I love the way it centers me. Without it, my body and my mind would be even more chaotic than they are now.

"Hey, girls," Camilla says, dropping her pink bag to the floor and removing her shoes.

"Hi," Sienna says, padding across the mat. They roll out their mats and take seats next to Joy and I, forming a haphazard circle. "What are you two talking about? You looked all chatty until we walked in."

Joy looks at me out of the corner of her eye with a smirk. "Do you two really want to know?"

"Maybe not," Camilla says, her brows pulling together. She looks at me with a puzzled look. "Do I, Mal?"

"I do," Sienna retorts. "Spill it."

"I want to do dirty, dirty things to Graham," I grin. Camilla flops back on the mat, her hands covering her face.

"I think I just puked a little in my mouth," Sienna says, looking at me. "Did you really just say that?"

"That's just the tip of the iceberg," I wink. "It's your fault. You're the one that got me the job working in such a confined area with him.

What did you think would happen, Sienna? Have you even looked at him lately?"

"Yeah," she says, wincing. "All the time. And I can't believe we're even having this conversation."

Joy sighs as she stands. "You're lucky you didn't hear her story from today."

Sienna's face twists in disgust as I stand, laughing. We all stretch quietly, each of us mulling over our own thoughts. Joy's obviously mirror mine because every time I make eye contact with her, I have to look away so I don't start giggling again.

"Are you ready to date again?" Sienna asks.

"I don't know. If I found the right guy, I'm sure I would," I admit. "But I don't even know what I'm looking for at this point. It's been so long since I thought about it."

"Have you talked to Eric?" Camilla asks. The sweeter of the two sisters, her voice is soft and comforting. She reminds me of their mother—prim and proper and nurturing. Sienna, on the other hand, is more lively. She's the one you could call at midnight and ask to sneak out and go for a drive. Camilla would've died before breaking the rules.

I hold my Warrior pose as long as I can, weighing my words before answering her. "I haven't talked to him. I doubt I'll ever hear from him again, to be honest." I release the pose and breathe. "I'm okay with that. It's the way I want it, actually. If he called, it would just set me back. I need to be focused on what I want and what I'm able to get."

"You can get anything you want," Camilla says. "You can go to school. Teach yoga. Change jobs or—"

"Move to LA with me," Sienna chimes in. "Cam is right. You can do whatever you want."

"You make it sound so easy."

"If you're thinking about dating, I know a guy," Camilla offers, ignoring her sister's glare, "that I think you might like."

"I'm sure you do," Sienna says.

"Don't start," Camilla fires back. "I don't say a word about your little friends-with-benefits thing with what's-his-name and I know him. I don't know why you feel the need to put down a guy you don't even know."

"Because I don't know him!" Sienna jumps to her feet, the purple ends of her hair swishing behind her. "You won't let me meet him. You made me promise not to even bring him up to Linc or Graham or Barrett. That says something, Cam."

"It says I don't want them to run him off before I decide if I like him or not! I need some room this time," Camilla says, taking a step towards her twin. "Once you all come into play, you either plant thoughts in my head or you scare him off."

"Only when we need to," Sienna says.

"I don't do that to you!"

"Because I don't need it," Sienna says, holding her ground. "You're the fragile one, Cam. You're the one we all have to watch out for."

"Hey," I say, a little louder than necessary. "Settle down, you guys."

Their faces fall, Camilla's eyes finding the mat and Sienna, the fierier of the two, shaking her head.

"I'm sorry, Sienna. Just give me some space, okay?"

Sienna holds her hand out and Camilla squeezes it. Their bond makes me smile.

"Anyway, you were saying something about a guy you know?" I ask gently. I don't really care, but I don't want this silence to last for too long.

"He's nice," Camilla says. "He just moved back to town too. Well, I guess he's always lived here, but he was gone for a while. Keenan Marks. Do you remember him?"

I shake my head. "Maybe vaguely. Short black hair?"

"Yup. I think you should let him take you out. He remembers you," she smiles softly. "I think y'all met before you went to Columbia."

My first inclination is to say no. But when I look at Cam's hopeful face and Joy's raised brow, asking me without asking me what I'm going to do about Graham, I realize I might be able to kill a couple of birds with one stone.

"Give him my number," I say, getting back into Warrior position. "We'll see how it goes."

EIGHT
GRAHAM

THE GREEN FLAGS COME OFF the file easily. Wadding them up, I throw them in the trash.

"Well done, Ms. Sims," I say out loud. The first error was intentional. I was just curious how well she paid attention to detail. Apparently, she's careful because the second two she found weren't on purpose and that's a problem in and of itself.

"Graham?" Mallory's voice rings through the intercom. It's sweet, professional as always. Anyone overhearing it wouldn't think twice, but I do. I hear the little tease, the slight taunt that lies just beneath the surface.

Besides her keeping me in a state of constant distraction, I hate to admit Lincoln was right: It is nice having her around.

"Yes?" I respond.

She smacks her lips together, the sound going straight to my cock. This is what I've been waiting on all day, the moment when she brings up what *almost* happened yesterday. Despite thinking about it all night and all morning, replaying the things I wish would've happened, I'm still not sure how I'm going to deal with it.

I want her. Of course I fucking do. I've admitted that to

myself. Intelligence, round ass, sharp tongue—what's left to be desired? But that's just the thing . . . it's all desire. It simply won't work. Besides, desire uncontained can really fucking burn.

The women I fuck aren't involved in my life in any way. They're acquaintances, women that know our time together is just that—a few hours here and there. It offers me freedom to work without the trappings of a relationship. It gives me autonomy to do what needs to be done. It's clean, organized, practical. Mallory Sims is none of those things.

So what happens if that box is opened? I already know she doesn't fit inside a mold. I can't just put this girl back in a box and I'm not sure where that would leave me. Her. Us.

I sit at my desk and stare at the phone, waiting to see exactly what she has to say. She's been very coy all morning. Polite. Detailed. Hot as hell. But she hasn't crossed a line or asked me about yesterday. Until now.

"Graham?" she asks again.

"I'm sorry. I'm here. What can I do for you?"

"Your mother is on line one."

Chuckling, I place my hand on the receiver. "Not what I thought you were going to say."

"Hmmm . . ." she says. "What did you think I was going to say?" The silence is filled with a heaviness that's undeniable.

"I can tell her you're busy."

"But I'm never too busy for my mother," I grin. "Send her through." I wait, relieved, to hear her voice.

"Good afternoon, Graham," she says sweetly in the phone. "Hi, Mother."

"I suppose you heard the news. Lincoln and Danielle are getting married at the Farm."

"I did. Barrett told me."

"Oh," she says, sounding surprised. "Linc didn't say anything to you at all? That's odd."

"He did," I grumble, turning away from my computer so I'm not tempted to check my email. "Barrett just spoiled the news."

"Are you helping get things together?"

Sighing, I look out the window. "I told him to send me contracts before they signed them. I'll have our attorney look at them and make sure we pay for them through the company."

"I hope your siblings tell you how much they appreciate you," she says.

"I just hope they all sign prenuptial agreements," I laugh. "Lincoln is all 'I'm in love and I'm not signing shit' right now and it's ludicrous. I like Danielle just fine. But that doesn't mean Lincoln doesn't need to cover his ass."

"Assets, Graham. Cover his assets," she corrects me. "I agree, but it's Lincoln's money to gamble with. I hate to say that, but it's true. He's a grown man."

"Sure he is. He'll have some grown man problems on his hands if this doesn't work out."

"You know, sometimes things aren't so black and white . . ."

"What's that supposed to mean?" I ask.

"It means that sometimes things get blurry. Lincoln loves Dani, Graham. If he believes in that, maybe we should too."

"I didn't say I didn't. I just said it was ignorant."

"Oh, son," she laughs. "I need to go. I have an appointment at the salon at four. I just wanted to check in and see how you were. Think we could do lunch this weekend?"

I glance at the pile of work on the corner of my desk. "I'm still really behind, Mom. I'll probably be in the office all weekend."

"What if I order you over here? Pull the Mom Card? Or tempt you with a homemade coconut cream pie?"

"I'll try. How's that?"

"Better than no," she sighs. "I love you, Graham. Make sure you're taking time for you, okay?"

"Love you, Mom."

I hang up the receiver and sit back in my chair. The hours upon hours of work I've been doing is starting to add up. I can feel it across the back of my shoulders, in my thighs when I stand. It's just an accumulation of stress and rigidity that's starting to wear me down a bit.

Swiping my coffee cup off my desk, I head to the coffee maker for a fresh cup. As I pass the door to my office, I hear Mallory's voice on the other side. Pausing, my hand on the knob, I listen to another man's voice. I'm not sure who it is, other than it's not one of my brothers.

I pop open the door, my jaw pulsing, before I realize what I'm doing. Leaning on her desk is a man in a brown work uniform, a package sitting between them. Mallory is leaned away from him, rolled away from her desk a few feet.

"Excuse me?" I ask, causing them both to jump.

"Oh, Graham!" Mallory gasps, her hand flying to her chest. She reads my pressed lips correctly and stands. "Can I get you something?"

Instead of answering her, I flip my glare to the delivery man. "Are you done here?"

"Yeah, I'm sorry," he stammers. "I just had a package to drop off."

"That looks accomplished. You can go now."

He bolts out the door like a flash of lightning. I give Mallory one quick look before retreating to my office.

My jaw still clenched, I don't bother to sit down. I won't be able to sit still. I've run off delivery guys before, ones that try to get out of doing their job by chatting up my employees. But this time, it wasn't about time management. It was because I was jealous.

I haven't felt that tinge of fury in a long fucking time, and I hate it just as much now as I did back then. I forgot what it felt like to have your blood boil in such an animalistic way, that caveman desire to mark your territory. Only thing is, she's not my territory. She's not my anything and she can't be. It would be like this every fucking day and everything would fall to pieces. This feeling is not what I want. It's not what she wants, either.

I feel her behind me. The air shifts, a lavender scent rippling around the room. My body is on alert as she comes closer. I don't have to turn around to know that.

"Graham? Is everything okay?" she asks.

"Fine," I say, shoving my hands in my pockets. "Did you get your package?"

"No," she says. "I got yours."

I fight the smile on my lips and continue to stare forward. I need to get a hold of this ridiculousness before it overtakes me.

"I have to say," she says as she comes around into full view, "I thought your package would be bigger."

"Is that so?" I ask, trying not to break.

A ruby red dress skims the curves of her body, a shiny necklace tucked in her cleavage. None of that is as spectacular as her smile.

This is the exact fucking reason I've avoided being around her today. My cock is hardening, my tongue nearly panting as I watch her body move in that damn dress. How did I ever think this could work? I'm a fool.

"It's a printer cartridge," she says. "I'll put it in the media room." We watch each other, the force between us stirring once again. I swear you can almost see it. "I just . . . You aren't upset with me, are you?"

"No." I force a swallow. "Of course not."

"Good."

She runs her hands down the front of her dress the same way I do my hair when I'm flustered. Her lip is in between her teeth, her eyes on the floor.

I lift her chin with the tip of my finger. My chest tightens from the moment I touch her and I know it's a mistake, but I do it anyway. "Mallory?"

"Yes?"

"I'm not sure I could be upset with you for anything," I say much more gravelly than I intend.

Her head tilts to the side, her cheek pressing against the sleeve of my jacket. Our eyes connect and it's like we're transported to another time and place, one where there are no rules, no fears, no histories or responsibilities.

"For the record," she says, looking at me with her big, whiskey-colored eyes, "I could be upset with you."

I half-laugh as my hand cups her jaw, my thumb stroking the soft skin of her cheek. My mouth drops open just a touch to let actual air in. "I'm sure you could."

"I might be upset with you right now," she whispers.

"Why is that?"

"Because you didn't kiss me yesterday."

I hold her gaze for a long moment, in a way to apologize, before dropping my hand away from her face. "I think that would only complicate things. Don't you?"

The words taste acrid as they fall out of my mouth, and the look she gives me feels even worse as it hits me in the chest. It's not resentful, not broken—for which I'm grateful. It's steely, a cage locking over her feelings.

"You're right. I do," she says, pasting on a smile and taking a step back. "I'm glad one of us has some sense," she winks and trots out of my office. I follow her, shutting the door with a snap.

"It's the right thing," I remind myself, heading back to my desk. "This is the best thing for both of us."

NINE
MALLORY

"HELLO?" I ASK, WITH A little more bite than I intend.

"Mallory?"

"Yes?" I pull out a handful of random items from my junk drawer and put them on the counter. "This is Mallory."

"This is Keenan Marks. Camilla Landry gave me your number."

I lean against the counter and sigh. "Yes, Cam said she was going to. How are you?"

"I'm good. You?"

"Shitty day at work, but otherwise..."

"I've had better days. This starting a new job thing sucks."

"Tell me about it," I groan. "Although I think my particular situation is unique, but whatever."

"Want to have dinner tomorrow and commiserate? Something simple, maybe a pizza or something?"

For a split second, I consider not going. I'm not in a date-going mood, not that I really am sure what that means considering I haven't had a real date in maybe ever. Besides, I don't think it would be fair to him. I'm not sure how he would compare to Graham and I know I'll compare. Fair or not, I will.

"Can I be honest with you?" I ask.

"I hope you will."

"I'm not sure what I'm looking for right now. I just got out of a relationship and I'm not even sure what I want. Does that make sense?" He blows out a breath.

"Well, I didn't know how to approach that topic, but same goes for me. I just got out of one hell of a relationship, and I just want to find someone to laugh with. Buy a pizza or a burger. Maybe catch a concert. So no pressure, Mallory. None at all."

I shut the drawer, confident I'm not going to find my missing pack of batteries. "Perfect! What time were you thinking?"

"Maybe six? At Backstreet? Do you know where that is?"

"Yup. I'll just meet you there."

"I'll look forward to seeing you tomorrow then."

"Same here. Good night."

I end the call and slide my phone across the counter top, watching it slam into a pile of napkins. They go fluttering in the air, half of them landing on the floor. I just watch with no intention of picking them up.

Keenan's call should've energized me. Dates are exciting, right? I'm not sure Eric even really dated me. Regardless, I'm pretty certain I should have some flutter of excitement. Then again, they usually don't come on the heels of having Graham Landry tell you he can't kiss you.

I look Keenan up on social media. He's cute, about my age, with short hair and big puppy dog eyes. He apparently plays a guitar and works at a bar. I vaguely remember him.

He does nothing for me. I'm sure he's sweet—he has some ode to his grandma on one of his pages—but there's no attraction whatsoever. Still, it will be good to get out of the house and to stop thinking about Graham. Who knows, maybe I'll fall breathlessly in love with Keenan and can thereby keep my job?

"Ugh," I say out loud, trying to sort my feelings. They're a big, messy heap and I can't even begin to dig out from under it.

My chest constricts, making it hard to breathe. If I had just not said anything, everything would be fine. I'd be looking forward to seeing him in a suit tomorrow and making plans with Joy for the weekend. Instead, I'm allowing him to command my thoughts.

He's going to fire me. I know it.

***

Graham

"WE'LL BE UP AND RUNNING soon," I say over the steam of my coffee. "I have a few calls to make today, a few things to run by our attorney, then we can sit down next week with Dad and make the final decisions."

"Sounds good. Thanks, G, for getting this put together. I appreciate it, man," Ford says, nodding over his mug.

"It's my job." Of course it's more to me than that, but it's not worth the time it would take to try to explain it. I sit my cup down and take the papers he hands me and stick them in the Landry Security file. "I'll send these to Mallory this morning and get her started on them."

Ford takes a long drink, watching me over the brim. "How's that going?"

"Fine."

"You're a terrible liar."

Chuckling, I lean back in my chair. "She's doing a fine job."

"I haven't been gone so long that I forgot how to decipher all your little nuances," Ford laughs.

"Back to the matter at hand," I say, bringing him back around to non-Mallory topics, "When do you want to launch?"

"As soon as possible. I'm going fucking crazy sitting around."

"You? Sit around?" I roll my eyes.

"It was a figure of speech," he says, standing. "I actually am taking Mom to breakfast today."

I stand, too, and watch him head to the door. "You're making me look like the bad son. Before you came home, I just had to compete with Barrett and Linc and that's not hard."

He pops open the door, looks across Mallory's to office, then steps back inside my office and closes the door. "How in the hell do you get anything done with her sitting out there?"

Glancing at the clock, it's three to eight. My stomach churns as I shrug. "I just try not to look."

"Yeah. Just don't look," he chuckles. "You're telling me you don't imagine her bent over the copy machine?"

"Not as much as I imagine her bent over my desk."

His laughter makes me smile. "If your goal is to simply *not look* at her, you're going to need to put on blinders today, brother. Fucking hell."

"You can wear them too, for that matter." I toss him a look, one that he reads correctly. His hands shoot up in the air, one still holding his cup of coffee.

"I'll just say good morning. It would be rude not to. Anyway," he grins cheekily, "what do you care?"

I fix my gaze on him until he shakes his head and gives me a little wave. He leaves the door open so I can hear him greet Mallory as he leaves. Her voice dances through my office, lifting my heartbeat as the volume of her tone softens. I find myself angling to listen to every last note, a sound I've craved since she left the office last night.

I'm beyond fucked. I have no plan for this. I have no clue how to navigate this minefield.

It's been a long time since I've pulled a true all-nighter, but last night, I did. All. Damn. Night. I laid in bed, sat on the sofa, worked in the den, even went for a drive just to try to distract myself from the look on her face when I told her I couldn't kiss her.

Something about watching her eyes lose their playfulness, feeling her physically distance herself from me, pains me in a terrible way. Seeing that look in her eye made me crave to hold her in my arms, to kiss her until I hear her whisper my name.

As if on cue, I hear her giggle from her desk. I smile even though my gut tenses. Lucky for me, I'm already sitting at my desk when she rounds the corner because if I were still standing, seeing her would knock me on my ass.

My pen clamors against the glass top as it tumbles from my fingers, my jaw going right along with it.

Holy. Shit.

A black dress that looks like it's wrapped around her in a hundred different pieces, winds tightly around her gorgeous body. Her hair is thick, wild, but strategically so. I see why Ford told me to wear blinders. "Morning," she says simply. "I was just coming to shut this. I know you like your first few hours of the day quiet."

"I've already been here a few hours." My voice sounds robotic and I try to shake out of this spell, but it's hard—in so, so many ways.

If this is her way of punishing me for not kissing her yesterday, she wins. Punishment doled out and accepted. I'll have blue balls all fucking day.

She begins to pull the door closed when she stops suddenly. "Oh, don't forget your nine o'clock meeting called late yesterday and moved it to nine thirty. I bumped your eleven o'clock appointment until after lunch so you're not rushed."

"What about my appointment at one?" I ask, feeling like I'm grasping at straws. My entire day's schedule is out of whack and I'm scrambling to wake up my computer to pull up my planner, all the while keeping one eye on her.

"I took care of it. They really didn't need to meet with you," she replies. "I faxed them the contracts to sign and asked them to courier them back by the end of the day. It'll be like you met with them, but will save you an hour." With a fake smile and a little shimmy of her hips that is for my benefit, she closes the door. And I just stand there, reminding myself I can't just go open it again.

TEN
MALLORY

I MAKE A KISSY FACE at my reflection, making sure the red lipstick and heavier eye makeup I just applied look good before snapping my compact closed. The little button is lit on my phone, indicating it's five o'clock and I'm officially off-duty. Graham usually comes out to say goodbye or see how my day went, but he doesn't today.

Smiling smugly, I put a fresh spritz of perfume on my wrists and dump my things back in my purse. Every time he did run into me today, he tried to seem unaffected. The fact of the matter is he tried too hard, because it was obvious. Good. Let's see how he reacts to this.

Switching out my office-approved footwear for a pair of black heels, I wheel around to face my computer. This will either work or it won't. Either way, I need it to fall one way or the other. He'll bite or he'll let go—I'm giving him the opportunity and will respond based on his reaction.

I can't handle this back-and-forth. If I have to force his hand a bit, I will. For the both of us.

I type out the email I've been constructing all day in my head.

To: Graham Landry, CEO
From: Mallory Sims, Administrative Assistant
Re: Employment
Dear Mr. Landry,
Due to recent events, I would like to deliver my intent to leave employment with Landry Holdings. I will stay as long as necessary to find an adequate replacement, however, I've come to believe our working relationship may not be sustainable.
I appreciate the opportunity to work with you and will gladly assist any way I can in transferring the position.
Thank you again,
Mallory

I hit SEND before I can rethink it . . . or before I can add "I wasn't wearing panties today either." I'm not sure how he'll take my announcement, but it's Friday, so I should be good to go until Monday morning.

I almost make it around my desk when his office doors fly open. He stands in the doorway, his eyes dark. "Can you come talk to me for a minute before you leave?"

"Sure," I say, my heart striking my ribcage with so much force I think it might stop beating. Following him in his office, he closes the door behind him.

"Have a seat." He motions towards the chair in front of his desk as he drops into his seat behind it.

Pulling myself together, I cross one leg over the other as casually as I can manage and smile. He bit. Now to see how hard. "What can I do for you, Graham?"

"You're quitting?"

"I take it you got my email."

He sighs, not out of exasperation, but out of annoyance. *That* annoys me.

"Does that not work for you?" I ask. He just narrows his eyes.

"Look, Graham, I don't want to complicate things for you. And I think I have," I gulp.

"You have no idea," he mutters. He shakes his head. "This is because I didn't kiss you yesterday, isn't it?"

"Don't be so self-absorbed," I say, although he's right. This *is* because he didn't kiss me, but I'm not sure how I would've felt, besides even more turned the hell on, if he had. Maybe it would've been awkward either way and we would've ended up here regardless. "This is about me wanting to work somewhere that I can understand my boss. Where I don't feel his eyes undressing me one minute and then having him act like it's a completely ridiculous thing to think the next."

"I've never acted like it would be ridiculous to kiss you." His eyes darken further. I shiver as he stares at me, slowly lifting himself out of his chair.

"I'll admit I like it when you look at me like that."

"How?"

"Like you are right now," I breathe. "Like I'm pretty or interesting."

"I do that because you are."

"But you look at me like that, you let me know what you want to do to me, then you refuse to follow through. You play with me."

"I didn't toy with you," he growls, coming around the desk. He stands in front of me, leaning back against his desk. Looking down, his face dances with early evening shadows.

"You did, but no more than I did you," I admit. "I'm no victim, Graham. But you don't play fair."

I'm acutely aware of the rise and fall of my chest. His gaze is so determined, so heavy, that it nearly stings. I want to stand, to even this power field a little, but I can't move. He makes it impossible.

"That's why you wore this today, to get to me," he maintains. "To drive me fucking nuts all day while you parade around, flaunting that body in my face."

"You thought this was for you?"

He's caught off guard, which only spurs me on.

"I hate to break the news to you, Graham, but I have a date tonight." I watch that bit of news settle over his features. He forces a swallow.

Uncrosses his arms. Narrows his eyes as his lips form a thin line.

"So, if you don't mind . . ." I say, standing and facing him. "He's probably waiting."

"Who is he?" he demands.

"Does it matter?"

"I wouldn't have asked if it didn't."

"Fine. He's a friend of Camilla's."

"Camilla did this?" he almost booms. "You're dating a friend of my sister's?"

"I'm going on a date with a friend of your sister's," I correct him, like he's crazy. "I'm not dating anyone."

"Where's he taking you?" he demands.

"So many questions . . ."

"For heaven's sake, Mallory," he says, throwing his hands up in the air, "Is he even taking you to a place that uses a damn fork? Does he have enough fucking sense to pay for your meal?"

Technically, you don't need a fork for pizza. I giggle, my way of releasing some of the anxiety that's rocketing through me from the way he's looking at me. "It doesn't matter to me where he takes me, Graham. It's the fact that he *wants* to take me at all."

"It does matter, especially when you're dressed like you want to fuck. Damn it, Mallory!"

I look him right in the eye, my heart pounding. "Maybe I do, Graham." I turn to leave, and he grabs my arm and spins me around. I catch myself on one of the chairs and gasp as he steps into my personal space. His cologne surrounds me, but this time, it's mixed with something else. Something muskier. Something edgier. Something purely male that I've never experienced before but know I'll never forget.

"You were making a point today." Graham takes the final step to close the distance between us, our chests nearly touching. "Point. Made."

I gasp a quick breath.

"Now it's my turn to make a fucking point." With that, his lips cover mine and I melt into his arms.

ELEVEN
MALLORY

THE CONTACT BREAKS SOME SORT of invisible barrier, not just the physical one. As our lips touch, the softness of his press against mine, his hands wrap around my waist. It's as if a green flag is waved and we're given the signal to go.

His kisses are deliberate. Each press, each lick, each time his tongue slides across my bottom lip is like a step in an intricate dance that I'm more than happy to let him lead.

I'm aware I'm being moved in a circle and feel the sharp bite of his desk dig against the back of my legs. When I pull back just enough to drag in a breath of air, one hand palms the back of my head, his fingers interwoven into my hair. He tugs back just hard enough to give me no choice but to look at him.

I'm putty in his hands, giving up some control in this moment. Strangely, I like it. No, I love it. It's such a turn-on because I'm allowing it. My choice.

"Is this what you want?" Each word is clear, his question emphasized by the look in his eye. Like he wants to eat me up. Like he wants to straight-up devour me.

I am sure. I've been sure since I walked in to Landry Holdings the first day. Logic tells me to consider every possible way this could end terribly. With a decided finger, I hit the override button on the voice in my head and do what I've been pledging to do—live a little bit. At least the consequences, whatever they may be, are based on something I did because I wanted to. And I damn sure want to.

"This is probably against some sort of company policy," I say, reaching up and working his tie loose.

"What do you care? You quit," he grins mischievously. His hands cup my shoulders, kneading them back and forth before dropping down the blades of my back. As they lower, palms flat against the fabric of my dress, I'm inched closer to him.

"I gave you my intent to leave," I utter. "That still makes me an employee."

"Consider the handbook amended," he blazes.

My breath is hot, my mouth watering to taste him again. I ache as he dips beneath the hem of my dress.

"Oh," I draw as he grasps the backs of my thighs. The feel of his skin on mine in such an intimate area, just inches south of the tops of my legs, has my hands shaking just a bit as I pull his tie off his neck.

"Your skin is so soft," he groans, his breathing rougher now, matching mine. "Damn it, Mallory. Why do you do this to me?"

I hold his tie up in the air, letting him see it, then toss it onto the desk behind me. "I feel even softer in other places," I promise.

His chest rumbles almost menacingly. "What am I going to do with you?"

Undoing the top two buttons, I lean in and whisper against his ear, "I didn't think you'd need a game plan laid out for you for this, Graham."

As I fall back on my heels, he steps forward, his cock solid against my belly. I let a slight moan escape, one he doesn't miss because Graham doesn't miss anything. He grins in reaction, his hands determined as they torture me on their slow ascent up the backs of my legs.

One hand slips between my thighs, gently moving them apart

and widening my stance. "I'm going to tell you one thing before this goes any further," he growls, his fingertips searing against my skin.

"What's that?" I nearly pant.

"I won't pretend this didn't happen once it does."

"If you could, I didn't do my job," I breathe. The anticipation of what's coming, of feeling him, of feeling him feeling me, becomes unbearable. Working frantically to undo the buttons lining his chest, I open my stance wider to give him access to whatever he wants.

As he reaches my opening, his pupils dilate. "You aren't wearing panties."

"You're quick."

He growls. Suddenly, I feel him all over me, touching me everywhere, like he can't explore my body fast enough. It staggers me as my senses try to analyze each and every touch.

His thumb glides over the opening of my pussy. He draws in a quick breath, gasping as he realizes just how wet I am for him. His hands skirt over my hips, palming my ass, the solidness of his cock digs into me as he nearly barricades me against his desk.

"Ah!" I moan as his hand lies against my vagina. It's just enough contact to ramp up my desire by a thousand fold, but not enough to get me anywhere I'm desperate to go.

He grins as I rip his shirt open, working my hips to encourage him to touch me for real.

His chest is hard, his abs forming definite squares under the tanned skin. I shove the shirt off his shoulders and then drag my fingertip from his sternum all the way to the band of his pants.

The look in his eyes is ravenous but everything else is calm. Deliberate. Methodical. But when I undo the button of his pants and scoop my hand inside, cupping his thickness, it's him that gasps.

Before I can do anything other than get a confirmation that he's as big as I imagined, I'm lifted up and sat on top of his desk. Things go sliding off each side, a container of paper clips smashing against the floor, spilling everywhere.

My chest heaving, I watch him draw closer until he's immediately in front of my face. "I'm going to have you right here, right now."

"If this takes much longer, I'm going to make myself come right here on your desk with you watching."

His hands falter at the waistband of his boxer briefs, his eyes flipping to mine. "Oh, baby. You're going to come and I'm most definitely going to be watching. But I'm going to be buried so deep inside you that you won't know where you end and I start."

I WANT TO COMPLAIN ABOUT the unhurried way he moves about his office, gathering his clothes, locking the door. The only thing keeping me from objecting is that he's naked and that sight is one I'll happily soak in for as long as I'm allowed.

He's long and lean, muscles cut into his flesh in a way I didn't expect. It's a delicious image—devilish smirk, broad chest, a V that makes me whimper. But it's what that V is pointing at that does me in. A verifiable nine-inch cock, hard as steel, the tip glistening with pre-cum.

If he thinks I was making a point by torturing him today with my dress, he's doing the same thing by making me watch him now. Once I realize this, it's game on.

When he turns back around, my dress is bunched at my waist. One heel-clad foot rests on top of his desk as I recline back on one hand. My other hand is toying with my opening.

He stuttersteps before stopping in place, his eyes glued to my fingers. I press the pad of one into my wetness and then hold it in the air. When his eyes reach mine, I press my lips together. "Looks like I'm a little wet for you, Graham."

"Stop." It's a command, an order, a mandate given in the form of a sexy rasp. But I don't obey. That would be too easy. Instead, I draw my fingertip up my slit until it lands on my pebbled clit.

"Ah," I moan, letting my head fall back, my hair swishing against the desktop. My eyes flutter closed, but jerk back open as his hand wraps around my wrist, his fingertips searing into my skin.

"I told you to stop."

"I heard you," I breathe.

"I will give you every bit of pleasure you have in this office. Understood?"

Instead of answering, I reach between us and palm his cock roughly.

Stroking it up and down, I grin. "Understood."

He bends forward and plants his mouth against mine. This time, there's nothing sweet or easy about it. Like a man that hasn't kissed a woman in years, he moves against me so frantically, so fiercely, I'm breathless. He draws my dress over my head and tosses it to the side, our lips only breaking long enough for the fabric to pass. I succumb to the relentlessness of his kisses, feeling myself weaken against him.

My ass squeaks against the glass as I'm guided towards the edge with a forceful hand on the small of my back. Silky strands of his hair slip through my fingers, and when I tug on a handful of locks, he finally breaks our kiss.

Our breathing ragged, my lips stinging from the delicious assault, he grins wickedly. "Lie back."

His palms resting heavily on my thighs, squeezing them in an almost massage-like fashion, I do as instructed. Through the haze, I mention I'm on the pill and hear him respond, although the specific words are a blur. Lying before him on his desk is the most vulnerable I've ever felt.

My entire body is on display, stretched out like an agreement to be manipulated. A flash of unease begins to rip through me, but when our eyes meet, it subsides as quickly as it came.

His breathing is as intense as mine, the hunger in his eyes burning as hot as the desire spreading like lava through my belly. But there's something else, a quiver in the cerulean blues of his eyes, that quells the anxiety of being studied by a man of his caliber.

"God, Mallory," he almost whispers, a slight shake of his head accompanying it. His finger touches the side of my face, the pad rough against my skin. He blazes a trail down the side of my neck, across my chest, and over the ridges of my stomach.

I see him swallow as he grabs his cock with one hand, my waist with another. He scoots me closer to the edge, his eyes turning wild.

If he can't hear my heartbeat, it's nothing short of a miracle. I can hear it pushing red hot blood through my body, elevating my temperature and need, pure *need*, to the boiling point.

His tip touches my opening, parting me just enough so I know he's there. I gulp, my eyes flipping to his face just in time to watch a slow, indecent smirk touch his lips.

"Come on, Graham," I beg through clenched teeth, gripping the edge of the desk until my knuckles turn white.

"Come on you? Or you want to come?" He swirls his hips, teasing me with his cock.

"Stop with the semantics," I say, wrapping my legs around his waist and inching him closer to me.

He laughs, clearly enjoying my frenzied state. "Maybe I could just stop altogether and kiss you. That's what you wanted, right? Maybe this is a little overboard."

"Fine," I say, starting to sit up. "Give me a kiss and let me get to my date. I'm sure he'd be glad to—Ahhh!"

My breath leaves me in a quick, hasty gush as he fills me completely. My legs shake around him, my eyes fluttering closed as I hear him chuckle. "What were you saying?" he asks cheekily. I don't get to respond before he slides out of me, the head of his cock stretching my opening, before he slips into me again. "I can't hear you."

"God," I moan, tilting my pelvis to give him more access to every piece of me.

His hands find my waist and guide my body off and on his. His length pushes through me, splitting my body open in ways it's never been pushed, kissing the back wall of my vagina.

It's a decadent, wonderful feeling—almost painful but not quite.

His speed hastens, his movements more decided, as he deepens his thrusts.

"Graham," I warn, my body squeaking against the glass. A thought begins to tickle my mind, wondering if anyone can hear us or see us through the windows. Just as that panic begins to settle in, his fingers squeeze me harder as he rocks himself against me.

My arms fly to the side, his stapler crashing to the floor in an unceremonious thump. In and out, he slides through my wetness, my thighs coated with how badly I want him. Need him. *Need this.*

"Open your eyes," he demands, kicking up the tempo another notch. It's nearly unbearable in the most blissful way. Everything is louder— my body against the desk, his against mine. Everything is hotter—the sex-scented air swirling around us, his cologne as it's heated from the sweat dotting his forehead. Everything is just *more* as I lose control and my knees drop to the side. "Eyes, Mallory. Open. There's no visualizing shit but me right now."

When I do open them, his are nearly burning a hole through me. I fight the urge to close them, to relish in all the feelings sparking through me like a fire show.

I release a moan, much louder than I anticipate. "Graham, I . . ." He smirks again, the pad of one thumb hitting my clit. He rubs small, firm circles against the overstimulated bud and it's like a match has been struck. There's no going back.

"I can't . . ." I suck in a breath of air, rocking my legs back so my knees are bent in the air. He pushes me towards the end of the desk as he buries himself in me over and over and *over*. "Graham!" I shriek, knowing I shouldn't, given the situation, but I'm in a state of total helplessness.

My body riots, tightens around him, a part of it wanting to desperately pull away and the other wanting him to slam into me harder—none of which I can vocalize. I just feel the burn, enjoy the explosion and the feel of his cock swelling as he pushes one final time.

I force my eyes to open and watch him lose control. As I fight the end of my climax, I watch him come apart inside of me.

His head thrown back, his mouth hanging open, is so, so sexy and causes a ripple of orgasm to course through me again.

My legs quiver involuntarily as he groans into the air. I try to hold myself in place for his benefit, but my body is too tired. My hips fall back to the desk as he opens his eyes and slowly pulls out.

We catch our breath, me still on the desk and him standing before me like a man that just conquered the world. Now, post-climax, I'm more self-conscious.

As quickly as I can, I swing my legs off the desk and stand on my shaky stems. I avoid his eyes, even though I know they're on me.

Tucking my boobs back into my bra and finding my dress on the floor, I finally raise my gaze to his. "That was better than a kiss," I say with a smile. I leave him standing in the middle of his office, his jaw hanging open, as I head into the bathroom I saw him go into earlier. As the lights flip on and the door closes behind me, I fall against the wall breathless.

TWELVE
GRAHAM

IT TAKES THREE TRIES TO get my belt secured. I don't even attempt my tie.

I may have gotten off, but I'm still fucking high on her. There is no after-sex dump, no bottoming out of desire that makes you feel human again.

The door opens and I pivot on my heel without thinking. She's standing in my office, no worse for the wear. The only indication of the last few minutes is a little plumpness to her lips and a ruffle of her hair.

The fact that she looks more beautiful post-coitus is disconcerting. An orgasm is supposed to bring you to your senses. It's supposed to quell the hunger, make you think logically and feel less needy. So why that isn't working in my favor now is worrisome. Why am I still considering kissing her, sitting her on the loveseat and asking about Columbia and business school and yoga?

Neither of us speaks. We stand, fidgeting, as we feel out the other. The twinkle of anxiety isn't hidden in her eyes, the shuffle of her heels against the floor another flag that she's unsure of where we stand.

I would offer her some comfort if I could find it. Truth is, I don't fucking know where we stand now either. I'd like to be able to see her Monday morning and not feel like . . . this. There has to be a solution.

"I'll make reservations at Zuva. My friend Fenton Abbott has been asking me to try his new restaurant anyway," I say, clearing my throat while I search for my discarded tie. "We can talk there."

Fresh air would do us both some good, maybe clear out the pheromones still swirling around my office. She doesn't answer, but when I look at her, she's smiling. Good sign.

"Let me find my phone . . ." Looking around my office, I see it lying against the wall.

"Graham?" She moves in front of me towards the door. "I already have plans tonight. Remember?"

My hand drops to the side. Surely I misheard her. "Excuse me?"

"I have plans. I told you that when I came in here."

"You're still going?" My temple throbs. There's no way she's going to some take out dinner with some prepubescent punk after what just happened.

She shrugs lightly. "Yeah. I told him I'd be there."

"Your cum is sitting in a pool on my desk," I say, motioning to the evidence. "And you are going on a date with someone else?"

Her brows pull together in faux confusion. "I'm not sure I understand why you care?"

"Are you serious, Mallory?"

"The question is are *you* serious, Graham?"

My jaw clenches. I wish I had my tie. I'd fucking tie her ass up on that loveseat and refuse to let her leave. Kidnapping? Maybe. But at least she'd have some sense fucked into her before I let her up.

How can she waltz out of here, to see another man no less, and leave me worked up?

"Did you think fucking me would make me not go with Keenan?"

Her audacity sparks something feral inside me. Stalking across my office, I stand just feet in front of her.

"I'm going to be late," she says, a tease in her tone.

"You're really going?" When she nods, I walk towards her until her back is against the wall. My hand slides between her legs and she parts them without objection. She's wearing panties now, which makes me happy.

Dipping my finger inside her still-soaked body, I slide it roughly through her slit. When I pull it out, it glistens in the light. "Be careful," I warn. "You still have me dripping out of you."

Her lips part and I watch her try to contain herself. "I'll keep that in mind." She pushes off the wall, her body coming so close to mine it nearly touches, before walking out the door without even looking back.

As the latch shuts, everything hits me all at once. The chaos of my office. The confusion in my head. Her juices on my desk.

Oh my God. I didn't use a condom.

I didn't use a fucking condom.

My hand slaps my forehead as I pace a circle. What am I fucking doing? How did I manage to lose that much control? *Fuck!*

Not only did I just fuck up epically, I just gave her the upper hand. I have to regain this and quick.

I scrub my fingertips down my face, hoping some sense filters back in my brain. This isn't just out of control. This is borderline psychotic.

I don't do this. This is Lincoln shit. This is the stuff Barrett used to call and ask for advice on how to repair it because he'd let the damage be done.

Damage be done. It's sure as shit done here in so many ways.

Picking up the strewn items and placing them semi-close to where they belong, I try to tell the anxiety in my gut to stand down.

I can fix this.

Taking a deep breath, I fall in my chair and don't look at the imprint of her round ass on the glass that covers the top of my desk in front of me. That won't help. Instead, I squeeze my eyes closed and imagine this is a situation Lincoln has presented me with. What would I say?

If this were one of my brothers, I'd tell them they're ridiculous. That they could have sex with any woman they want. Why do they have to pick a woman they work with, a woman with so much access to all the things that are important to them? Why compromise business with pussy? It's weak. It's stupid.

I'm fucking stupid.

I'd tell them to break things off slowly, but to get out of the situation as quickly and harmoniously as possible and then not get into it again. I'd probably call them reckless and rash a few times for good measure.

Yet, when I open my eyes and all I see is her, I know it's not going to be that easy. I need her help.

Chuckling, I roll my eyes. I'm so lying to myself.

When I imagine her smile, I know I'm screwed. And when I remember that she's with another guy, I know I'm in way over my head and I have to get out of it before I drown. I have to regain control. I need this on my terms.

Wheeling my chair around, I open her email from earlier. My fingers begin clicking the keys.

To: Mallory Sims, Administrative Assistant

From: Graham Landry, CEO

Re: Employment

Dear Ms. Sims,

Due to recent events, I'm declining your request for termination of employment with Landry Holdings. You are expected to be at your desk by eight o'clock on Monday morning.

Mr. Landry

"THAT'S IT," I SAY, SHUFFLING the papers until the full Gulica Insurance file is on top. This quote is our coup, a rate nearly a third of all other competitors without having to resubmit our financials. It's huge for Ford, cutting his start-up costs in half.

I stretch my arms overhead. Picking up my glass, the last swallow of an Old-fashioned in the bottom, I carry it through the house and into the kitchen.

The sky is dark as I peer out the window over the sink. My stomach rumbles, protesting the cluster of nerves that's been wound in it all evening. Half of my attention has been on Landry Security, the other half on Mallory.

The glass hits the bottom of the sink with more of a thud than strictly safe. Both hands grasping the ledge of the farmhouse ceramic, I bow my head.

It feels like I'm torn in half, part of me living the life I know and the other being pulled away by some crazy need. Need for what, I don't know. I've never had this problem before. I'm great at tuning out the noise and focusing. It's my forte. If only I could focus right now on what I should. Namely, not her.

There's nothing clean about this. As a matter of fact, it's so fucking tangled that I can't manage to straighten it out no matter how much I try.

"Hello?" I say, answering my phone after the second ring.

"Hey, Graham. It's Camilla."

"You avoid my calls left and right and then call me randomly on a Friday night. If you called to tell me you've gotten yourself in trouble, I really don't want to hear it tonight, Camilla."

She laughs through the phone. "I'm not in trouble. I was just seeing how your week went."

Spinning around, I let my back rest against the marble counter. It feels good against the scratches in my skin from Mallory's heels.

Just like that, I'm fighting a hard-on. "Graham?"

"I'm here. Just getting a drink," I lie. "This week went well.

Should it have?" I give her a second to consider where I'm going with this.

"Mallory said she offered to quit today."

"I didn't accept it."

"She said that too," she laughs. Her words calm the acid in my stomach just a bit. "I don't think she meant it. What do you think of her?"

"I'm not discussing this with you, Swink," I say, using the nickname our grandfather gave her years ago because she's so nosey.

Camilla sighs. "You want to know what I think?"

"Not really."

"Graham! Stop it and listen to me."

Rolling my eyes, I switch hands. "I am. I'm listening to you meddle." My jaw clenches. "Want to hear what I have to say about you setting her up on a date tonight?"

"Oh, did that bother you?" she asks sweetly.

"Why do I suspect that's why you did it?"

"Because you're not stupid," she laughs. "Look, Ford and Lincoln have both said you like her. And," she says loudly over my objection, "I'm friends with her, G. I know . . . things."

"I know if you pull that again, your check from Landry Holdings next month will be late."

"You wouldn't dare!" she giggles.

"Try me. Now I have to get back to work since I've gotten nothing done this week."

"That's telling," she mutters.

"That's telling that something needs to change. I have Lincoln's wedding to monitor before he fucks up his life. I have Ford's security business to take care of, Barrett's odds and ends he left behind here to deal with," I sigh. "I have investment meetings all week for our portfolio and a land deal Dad wants to look at early next month that I have a lot of prep work to put in. Sienna is wanting to pull a part of her money out and invest in some fucking hat line that will be a total fucking loss, and I have to deal with Mom trying to convince me to let

Sienna spread her wings. Then I have your bullshit, creeping around God knows where—"

"Stop it."

"I could if you'd just be open with me about who you are seeing."

"Who says I'm seeing anyone?"

I look at the ceiling in exasperation. "You said yourself I'm not stupid. Dad wants me to hire Parker to follow you around and—"

"You wouldn't!"

"I haven't," I warn, "but I will if you don't 'fess up soon."

She gruffs through the line, mumbling about me being overprotective, but it's nothing I haven't heard before. Finally, she sighs. "Why don't you go take a bubble bath or something? Take the night off."

"I don't have the luxury to be unproductive, Camilla."

"Easy there, big guy," she says softly. "I didn't say you did. I'm just saying . . ."

"Saying what?" I bark at my sister, then immediately feel guilty. "I'm sorry. I'm just stressed out."

"I can tell."

Silence stretches between us and I kick myself for letting things get like this. This isn't me. I manage shit. Shit doesn't manage me.

If I break, it all falls apart. If I fail, we all go down.

"When is the last time you did something you wanted to do?" she asks. "Not for work or for any of us, but for you?"

Pulling the phone away from my ear, I see an incoming text from a number I don't know. "I don't know, Cam. What's it matter?"

"You need to take care of yourself," she insists. "You act like you're this . . . stoic guy that doesn't need anyone. And maybe you don't, I don't know. But you need to enjoy your life. Find some balance."

"I'm balanced. My scale just looks different than yours."

"Balance is balance, Graham. It means what it means."

This is brewing into a fight, one I don't want to have. Not just because it's Camilla, but because I just don't have the energy. Or the temperament. "I'm not in the mood to have this conversation," I tell her.

"Can I offer you a suggestion?"

"Sure," I sigh. "Then I need to go." I pull my phone away from my face again as an alert beeps through.

"Give Mallory a chance. She really needs this job, Graham, and I know she's smart and—"

"It was her that tried to quit," I remind her, my frustration going up a few notches. "I didn't try to fire her. But, come to think of it, maybe I should've let her. It would resolve a few things."

I'm right. I should've. But the thought of not seeing her on Monday morning gives me a feeling I'm not willing to deal with yet. I need to wrap my head around this before I go making huge moves. Well, bigger moves than I did today. Or sinking inside her again . . .

"Maybe you should consider why you didn't," she says gently.

"I need to go, Cam."

"Come have lunch with Mom and I tomorrow."

"I'll try," I say. "I'll talk to you soon."

Before she can pull me in a different direction, I end the call. Flipping to texts, I see the same number has hit me up a few times. I click on line.

There are four messages in green.

I got your email. You can't just "decline my request" without talking to me about it.

Although, I find it telling that you want to keep me around. I'm good, huh? ;)

Just in case you were curious, we used forks. Real metal ones.

We had a meal and went our (separate) ways. My thighs are still kind of stuck together. Guess I'll grab a bath and consider your REQUEST that I stay with your company.

My fingers are striking the keys on my phone before I can consider it.

It wasn't a request. Don't be late.

Her response pings immediately.

Her: What if I am?

Me: I'll make you work over.

Her: Does any of that include desk work in your office? If so, I'll see you at ten after eight.

My hand goes to my cock as I imagine her on my desk, splayed out just for me.

Me: I'll say you performed well for your first week.

Her: I'd say it wasn't terrible working for you.

Me: Wow. Thanks for the vote of confidence.

Her: Could've been worse. Could've been better.

Me: Any tips going forward?

Her: Use your mouth more, Mr. Landry. It's how deals are made.

THIRTEEN
MALLORY

THE SUN SHINES BRIGHTLY, WARMING my skin as I walk through Xavier Park with a mug of hot tea. I love Sundays, always have. The world sort of slows down for a second. People are happy from sleeping in or from going to church or hanging out on the sofa in their pajamas.

It's a little treasure of life I'd forgotten about. With Eric, Sundays were a day to clean the house, iron clothes, change plumbing. There was never a leisurely breakfast or a trip to the country or a morning in bed with toast and television. I didn't even realize how much I missed Sunday mornings until I got back to Savannah.

My phone stuffed in my pocket, I watch the geese on the lake and the kids playing on the swing sets and slides with their parents sitting at picnic tables, reading the paper.

It all makes my heart happy. The fresh air. The peace. The memories of Graham.

Keenan and I hit it off on our date, if that's what you want to call it, but only as friends. By the third slice of pizza, we were joking about how pathetic we were, each clearly hung up on someone else.

I haven't felt this happy in as long as I can remember. Maybe it's not so much happy, it's content. Optimistic. I'm not sure why the world looks a hint sunnier today, but it does.

My thigh vibrates, my ringtone jingling in my pocket. I pull it out and see Graham's name on the screen. Hurrying to a vacant table, I set my tea down and smile ear-to-ear as I answer it. "Hello?"

"Good morning," he says. "I'm sorry to bother you today."

"It's no problem."

"I took the entire Landry Security file home and I can't find the Gulica quote."

"It's in the red paperclip. The top page is a yellow sheet, I think. Something from . . ."

"I got it," he says. The way he says it makes me wonder if he didn't have it all along. "Thank you. Good memory."

I climb on the table, picking up my tea. I love the sound of his voice.

It warms me from the inside out. "You're welcome."

"So . . ." He takes in a quick breath. "What are you doing today?"

"I'm at Xavier Park. Just walking around, drinking some tea," I sigh happily. "I love Sunday mornings. What can I say?"

"Strangely, I do too," he chuckles. "People are less assholish on Sunday. It's like religion hits them or something."

"My thoughts exactly."

We laugh together, the kids behind me giggling as they run from the swings to the slide.

"When I was growing up," Graham says, "my grandmother used to make a big Sunday dinner. We'd go to church and then to her house and she'd fry chicken or pork chops or make egg salad sandwiches. Us kids would run around her yard, raising hell, then we'd eat and watch football or take a nap or something. Those are some of the best memories of my life."

"I'd just wake up and eat cereal and watch cartoons. My parents worked on Saturdays, so we'd have to go to a babysitter. Sunday was the day we got to stay home and sleep in. It was our lazy day. But you probably know nothing about being lazy."

"Not really," he chuckles. "But I do less on Sundays than I do the rest of the week. I may not take it completely off, but I do sleep in."

"Until when? Five?"

"Six," he protests. "I slept in until six today."

"Slacker," I tease. "I see you taking the day off. That's why you called me to see about papers, right?"

"You got me."

I take a sip of my tea, the honey at the bottom of the cup oozing to the top, touching my lips. "Tell me you at least had something crazy for breakfast."

"Define crazy."

"Kid's cereal. Stuffed French toast. Biscuits and gravy."

"I haven't had kid's cereal since I was a kid."

"Why not?"

"Because I'm not a kid."

"That makes no difference," I point out. "Those chocolate pebbles are the best thing ever. Let them sit in the milk until they're a little soggy and ... oh my goodness."

"I used to like the fruity ones. Only as soon as they hit the milk, though. I hate them soggy."

A smile touches my lips as I imagine Graham as a little boy, eating cereal as fast as he could. It's adorable, probably even less adorable than it really was.

"Well, I had chocolate chip pancakes with butter and syrup," I tell him. "Not much more adultish than chocolate cereal."

"I haven't had pancakes in forever."

"Who are you?" I joke. "What do you even eat?"

"I had a blueberry muffin this morning. And a bowl of oatmeal."

"So boring."

He laughs. "So true."

"Maybe I'll bring you some pancakes tomorrow morning. I feel like you're deprived."

"Oh, so you're coming in to work tomorrow, huh?" he singsongs. "Good to know."

"Someone didn't accept my intent to resign."

"Someone was bluffing with her intent to resign."

I blush because he's kind of right. I didn't want to resign, but I absolutely would have if it would've made things easier. But talking to him today doesn't feel awkward. Maybe it even feels easier.

"I wasn't exactly bluffing."

"You were," he says simply. "But I'll tell you something."

"What's that?"

"I like the way you bluff."

"I like the way you do a lot of things," I say quietly.

"You're pretty well-versed in a number of things as well."

Standing, I head towards the lake and consider my next move. I'm not sure where to go with this, so I change the subject.

"One thing I don't do well is ski," I say randomly. "I wish I could."

"Where the hell did that come from?"

"I'm looking at the lake and thinking about the last time I water skied. It was a couple of years ago and I thought I was going to drown. I never did stand for more than a few seconds."

"We go out every summer and fuck around," he says. "I love to water ski. Snow ski. It takes focus and quiet and most of it is in your mind." He pauses for a long moment. "Maybe someday I can give you a lesson or two."

"That could be a summer bonus. Three free ski lessons."

"I never said they were free."

Taking a sip of my tea to wet my throat, I try to wrap my head around what that means.

He groans into the phone. "My father is calling. We're working on a charity thing for Lincoln, so I really need to take it."

"Go," I say. "Take it. I'm glad you found the paper you were looking for."

"Me too."

The way he says that makes me think it was never lost, but I'll never be sure.

"I'll see you tomorrow," I say. "At eight sharp."

"Goodbye, Graham."

"Bye, Mallory."

FOURTEEN
MALLORY

I WOKE UP WITH A smile. On a Monday. This surely means the world is ending.

My tea in hand, my hairbrush standing in for a microphone in the other, I dance around my apartment singing nineties music while I get ready for the day.

While my moisturizer sinks in, I check my email. My inbox has a few junk mail pieces, but buried between them is a notification from the local university. I click it, humming the chorus to a song about opinions being like assholes.

It's a breakdown of their undergraduate degrees and an online form to begin the application process.

Turning the music down and placing my tea on the counter, I go back to the form. Could I do this? Am I ready for this?

It was great in theory when I sent in the request form, thinking it would get lost in online traffic and I could say I tried. But it's here. Looking at me. And all of a sudden, things seem real. And terrifying.

What if I do it and fail? What if I get in it and hate it? What if I can't hack it?

What if I really am the little poor girl from the trailer park with parents that can already say, "Told ya so"?

Exiting out of the program, I down the rest of my tea and then head back to the bathroom. As I flip through my lipsticks, I think about Graham. He's unlike Eric or the guy I dated briefly before him when I was eighteen. Graham is mature. Confident. He's in charge, but not in a stroppy way. After you break through all that obsessive and relentless attention to detail and being a total control freak, he's fun. I bet he's even sweet. Plucking out a new tube I got yesterday, I know it's the right shade. Red. *I'm definitely going with red.*

It's the color of ripe cherries and I love it. I count to thirty, not letting them touch, and do another layer. Once that's dry, I swipe on some gloss and check out the entire ensemble in the mirror.

It's just what I was going for. Professional and studious, yet just a little sexy flair with the red lips, slightly off-the-shoulder top, and the highest heels I own that are daytime appropriate.

A bubble of anxiety rustles in my abdomen and as hard as I try to ignore it, it's there. I feel it, nestled heavily in my stomach. I'm not sure what part of it I'm most nervous about. He clearly wants me to come back to work, but I'm terrified it will be weird even though talking to him yesterday helped.

Then it hits me. That's why he called me. To make it less weird.

A full-body shiver takes over and I force the scent of him out of my thoughts. I can't. Today, I'm determined to be Mallory Sims, Administrative Assistant extraordinaire. I will resist his power. I will not succumb to his prowess.

Yeah, right.

He fucked me on his desk. I've seen him naked. He's felt me in ways only three men in my life have.

I don't feel ashamed or guilty. Eric would call this "whore-ish" behavior, but it doesn't feel that way at all. It's fun. Liberating. It makes me feel wanted and I like it. A lot.

I just need to keep that in check.

Leaving the bathroom, I try not to trip over the cord to my curling iron.

Ten minutes later, I'm in my car and on my way to Landry Holdings to see what will happen. I'll just read his cues and go from there.

***

"You're not late."

I jump at his voice, although I knew he was watching me. His door was open when I arrived and I pretended not to notice.

When I look at him, leaned against the doorframe, every bit of willpower is out the window right along with any lockdown I may have thought I had on my libido.

Fitted black suit pants and jacket with a light blue shirt and straight black tie make him look like the CEO he is while teasing me with what I now know is beneath. The sexiest thing he's wearing, though, is a smug look on his handsome face. Monday morning has never looked so good. "Good morning to you too," I say, rolling my eyes like I'm not affected by him. "Glad you noticed my punctuality."

"And here I was hoping you'd be late and you disappoint."

My belly clenches. "I can't work over tonight. I'll aim for disappointment tomorrow."

"Why is that?"

"I have places to be."

He strolls predatorily to the front of my desk and plants his hands in front of me. Leaning in, his eyes picking up the blues in his shirt, he narrows them. "And why is that?"

"I have plans." I enunciate every syllable, letting my lips fall in a pout. He notices. The wheels turning in his head, he thinks for a long moment before responding.

"And what may those be?" he asks.

"Do you really want to know?"

"You're damn right I do."

I lean in so close I can feel the heat of his breath on my face. "I teach yoga tonight, Mr. Landry. Is that all right with you?"

"Is this a co-ed class by any chance?"

"Why? You wanna come?"

His chest rumbles, his gaze turning wicked. "Oh, baby, do I ever."

"I—"

A sound booms behind Graham, interrupting me. Graham shoves off my desk and I look around him to see Ford walking in.

"Did I interrupt something?" he grins.

"Just letting Mallory know you and Dad are coming in this morning to go over the final security plans. She's making sure my morning is open until lunchtime." He glances at me and I nod. "What time is Dad coming?"

"He should be here any minute." Ford stands alongside his brother and smiles knowingly at me. "How are you?"

"Good." I return his smile and keep it as un-noteworthy as possible. As much like my thighs aren't burning to be separated by his brother as I can manage. "How are you this morning?"

"Not as good as you, I don't think." He tosses me a wink before looking at his brother. "I'll wait in the conference room. Are we using the one down the hall?"

"Yeah. I'll be in there in a few minutes. Let me take care of a few things and grab the files."

"You go take care of those things. I'd hate for you to be distracted." Ford leaves, chuckling under his breath.

Once he's gone, Graham shoves his hands in his pockets and turns around. He studies me carefully, like he's not sure what to say.

"Graham, listen," I begin, "I'm sorry about all this. I mean, I'm not sorry. Friday was amazing. I might have . . ." I start, then stop.

"You might have what?" he smirks.

"Nothing," I smirk back. "On a serious note, I don't want this to blow back on me. I need this job. I like working here. Maybe we could transfer me to another department or something."

He bites the inside of his jaw. "No," he says on an exhale. "That'll never work. I think that would cause more problems than just leaving you here, actually."

"Really? I was thinking maybe it would just put us out of sight, out of mind."

"I didn't see you all weekend and I couldn't get you out of my mind," he admits guiltily.

Forcing a swallow, I try to keep myself steady. The air thickens around us, white noise flowing past my ears. "I couldn't get you out of mine either."

"We've found ourselves in a predicament." He sits on the corner of my desk, his face sobering. "I need a little bit of time to get this figured out. I need you to work here. You fit in our company perfectly. But I do need to concentrate and I don't know how to swing that."

Our gazes hold on to the admissions, the energy between us crackling. His features soften and I want to reach out and touch his face, feel the smoothness of his cheeks, but I don't.

"Is my schedule clear today?" he asks.

"I cleared it on Friday. Ford called and mentioned the meeting, so I went ahead and rearranged things. I also dug out a few files I thought we may need based on my conversation with your brother."

Graham's brows shoot to the ceiling. "Very good." He stands and disappears into his office. When he returns, he motions for me to follow. "This should take most of the morning. Take notes, ask questions if you don't understand something, and try to breathe." He leans in and smiles. "Don't forget to breathe."

"Will do. And Graham?" I ask when his hand hits the door.

"Yeah?"

"I want you to know something."

"What's that?"

"You look incredible today."

The corner of his lip tugs up. "Thank you. So do you."

"I'm not sure how I'm going to handle this visual and then seeing you in action. I might have to, you know . . ." I wink.

His eyes blaze, his hand falling off the door. "You wouldn't dare."

"No, probably not," I shrug playfully.

"Don't you even think about it."

"Well, it wouldn't technically be in your office, so it wouldn't be against the rules."

"The rules are now amended to include all Landry property," he declares.

I sigh, looking at him through my lashes.

"Mallory, for the love of God, stop fucking with me. I need to concentrate." The door flies open and we start down the hall. Employees step to the side as we make our way down, mutterings of "Good morning, Mr. Landry" with a few swoons from women clasping notebooks to their chest can be heard as we pass by.

Once we reach the end of the hallway, he turns to me. "Behave." Before I can answer, the door is open and inside we go.

FIFTEEN
MALLORY

A LONG, MARBLE TABLE THE color of sand extends the length of the conference room. Ford and his father sit across from each other, Graham and I sit at either end.

The security meeting has lasted three hours, most of which I've sat and watched Graham in action. His brain works so fast, his intelligence so apparent, that I'm awestruck. I've worked with bright men before, but nothing like this. He's on another level with facts, figures, insight that blows my mind. How does one man, at his age, no less, have so much knowledge?

Everything Ford or Mr. Landry ask, Graham has the answer. He seems to have thought and researched this from every possible angle and I'm beyond impressed.

And beyond turned on.

"All we need to close up this piece are the numbers for the insurance. Do you have them?" Mr. Landry asks, turning to Graham. He starts to flip through his files, his forehead crinkled perfectly.

He doesn't have them. I do. In our little banter this morning, he left them on my desk.

"You had me bring them, Graham," I say, sliding the file to his father. "Remember?"

A look of relief washes over his face. "Thank you, Mallory."

"You're welcome. Also," I say, pulling out a notepad, "I found this in Linda's drawer. It looks like there were notes taken by someone at some point in a meeting about training courses and different licenses."

"We've been looking for that!" Ford exclaims as I scoot the legal pad down the table to him. "We've looked everywhere. With Graham's assistant merry-go-round, we didn't know where these went."

"They were in a file buried in the back of my desk," I explain. "There's no notation on them at all to indicate what they're for. I just knew because I've been working with you all on this."

Mr. Landry peers at me much the same way Graham does. "How long have you worked here?"

"Not long," I reply, looking at Graham. He's almost beaming at me. "A couple of weeks."

"I like you," he says, almost like an afterthought as he flips through the file. "These insurance numbers look great. Let's get some lunch and then get started on location. I really like that one downtown, but I know Ford prefers the one on Woodrose Avenue."

They all start to stand and I clear my throat. "I hope it's not out of line, but I ordered you all lunch. It should be here in about twenty minutes."

"You did?" Graham asks.

"You told me this would last through the morning," I shrug. "Not taking a lunch break will expedite this. That's what you want, right, Ford?"

"Yeah," he says, grinning at me. "Thanks, Mallory."

"No problem."

"Graham, if you ever want to get rid of Mallory, I'll take her." Graham flashes his brother a look that only makes him laugh.

"I was kidding," Ford says, "but not kidding. If this doesn't work out," he says, looking at me, "I have this company I'm starting..."

"She's employed," Graham says.

"Boys," Mr. Landry interjects, silencing them both, "she's sitting right here." He looks at me and smiles. "And she's not stupid. If you need a job, I'll hire you."

We all laugh before they return to their discussions about location and square footage, and I find myself spacing out while I watch my boss. His fingers twist a pen, flipping it back and forth, while volleying ideas with his family members. The way they defer to him, ask for his opinions, the way he's ready with a plan for every possible path is such a turn-on.

I take my hands off the table and place them in my lap.

The movement gets Graham's attention, but he doesn't miss a beat. He continues his little speech on utility prices, his eyes trained on mine. I hold his gaze, widening my eyes, teasing him. I could never go through with this here, not in front of his brother and father. But he doesn't know that. And this is fun.

Graham's head cocks to the side in a silent warning, and I can't help but smirk. I wiggle my eyebrows and watch his lips press together. He clears his throat, shifting in his seat.

I form an "o" with my lips and wink at Graham. That does it. In one swift movement, he stands. His brother and father lean back, puzzled.

"Is everything okay?" Mr. Landry asks. "Graham?"

"I need to get something from my office. Excuse me," he gruffs, storming out the door.

I bolt upright, not sure what to make of that. When they look at me, I shrug. "He didn't have a lot of coffee this morning," I offer weakly.

Ford chuckles. "He seemed a little preoccupied when I got here today. I think he was focused, and I know when I'm thinking about work like that," he grins cheekily, "coffee gets easily overlooked."

"Graham does have a drive that's hard to find," Mr. Landry offers. Ford tries to stifle a laugh. "Would you agree, Mallory?"

"Most definitely," I giggle.

"He's acting odd today," Mr. Landry comments to Ford. "Is he acting all right with you?"

"He's fine, Dad. Don't worry about him."

"I don't, usually," Mr. Landry says, shaking his head. "He has his shit together more than any of you, which concerns me today when I see him like this. I—"

He's interrupted by a buzzing sound loud in the air.

"Mallory, would you see me in my office, please?"

Graham's voice is clear and not without a brusqueness that's impossible to miss.

"Sure. I'll be right there." I stand, smoothing down my dress. The intercom disconnects with a thump. "I moved the creamer on him," I joke. "I'll be right back, gentlemen."

I feel their gazes on my back as I exit and weave through the people standing in the halls on their lunch break. Once I enter my office, I see his doors are open.

A feeling of anticipation lingers in the air. I approach the doorway and find him standing next to his desk, his tie loose around his neck, his hair ruffled. His jaw is set as his gaze sweeps over me.

"What the fuck are you doing?" he asks.

"I was still taking notes. I was doing my job."

"You were fingering yourself."

"You don't know that."

He storms towards me, grabbing the edge of the door and slamming it behind me, locking it with a flourish. "If I touch you now, will you be wet?"

"Like that has anything to do with if I was touching myself or not," I say. "Just looking at you—"

I'm against the wall, the force causing the painting over the love seat to shake. His lips are all over mine, my jaw, down my neck to my chest. "Oh, God," I moan, soaking in the way his hands roam my body—my arms, my cheeks, down my chest and then over to my sides. In a swift motion, his hands are palming my ass and lifting me.

Instinctively, I wrap my legs around his waist as he picks me up, pinning me against the wall. He kisses me senseless and I go right back at him, working frantically at the buttons of his shirt.

I'm whirled in a circle as he walks me backwards. I jerk his shirt free from his pants and fumble for the last button. Before I can get it undone, he drops me on the loveseat.

Lying back, my breathing all over the place, I look up at him. His hair is sticking up everywhere, his jacket half off, his shirt completely askew like he was just mugged. It's hot as hell.

He gets on his knees, dragging my left leg and tossing it over his shoulder. A grin lifts the corner of his lips.

"You need a release, baby?" he asks.

My legs are spread, my pussy wide open for him. It seems like I should care, that I should feel some sort of self-consciousness, but I don't.

I just don't.

"Your dad and brother are in the conference room," I say as clearly as I can.

"You don't think Ford knows what's happening in here?" He drags a finger up the inside of my thigh. "He'll keep Dad busy." His finger drifts over my opening, touching it just lightly enough that I shiver. "This is what you wanted, isn't it?"

I can't answer him. I can't even look at him. All I can do is lie back, my dress straddling my waist, and wait for any touch he'll give me.

I don't have to wait long. His palm lies flat along my stomach, his thumb finding my clit. The push, steady and firm, is enough to almost make me yelp.

"Shhh . . ." he snickers. "It's the middle of the day, Ms. Sims. You don't want an audience, do you?"

"I don't care," I say, bucking against his hand.

"No, but I do," he replies. "I don't want some fuckhead making copies to hear you moan my name. And you *will* be moaning my name."

He swirls the pad of his thumb over me before grabbing my hips and planting his face between my legs.

"Ah!" I moan as he sucks me into his mouth. "Oh, God, Graham."

"Told you."

I think I'm going to melt against his face, completely lose control from the contact of his tongue parting me. When I look down and see that he's watching me, I nearly die.

Grabbing his hair, I pop myself up as much as I can and watch this man's face between my legs. "Do I taste good?"

He hums against my opening before flicking his tongue against me.

The sensation is incredible.

He slides his hands under me, lifting my hips so my pussy is angled right at his mouth. I can hear him sucking me, lapping against me, stroking me with his tongue. Just when I think I can't take it anymore, he inserts a finger, twisting it in a "come here" fashion.

"Graham," I groan, short of breath. My hands weave through his hair, pushing his face into me.

Another finger goes in, the rigidity of the digits such a contrast to the softness of his mouth. He strokes in and out of me, this powerful man in a suit kneeling under me.

"You like that?" he asks, drawing his fingers out and shoving them back in. "Does that make you want my cock?"

"Yes," I moan, begging for more friction.

"Too bad."

I want to argue, to beg him to undress and climb on top of me, but I can't form words as his strokes bring me higher and higher.

"The next time I tell you not to do something, fucking listen."

"I just . . . I didn't. I . . ." My head falls back, my hands finding my breasts and cupping them together. "Oh. My. God."

"Be quiet or I'll stop."

Biting down on my lip, my back arched, I feel myself start to near the edge of no return.

"You drive me fucking crazy," he says, his tone completely controlled. "I don't know what to do with you."

"Do this to me," I beg. "Please."

He smirks. "I'm going to make you come now. I'm going to watch you completely lose control on my hand. I want you to remember who controls this, got it?"

He's purposefully not getting me off, holding back just enough so I can't come until he says so.

"Graham," I groan, my insides clenching, trying desperately to get enough friction to burst apart. "Please."

"Who is in control of this, Mallory?"

"You," I bite out.

"Who says when you come?"

"You fucking do," I huff, spreading my legs farther. "Now do it."

"You take orders pitifully," he says, but gives in, and within four strokes, has me coming all over him.

SIXTEEN
GRAHAM

LINCOLN'S PRENUPTIAL AGREEMENT IS IN my hands. It takes all of three seconds to read it.

A heavy, bold X strikes through each page with an arrow indicating I should turn the document over on the last one. I do and see this scratched out in Lincoln's handwriting:

> I, Lincoln Fucking Landry, will not make my girl sign some stupid piece of paper letting her know if she leaves me, she can't have my money. Truth is, if she goes, she may as well take all the cash I worked so hard for because who would give a shit at that point? (And I have you. You can make me more.)
>
> I know you're making that face you make when you think I'm making a really bad choice (worse than the time I used duct tape to keep the braids Sienna put in the dog's hair in place), but I got this. Relax. I mean, if I'm wrong, you will be right and we all know how much that makes you happy.
>
> Thanks for looking out for me, G. You'll be my best man, right?

I don't know whether to laugh or call him and rip his ass. This is utterly stupid, to not protect your interests when combining your life with someone else's. But it's Lincoln, and as much as I hate to admit it, I'm not entirely surprised he's going this route.

Mallory's voice trickles in through the door I left cracked open for that sole purpose. Having her out there is a godsend professionally. Sometimes I sit at my desk and listen to her make phone calls, take care of issues, deny people entry to my office in awe. Linda was good. Mallory is great.

If that's all it is, I'd be fine. But it's not. I know it and I can't fix it and it drives me absolutely mad.

Hearing her a few feet away does the same thing for me that watching Vanessa teach Philosophy did in college. There's nothing sexier than a woman with a brain, but it's more. It's an unraveling of my wits, a chipping away at my concentration, a veering into the dark, unchartered waters of a place in my life I'm not ready to go.

I wasn't ready with Vanessa. I had so much to do, so many balls to juggle, but I tried. As they fell to the ground and shattered, I knew things would never look the same to me again. I'd lose the ability to see things through rose-colored glasses. My naiveté was stripped the day her truths were told.

As I sit, one leg resting on the knee of the other and feeling the warm sunlight shine on my face, I listen to Mallory and feel my walls crumble. They aren't barriers to keep people out; I've let many women inside over the years, just in carefully timed, preconceived ways.

I couldn't do that with Vanessa. It was all or nothing, just like I fear it would be with Mallory. The loss of complete control, and I can never do "all" again.

"Graham?" A knock at the door raps through the room and I glance that way. Mallory is standing there, her head resting on the doorframe, a soft smile touching her lips. "It's five. I'm going to head out."

"Come in here for a second." I sit up and watch her move across my office, a feeling of warmth drifting through my core that unsettles me. "Besides your little outburst, I'm really proud of how you did today with my father and Ford. You made me look good."

Her cheeks flush. "I just made sure all of your ideas and plans were in line. Today was all about you." She sits on the edge of the chair across from me.

"Today was about Ford."

"You should celebrate. Maybe with pancakes."

"You didn't bring me any or I would."

"I didn't have time," she scoffs. "I'm not a super morning person, even though today was actually decent."

"I love mornings. Every day is a fresh start."

She shrugs. "I guess I've not always had a lot to look forward to."

"I'd venture to say," I tell her, leaning against my desk, "that you have a lot to look forward to. Your whole life is in front of you."

"True." She says it, but she doesn't believe it.

"Yes, it's true," I insist. "You can get up every day and decide what you are going to accomplish, what goals you're going to work towards. Think about that. Every morning is an opportunity to change what you aren't happy with."

"My head hurts," she laughs. "Today was a long one."

"You have yoga tonight. Is that right?"

She nods. "I do. I need it. I'm teaching an all-girls class. But if you want to come, I'll make an exception."

"No yoga for me," I grin. "Come on. I'll walk you to your car. I know how much you hate being late."

I gather my things, listening to her ramble about essential oils and yoga, and we walk to the elevator. I don't listen to the words, just hear the delight in her voice. This is what I've found myself craving, more than anything else, late at night when I'm home alone.

The elevator is packed. We squeeze in and ride to the executive parking floor. When we exit, it's empty.

Her shoes tap against the concrete as we make our way to a small, four-door, red compact car.

"This is it," she says, unlocking it with a key. "Yeah, I know," she sighs.

"I didn't even know car doors could be opened with keys anymore."

"This one can," she laughs. "I had a newer car with Eric, but I couldn't afford the payments so I left it with him. This beauty gets me where I'm going."

"Does she?" I give the vehicle a quick once-over as discreetly as I can. It's probably more than ten years old and looks like something a greasy haired used car salesman would sell you, only to have it break down a week later. "How long have you had this?"

"A couple of weeks. It's fine. Not fancy, but good." She looks at the floor and I realize she's embarrassed.

"Hey," I say, lifting her chin so she's looking at me. "Don't."

"Don't what?"

"Get that look on your face."

"Don't feel pity for me," she says, brushing my hand away. "I'm driving this hunk of metal because I choose to. That alone, that I made the choice to do this, means a lot to me."

I look at her in disbelief. How many people do what she did? Realize they deserve more and leave behind everything they have for a life that's harder, at least materially?

"I respect that," I say, my tone somber.

"Yeah, well, I'll remember how respectable it is when I'm trying to figure out how to add windshield wiper fluid."

Tossing her bag in her car, I hear a crunch. There are a host of takeout bags and Styrofoam cups littering her passenger seat and floorboard.

"That bothers you, doesn't it?" she giggles.

"I know what you're getting as a Christmas bonus."

"What's that?"

"Your fucking car cleaned. Just . . ." I can't take it. Stalking back to the elevator, I grab the plastic garbage can and haul it across the parking lot. It squeals as the bottom rips along the pavement.

"Graham!" she shouts over the ruckus. "What are you doing?"

Shaking my head, I nudge her out of the way. "My God, Mallory," I groan. Bag after bag, cup after cup, napkin after pieces of plastic that are semi-damp, get swiped up and dumped into the can behind me.

I'm leaned across her console, the crunch of the debris muddling the sound of her objections. The carpet is a mess and there's a weird smell that reminds me of bacon, but at least you can *see* the carpet now.

Making a face, I climb out of the driver's seat and dispose of the last items in my hands. "*That* is a fucking disaster. Park in the front tomorrow morning and I'll have someone shampoo it out."

"You will not!"

"Oh, I will. I'll consider it a gift to humanity."

"You're such an ass," she says, smacking my chest. I catch her hand and pull her to me. It's automatic, such a natural move that it catches us both off-guard. "There are probably cameras out here, Mr. Landry."

"What's that supposed to mean?"

"That means I know that look in your eye."

"You're safe," I sigh. "I can't throw you on the console of your car. I'm afraid your face would get stuck in syrup or something."

She rolls her eyes and climbs inside. "I'm going to be late to class. I'll see you in the morning."

I close the door behind her and step away so she can pull out. She gives me a little wave and a beep of the horn as she drives, entirely too fast, out of the garage.

As her taillights get farther away, a sense of loneliness begins to filter my way. There's no longer the smell of lavender, the sound of her making fun of me, or the twinkle in her eye that makes me want to ask her a question so she'll talk to me.

Tension stretches across my shoulders, tugging my muscles tight. With the stiffness comes a pulsing sensation behind my left eye, indicating that I'm on the cusp of one hell of a headache.

Everything is out of order. The pieces of my life are strewn around worse than the contents on her floorboard, and I can't shuffle them back in place fast enough. My desk is still loaded with papers, Lincoln's refusal to be sane, and Ford's security company to deal with. Typically, I wait for this moment—everyone gone, everything quiet, and I can really dig in. Now I can't because I have another, potentially worse issue at hand: I need Mallory around as badly as I need to put distance between us.

The pull coming harder in my temple, I head to the elevator and press the button. While I wait, I type out a text.

Me: *Thank you for asking me to be your best man in such a brotherly way.*

Lincoln: *Don't kid either of us. You love that I picked you over Barrett and Ford.*

Me: *Well, it only makes sense to pick me.*

Lincoln: *How do you figure?*

Me: *I'm the one settling in to spend the evening getting a plan together to save your ass in case everything goes south.*

Lincoln: *Do me a favor?*

Me: *What, Linc?*

Lincoln: *Get a drink. Because as wound up as you get, you'll be dead before I'd need you to implement that plan and then I'd really be fucked.*

Me: *Always about you, isn't it?*

Lincoln: *Hell, yeah. Oh—Ford said you got it on in the middle of a meeting today. Can I say I'm super proud of you?*

Me: *Talk to you later.*

Lincoln: *Wait! You can't jump my ass and then ignore me. This is the day Graham proves he's human. Let's discuss. Should I grab some pizza and meet you at the office?*

Laughing, I turn my phone off and slip it in my jacket. I step in the elevator and head to my office, hopefully to work and not to think about Mallory.

***

Mallory

"THERE YOU ARE!" JOY CHIRPS.

I hurry inside the yoga studio and toss my things against the wall. Tonight's class, thankfully, is one of the smaller ones and no one is early.

"I was thinking you weren't coming," Joy remarks. "You said you were on your way forty minutes ago."

"I . . ." I plop on the mat and look at my friend. "Does it really matter what made me late?"

"Nope. It's how you roll. I take that back," she snickers, "it's unless you were getting all hot and sweaty with Bossman. In that case, I want every detail. Do not leave anything out."

Rolling onto my mat face-first, I pretend to stretch out my lower back. It does feel good, but it actually gives me time to figure out how to keep my face blank around Joy.

I could tell her about Graham. If it were anyone else, no doubt I would. I always have. But this time, I want to keep it for me. This time, it feels . . . *different*.

I'm not sure what it is, although it certainly doesn't feel like just sex. Not quite. Sex is insertion. An act and then it's done. It's not walks to my car. He could have me without the little looks during the day, without taking the trash out of my floorboard. But what does that mean? I have no idea.

"How did things go today?" she asks. She's prodding for information, the tone in her voice giving her away. "Anything new with Graham?"

"No, nothing's new with Graham," I sigh. "He's my boss, Joy."

"So something did happen!"

"What on Earth are you talking about?"

"You're defensive. The last time we talked about this, you were all, 'He's so hot!' Now you're acting like I'm ridiculous for bringing it up. That means you're deflecting."

Heaving a breath, I roll onto my back and look at the spackled ceiling in desperate need of a paint job. "Things haven't been purely professional," I admit.

"I knew it!" she shrieks. "My God. Is he as good as I think he is? He is, isn't he?"

"Joy . . ." I almost whine. I feel like she's forcing me to talk and I hate that. "Can we not talk about this?"

"Why?"

Struggling to sit up, I try to come up with an explanation that she can understand. That I can understand. "Have you ever not wanted to talk about something until you can get your head wrapped around it?"

"No," she mutters. "I always call you and have you help me figure it out."

I toss her a pathetic smile. "I know. I do you too. But I don't know what to make of this and I'm really afraid getting your input is going to make it harder."

"I give good advice."

"You do," I laugh. "But everything when it comes to him is pro-Graham. I don't fault you for it. Look at him," I shrug. "But I need to make sure I'm looking at this pro-Mallory. Does that make sense?"

Joy grabs her water bottle and squeezes some in her mouth. "It does. But you know I'm pro-Mallory, right?"

"Always." I stand and stretch my arms over my head. "I'm going to the bathroom before everyone gets here."

Jogging across the mats and through the doors to a vacant hallway, I stand with my back against the cool brick. My mind goes to Graham, like it does anytime I'm not specifically thinking of something else.

I like him. I like him way more than I want to admit. Even more problematic, the more time I spend with him, the more time I *want* to spend with him.

But am I getting jaded by the TDH—tall, dark, and handsome? Am I wrapped up in the Landry spell and not seeing things like a logical human being?

He's my boss. A CEO. I'm a drop-out with no plan. What could possibly come of this long-term? Not much. Besides orgasms.

There's nothing wrong with having fun with Graham. We're two consenting adults. But I need to remember that no matter how easy it is to become infatuated with him, I have to keep my head clear. I can't get wrapped up in this and then be gobsmacked when it doesn't work out. There's nothing to work out. This is fun. Just fun.

"What are you doing out here?"

I look up to see Sienna propping the door open with her hip. "Hey," I say, shoving off the wall. "I was just taking a couple of minutes to regroup. Joy can be kind of overwhelming."

"She really can. I love her to absolute pieces, but she just attacks!" she laughs. "You okay?"

"Yeah. I was just thinking," I say, going through the open door and leading Sienna to our mats. "After I figure everything out, I think I want to start my own yoga studio."

"I think that could be cool," Sienna says. "It's a big thing in LA. You know, you could always head West and come live with me. Free rent. Free food because my mom orders groceries to be delivered to my house. Is that not crazy?"

"Sounds fun," I note. "I just . . . I think I need a little time on my own. I've never had that. It has to be good for a girl, doesn't it?"

"Sure. But it's also good for a girl to know people around her care about her and are there for her." She faces me head-on so her back is to Joy and Camilla. "You're okay, right? I know you don't want to talk about everything in front of them, but I also know how working for my brothers can be. My mom made me intern at Landry Holdings one summer in high school. She called it 'character building.' I called it hell."

I laugh, imagining her purple-streaked hair and pink nails fitting in at the office. "It's not for everyone."

"No, it's not." She peers in my eyes, much like her brother does when he's trying to read my mind. "I haven't seen you have this much pink in your cheeks since you got home. You look happy, Mal."

"I am." A flutter of butterflies kicks up in my belly and I can't wipe the cheesy smile off my face. "It feels good to be in charge of my day. To really have options in front of me and know I'm the one that gets to decide what I do. And who I do," I wink.

"I don't want to know." She tosses a toned arm around me and rests her head against mine. "You know what? Fuck Eric."

"You know she's probably thinking about fucking your brother," Joy chimes in, making us laugh.

SEVENTEEN
GRAHAM

MY GLASSES BOUNCE OFF THE papers and rattle as they fall off the stack and land on the desktop. "Ugh," I groan, covering my face with my hands and massaging my temples.

I can feel the start of a major headache stretching across the front of my face. There isn't enough stretching or miles with Ford to work out the kinks from today.

Not helping matters is that I got maybe three hours sleep last night. Maybe three. Probably not. After dinner with my mother, a brainstorming session with Barrett, listening to Sienna present reasons why she should be allowed to start her own company since Ford is, and then finding a huge error in the bid for equipment for Landry Security, there was not enough time in the day. Especially when I used whatever remaining seconds left, and a quarter of the ones I didn't have to spare, thinking about Mallory. It's not as bad when we're at work. She's here. I'm here. She's within reach, however stupid that sounds. Not that I can reach, but just knowing I could and no one else has access gives me a sense of comfort.

Add that to the top of my stress load.

"I can't be worrying about this," I grumble.

She came in here like the chorus of a song, blasting her way into my life and falling into my arms. And I, the stupid motherfucker I am, didn't let go. I say I couldn't, but I could've. I should've. But I didn't. The worst part is—I know why. Her damn eyes.

I've only seen one pair like that in my entire life. Although those were green and Mallory's are gold, they're the same in the ways that count. The only two eyes that look at me and see . . . me. The whole package, not just a piece of it. That's what makes her irresistible. That's what makes me insane. That's what makes this whole damn thing perilous.

"Hey." I look up and see her poking her head around my office door. "Do you need anything?"

Of course I do. I need so much that I can't have. The things I need are the things that will ruin me.

"I'm good," I say, giving her the best smile I can manage.

Her nails tap against the wood before she steps inside and pulls her brows together. "You're not okay."

I lean forward on my desk, folding my hands in front of me. My smile now is genuine, a warmth spreading over my core. Not because she's beautiful or sassy or giving me that look that I've come to find so amusing. But because she . . . cares.

"I'm okay, Mallory."

She shakes her head. "You've been quiet all day, weirder than usual."

"I'm weird?" I chuckle.

"Yeah," she says, exasperated. "You look like you're walking this line all the time, like you're afraid someone will see you move a certain way or say a certain thing and ruin everything. But today . . . you haven't said more than ten words to me."

She attempts to make me believe this doesn't bother her. The sadness just below the surface is enough to take all that warmth I felt two seconds ago and drown it in a pit of ice water.

"I'm sorry," I say. "I just . . . today's been Hell."

"Can I help? Tell me what to do and I'll do it."

"Just keep doing what you do."

I hope she hears the professional aspect of that and not the edge of the rest. Not the fact that I'm starting to rely on her presence, her smile, her laugh more than I even care to admit.

"I'll be right back," she says, spinning on her heel and walking out.

I hear things rustle before she reappears.

In a grey dress with pockets on the sides, she looks like a professional administrative assistant . . . with a can of soda in one hand and a protein bar in the other.

"What are you doing?" I lean back in my seat as she sets the items in front of me.

"You need a pick me up. Here, eat this."

"Do you not see the irony in a sugar-filled soda and a protein bar?"

"It's called balance," she sighs, circling behind me. Her fingers dip beneath the collar of my jacket and tenderly grasp the back of my neck. "You need a little balance and a little relaxation." She works my muscles back and forth, her thumbs rolling up and down my skin. "You are so tight."

"That's my line," I crack, moving my head side-to-side to give her more room. "God, that feels good."

"That's *my* line," she laughs.

Working out the knots that I didn't even realize were so apparent, I nearly melt in her hands. I can't remember feeling like this before. Ever. Any time a woman has touched me, it's for a purpose—an end result with her as the beneficiary at the end. This? This is just for me.

"You could use some yoga in your life, Mr. Landry."

"Not my thing," I say, almost cringing as she really gets deep into the tissue.

"It should be. At least some of it. It's really amazing," she sighs. "My first-of-the-month resolution is to find balance."

"Your what?"

"Everyone does New Year's resolutions. I always fail by day three. There's just so much pressure because everyone knows you're supposed to be walking ten thousand steps or not eating cake. It's horrible."

"I'd never vow not to eat cake," I remark. "That's absurd."

She laughs, giving me one final squeeze. "I tried it once. I failed, hence these hips." As she walks in front of my desk and sits across from me, we exchange a smile.

"I happen to really like those hips."

"Anyway," she blushes, changing the topic, "I'm doing a resolution each month. It's just something I want to work on and get better. Each month is roughly thirty days and that's how long they say it takes to make a new habit."

"So your new habit is balance?"

"Yes."

"And here I was hoping it would be me," I whisper. The words leave my mouth and I regret them. I mean them, absolutely, but I don't want to lead her on that this can be a habit. It can't. It has to end at some point or find some way to fit in boundaries and I'm not sure she's boundary-able. That's a completely different obstacle I can't figure out how to clear.

Thankfully, she ignores my comment. "I think *you* need balance," she says. "You do, do, do for all these people. I only know the tip of it, I'm sure, but you are the center of your entire family, Graham. And then you run this company like it's your baby."

"It *is* my baby," I correct her.

"That's what I'm saying," she sighs. "When do you get to do Graham things? When do you relax? When do you get to be you and not in a suit?"

"I'm not sure what planet you're on, but I look damn good in this suit."

"Stop changing the subject!"

"While I'm honored you care so much about my dress code, I can assure you I'm fine. I'm doing what I love. This life I have, it's one I created after a lot of thought and planning. There's nothing else I want or need that I don't already have."

Her face falls and I feel like a complete motherfucking asshole. I didn't see the shit I was stepping in, just explaining myself like I would to anyone. Except, she's not just anyone. I don't know who she is, but if I said she wasn't any different than Barrett or Linda, I'd be a liar.

Although the next words are the complete opposite things I need to be saying, they're falling out of my mouth before I can stop them. "Let's go to dinner."

She shoots me a look that tells me just how confused she is. "What?"

"We worked our asses off today. Let's go get some nourishment."

"Graham..."

"You said we both need balance," I point out, straightening my jacket back out as I stand. "Let's get some dinner and some cake to offset the bullshit that happened in here today."

Her eyes light up and it calms the anxiety building over my inability to think before I speak around her. Still, she doesn't answer.

"Come on," I goad, flicking off my computer and holding my hand out to her. "Let me take you to dinner."

"I only go to dinner with men that take me to places with real forks," she teases.

"I don't think forks are your problem," I say, feeling her soft palm rest in mine. "I think finding real men may be your issue."

She shoves me with her free hand, and I find myself laughing out loud as we exit the office.

EIGHTEEN
GRAHAM

"CAN YOU BELIEVE I'VE NEVER been here?" Mallory looks at me with wide eyes as we near the entrance of Dalicon. "I almost forget it's even here. It's just tucked back here so neatly."

"This is one of my favorite places in Savannah," I tell her. I give my name to the hostess and she whisks us through the restaurant. With the large, wooden beams crisscrossing the ceiling and warm walls set off with dark floors, it's a very relaxed place. The burnt orange paper lanterns and wall art give it a slight air of sophistication that I love.

Once we are settled into a little table in the corner and have ordered wine, Mallory seems to relax. "This is stunning. I just want to look around and that says something—I always want to eat!" she laughs.

"Soda and protein bars?"

"No," she says, but stops when the waiter appears at our side. He starts to hand her a glass. As he does, he's bumped from behind and a splash of wine lands in Mallory's lap.

"I'm so sorry," he says, resting the serving tray on a vacant table and rushing to Mallory's side. "Oh my gosh, I'm so sorry. Here, let me get you something."

As I start to extend a hand with my linen napkin, I'm stopped by her laugh. "Please," she gushes to the waiter. "It was an accident. It's no problem, really."

"But, madam, I am so sorry. I should be more careful. I've just ruined your dress."

"Please . . . Donnie," she says, eyeing his name tag. "It's really no big deal. It'll clean. And if it doesn't, it's a dress. I'll survive."

"Are you sure? Absolutely sure?" he asks, stunned. "Can I at least get you an appetizer? Let me do something."

I tune out, unable to really focus on anything but the pure kindness in her eyes. Before long, she has him laughing along with her and I'm speechless.

"Sir? What can I get you?" Donnie asks.

Shaking my head, I indicate off the menu what I want and once he's gone, I smile at Mallory. "That was pretty fantastic."

"What?" she asks, dabbling the wet spot with a napkin, completely oblivious to what I'm referring.

"How you handled that."

"How was I supposed to handle it?" she asks, resting the linen next to her plate.

"Most women would've freaked out over that. You were worried about Donnie boy."

She takes a sip of her wine. "Accidents happen. God knows I've had my fair share. You heard the story I was telling him about the time I dumped an entire tray of margaritas in someone's lap. You just have to let some stuff go. Or maybe you just realize that once you've been in their shoes."

"You were a waitress?"

"Yeah. I've done dishes, worked as a cashier once at a grocery store. That was the worst job I've had, actually. People just look at you like you're garbage," she frowns. "I've worked in a beauty shop, cleaning up tanning beds after the people leave and sweeping up hair and stuff."

"When? High school? Now?"

"My whole life," she shrugs. "I did a lot of those while I was in high school. I'd go to school and then work the hours I was allowed under the law. And then, sometimes, I'd work at another place and they'd just pay me under the table so I didn't get in trouble with school."

"That must have been really hard," I note, thinking about how hard I thought it was going to school and helping Dad out on the weekends.

She smiles. "It wasn't easy. But that discipline got me where I am today." Her finger runs around the rim of her glass as she thinks. "It's where my work ethic comes from. If I wanted a tank of gas or car insurance, I had to get the money for it. If I wanted the fancy jeans with the sparkly pockets, I had to hustle for that. It sucked then, but I'm not afraid to work now for what I have. Or what I want." She looks at me, her eyes shining in the dim light. "That's why I respect you so much, Graham. I see your work ethic and I admire that. There aren't a lot of people that will just do the job, you know?"

"Yeah, I know," I chuckle. "I replaced your position about fourteen times before you showed up."

The waiter places our food in front of us. He takes a minute to chat with Mallory, making sure she's completely happy and comfortable. Watching her get doted on is amusing and witnessing her sweetness shine with Donnie is special. It's not something I've seen often.

"So," I say, "what do you want to do with yourself? You don't want anything in the field of medicine, that we know. What are you thinking?"

"Honestly?" She slices her chicken breast carefully, her lips pressing together. Finally, she shrugs. "I don't know."

"How do you not know?"

Her hair swishes back and forth as she shakes her head. "I tell Joy I'm having a mid-life crisis," she half-laughs. "I've spent my entire life, since turning eighteen, doing what I needed to do or what Eric wanted me to do."

"I don't think I like him."

"I don't. So that's two of us," she sighs. "I let him manipulate me. In the moment, I didn't realize it, but I see it now."

I set my silverware on the edge of my plate and look at her. "What happened with him? Do you mind me asking?"

Her fork drops too. "When I told him I was dropping out, he went ballistic. He said I was a liability to him, a nobody that would never amount to anything. There was something in the way he said it that time—"

"He'd said those things before?" I bite out, feeling my irritation soar.

She shrugs, trying to play it off. "Maybe. But that time . . . he just made me feel really bad. I don't know why it was different that time than before. It was just a really ugly argument."

"Explain ugly," I say, narrowing my eyes.

"No," she says, reading between the lines. "Nothing happened. God, no. He's still alive. If he would have hurt me physically, I'd be locked up."

"Mental abuse and physical abuse are no different."

"I know," she whispers. "But I made a decision that day that I'd had enough. I was at this point where I felt so . . . put in a corner. Does that make sense? Like my whole life was being scripted by someone else. I'd never done anything I wanted to do."

I fiddle with the corner of my napkin.

"And it's not like he even promised me the world for hanging in there. He told me flat-out we had no future."

"He sounds like a complete tool."

"Apparently I'm just the dating kind, not the kind for marriage." Her eyes flick to mine with a sadness that slays me. I reach for her hand.

"You know what I think?"

"What's that?"

"I think he's right."

Her gaze drops to the table, her shoulders slumping. I grin.

"You are just the dating kind for a guy like that. He doesn't deserve to keep you long-term."

The corners of her cheeks start to bend, but she doesn't smile. I work harder for it.

"You are young. Beautiful. Smart. You have the whole world at your feet, Mallory. Why would you stifle your potential by staying with someone that wants to keep you in a box?"

She perks up, the smile I'm dying to see starts to slide across her cheeks. "You think so?"

"I know so. Now you just need a plan and I happen to be an excellent planner," I chuckle. "What do you want to do with yourself ?

"I was telling Sienna the other day that I might open a yoga studio someday."

"And . . ."

She shrugs.

"That's it?" I ask. "You want to maybe open a yoga studio at some point in the future?"

"Yeah, that's it," she says defensively. "Look, Graham. I'm starting all over. I know that's hard for you to understand, being who you are, but I'm doing the best I can to basically recreate dreams and decide who I am in the midst of my life."

"Hey," I say, reaching for her hand and placing mine on top of it. "I didn't mean anything by that. It came out as a jerk thing, and I didn't mean it like that at all. I was wrong."

"I know I get protective over myself right now. I just am so afraid I'll slip and end up in some position where I'm cut down."

"I'd never cut you down. The only people who cut others down are those threatened by their height. The higher you get, the more lovely I think you are."

Her cheeks flush. Her hand rolls over and she squeezes mine. "That's very nice of you to say."

"I only speak the truth."

She relaxes in her chair. "Tell me about you, Graham. What are your life plans?"

"I just want to keep doing what I'm doing until I can't," I say simply. "This business is my life. Growing up, I just wanted to be my dad. Not emulate him or pretend to be him—I wanted *to be* him. When he stepped back and made me President of the company, it was the proudest day of my life, you know? My father sort of passing the torch."

"That's awesome," she grins. "But I feel like everything you do and say has to do with the business. What about outside of that? You have this huge family. Do you want that too?"

I bring my hand away from hers slowly. "I don't think I'll have a family as large as mine, no. I mean, there are six of us and I'm not getting any younger," I chuckle.

"But do you want kids? Is a family a part of your future?"

Taking a sip of wine, I consider her question. More than that, I consider it in context of who she is and who I am and what this is between us. Or what it could be. And what I'm capable of letting it be. "Maybe someday," I say, figuring that's fair enough. "I'm not averse to having a family. Clearly, I love having a big family and I think that having children is always a blessing. But it's not something I think I'm ready for right now, nor do I think I'll be ready for it in the foreseeable future."

"I didn't think so," she almost whispers. Her features glow as the candle in the middle of the table dances back and forth. She tosses me a smile that she has to try too hard to look natural and takes a sip of her wine.

"What about you?" I ask, already knowing the answer.

"A family? Someday, yeah, absolutely. I hope to have a family of my own. I'm not sure what the point of life is otherwise." She glances at me softly. "I'll be honest—I like being in a relationship. I liked the teamwork aspect of it and making dinner and going grocery shopping. I grew up watching my parents do those things together. They enjoyed that, looked forward to it. Maybe it was all they had together, I don't know. It just seems like a part of life that really makes life . . . life."

"Well, my parents certainly didn't grocery shop together," I say, trying to imagine my dad with a shopping cart. "But I can understand what you're saying. For some people, relationships work." I look her square in the eye. "They just aren't for me."

My chest tightens, my steak threatening to come up as I watch the fire in her eyes start to wane. A part of me wants to grab her hand and tell her I want to have her in my life in some capacity, what that is, I don't know. But that wouldn't be fair. To either of us.

"I'm going to use the restroom," she says, scooting her chair back.

"I'll order the cake."

"What?"

"Cake, Mallory. We're having cake," I say, trying to win back that smile.

"Make it vanilla with vanilla icing."

"Really?" I ask. "Their dessert menu is two pages long and you're getting vanilla cake with vanilla icing?"

"I figure vanilla has fewer calories than chocolate. This is balancing out the three sodas I had today," she winks and takes off, leaving me chuckling behind her.

***

Mallory

I FOLLOW GRAHAM THROUGH A short hallway and into a wide open kitchen. Dark wood floors and cabinets make the large stainless steel appliances pop. Light flows in from the bright moon outside the windows, but the room also glows from soft lights under the cabinetry.

His house is in a subdivision bordering a golf course, which surprised me when we arrived. I expected him to live somewhere more private, maybe even out of town, but he doesn't. Still, it's incredibly peaceful here, almost like you leave the city and step into another place altogether. It smells of his sandalwood cologne mixed with something crisp. Clean. Intoxicating.

Graham takes my coat and lays it over the back of one of the tall stools lining the island along with his suit jacket. "Can I get you a drink? Something to eat?"

"We just had dinner," I remind him.

"I know. It's just years of manners embedded into me by my mother. Never invite someone over and not offer them food and a drink."

He watches me in the way he does for a long moment. I feel the ripple of uncertainty that's been wedged between us since our talk of the yoga studio and families. Dessert was nice and our conversation flowed like normal, but I could feel something a little heavier on our minds.

The car ride here was quiet, soft music playing in his SUV, the only words really spoken were him asking if we could swing by here for some papers before he returns me to my car at Landry Holdings. Now, looking at him over his kitchen island, I'm not sure what to think. Maybe he doesn't either.

"Thank you for going with me to dinner tonight," he says finally.

"It was nice. Thank you for asking me."

He roughs his hand down his face before reaching for my hand and leading me to a set of French doors. He slides them open and we step out onto a patio.

The air is chilly and I shiver. He immediately pulls me into his side and runs his hand up and down my arm. "We can go back in," he offers.

"I just thought you'd like it out here. Watch this." Grinning, he goes to a large stone fireplace and flips a switch. Flames begin to dance inside.

"That's awesome," I laugh, curling up on the love seat facing the fire. The fence has a row of thick pine trees on the inside, creating a barrier from the homes on either side and the golf course behind the house. It creates a little nook of privacy that feels like a fairytale. "I could get used to this." As he sits beside me, the flames shooting shadows over his face, I realize just how breathtakingly handsome he really is when the stress of the day is gone. "This is how you relax, isn't it? Sitting here by the fire."

"Sometimes." With a gentle hand, he takes my arm and pulls me against him. My breath catches in my throat at the contact. It's more intimate, more connected, than I've been with him before, and on top of our conversation earlier, I'm not sure what I think of that.

My head on his chest, I gaze past the patio and onto the golf course. "Do you golf?"

"A little. It's a good place to hammer out business deals," he says. "Dad golfs pretty well. Barrett hates it. Linc is an asshole to golf with because he's so fucking good and doesn't even try."

"What about Ford?"

"Ford can. I mean, he's decent. He just doesn't really spend his time on those things." His hand runs up and down my arm again. If I didn't watch it, I could pretend this was more than it is. "Ford takes serious things seriously and fun things for what they are. He really is probably the best out of us all."

"I don't know . . ."

"What do you not know?" he says, angling his head to look at me.

His eyes shine in the low light.

"I happen to think you're the best out of them all."

He chuckles, letting his hand fall to the small of my back. "That's nice of you to say."

"It's true. Barrett is so charismatic, Ford charming, and Lincoln is so . . ."

Graham flips me a look, almost a warning. "He's so what, Mallory?" he goads me.

"So *Lincoln*," I try, giggling. "But you are all of those things."

"I don't think I'm charming."

"You are *so* charming," I smile, tapping his cheek until he faces me. "And kind. You think of everyone but yourself, which is why you need yoga," I wink. "Want to know my favorite thing about you?"

"No. This is starting to make me uncomfortable," he cringes.

"I don't care," I whisper, teasing him. "Besides seeing you naked and being on the receiving end of your smile, my favorite thing about you is how smart you are and how passionate you are about the things that matter to you."

He huffs, clearly embarrassed, and looks away.

"Do you want to know what my favorite thing is about you? It might surprise you," he says, tapping my nose. "It's not how insanely gorgeous you are or how good you are at your job or how I can talk to you about anything and you know a little something about it."

My cheeks flush and I try to look away, but he doesn't let me. Instead, he holds my gaze in place and smiles.

"My favorite thing about you is your heart." He says it so simply, so matter-of-factly, that it takes a second to process it. "At first when you would ask me how I am in the morning or if I needed something before you left work, I'd assume it was a part of your role. But I've come to learn you *really* are asking. You really do care if I'm okay."

"And if not, I'll bring you a soda and a protein bar," I say, nestling my head against his chest as the warmth of the fire snuggles me in.

"I love that you care, Mallory. And it comes from such a good place. You don't ask because you want something from me. Just like Donnie tonight. You were worried he was upset. That's pretty incredible."

"That's called having a heart."

"That's called being a lady." He wraps his other hand around me, fastening them at my hip. "This is nice."

"Mhmm . . ." I say, unfastening a couple of the buttons on his shirt and slipping my hand inside. His tight chest, rough and warm, sends a blast of energy right through me. "You know what?"

"What's that?"

"I thought you were going to say your favorite thing about me was my punctuality."

He laughs and I can feel the reverberation in my hand. His heart quickens. "No, but I could've said something else."

"Like what?"

"Like the feel of your pussy wrapped around my cock."

His words, coupled with the grit in his tone, makes me weak. As he stretches back, I see the bulge in his pants, and I know, right or wrong, ready or not, I'm going to come.

"I know what you mean," I say, skimming my palm down his chest and cupping him. "I love the way my body stretches as you put the tip of your—Ah!"

Before I can finish my sentence, I'm flipped on my back. Graham hovers over me, his eyes dancing with mischief.

NINETEEN
MALLORY

GRAHAM'S TONGUE DARTS OUT, SKIMMING his bottom lip. He's pinning me against the loveseat with a hand on either side of my face. "You drive me crazy," he says, narrowing his eyes. "I try so hard to be on my best behavior around you and you just whittle me down. Every fucking time."

"Well," I tease, wrapping my legs around his waist. "I think your 'best behavior' is subjective."

"You know what I mean."

"And you know what I mean."

My heels locked at his back, I squeeze my thighs around his waist and pull him closer to me. His lips hover over mine but they don't touch.

"What exactly do you mean, Mallory?"

I wind my fingers in his hair and tug gently. "I mean this is the Graham I like best. I like seeing you like this."

"Struggling to keep myself together?"

"Exactly." Lifting my head, I flick my tongue against his lips. I can feel the heat of his mouth, the taste of his desire. "Don't try so hard," I whisper.

"It's futile anyway," he says. I barely hear the words as he pulls back. "Stand up." He climbs off the loveseat, stripping off his shirt. "Now."

My stomach clenching at the intensity in his eyes, I'm on my feet before I realize I've moved.

"Take your dress off. Everything. I want you completely naked."

The air brushes against my skin as the linen covering my body pools at my feet. As I step out, I watch Graham and almost gasp.

He's standing in front of me, his cock in his hand, watching my every move. "Bra. Off."

With a shaky hand, I unclasp the back and throw it at him. He catches it and presses it to his face.

"Now what?" I stand before him, not a thing on my skin. My hair drapes around my shoulders, and despite the fact I'm standing completely naked outside under the watchful eye of this sexy CEO, I don't feel a bit nervous. Just . . . admired. That feels better than any orgasm, any accomplishment, any nice words ever spoken to me.

Graham sits again, his legs spread. He's in complete control, managing the situation not with words or power, but with his eyes. That's all it takes. He strokes his cock up and down, all the while not breaking eye contact with me. The flames of the fire dance beside us, the heat tickling my chilled skin.

"Come here," he instructs.

I take the few steps to him, but before he can say anything more, I drop to my knees.

"Mallory . . ."

Gripping his cock at the base, I look him dead in the eye and flick my tongue against the head. His chin lifts, the muscles in his neck flexing as I stroke his length, letting my tongue trail down his shaft.

He clutches the armrest, his arms tensing and giving me some serious arm porn. I can feel the knot in my core igniting faster than I can attempt to control it, burning hotter with every minute.

I pull his swollen head into my mouth, sucking it like a lollipop.

He growls, lifting his hips in reaction. I take him as deep as I can, then pull him out to the tip, flicking it with my tongue.

"Fuck, Mallory."

Taking his balls in my other hand, I squeeze them just enough to let him know I have them. As I pump him into my mouth, I feel him harden even more as my hand slides up and down him. He's so thick I can barely get my entire hand around him.

Although my body screams for attention, my clit pulses between my legs, watching him react to me is worth the torture. His eyes squeezed shut, his frame trembling under my control, is unbelievable.

Just as I find the tempo I know will have him losing control, he reaches forward and takes my face in his hands. He guides me away, his cock making a popping sound as it releases from my mouth.

Falling back on my heels, I wipe my mouth with the back of my hand. "Why did you stop me?" I ask, catching my breath.

"I'm not getting off in your mouth. Stand up."

As I get to my feet, he rustles in his pants behind me. I hear the tear of a package. When I turn around, I see him rolling a condom down himself. I flash him a confused look because we didn't use one last time. "I always use a rubber," he says. "You caught me off guard last time."

He tosses the wrapper on the coffee table. "Now bend over the love seat. I want your ass up in the air."

Climbing up, I rest my arms over the back of the loveseat. The wicker bites into my arms. Widening my knees and tilting my hips up, I feel the chill of the air on my heated pussy.

Looking behind me, I see Graham standing a few inches away.

"I could look at this all day every day." He puts a hand on the globe of my ass. "This is perfect." He smacks it lightly, just enough to sting. When I yelp, he laughs. "Just a warning, sometimes people are out on the golf course at night walking their dogs. They can't see us— that I promise. But they can hear us. You might want to keep it down." He snickers, getting behind me and wrapping an arm around my front. One finger touches my clit and I gasp. "Or not."

His cock slides into me in one swift thrust.

"Oh my God!" I bend forward again, my hands winding over the wicker. My hair all falling to one side, I lean back against him. He pulls almost completely out and then pushes all the way inside me again. "Fuck, Graham. Do that again."

He does. Once. Twice. Three times. By the fourth time, I've moved my hips so the tip of his cock hits my G-spot perfectly. He's so damn hard, so solid, that every penetration is almost an action itself.

One hand digs into my hip. The other reaches around me, applying pressure to my throbbing clit.

"My God," I groan through clenched teeth.

"What do you want, Mallory? Do you like this?" He pushes into me harder. "Is that what you want, baby? You want me to fuck you so hard you can't think of anything else?"

My breasts bounce, my head dipped, as I push back on him. He growls behind me, the intensity of his thrusts coupled with the expertise of his fingers, is sensation overload.

"Ah," I cry, leaning back. Working my knees farther apart so he can go even deeper, I think it can't get any more intense. Until he works one hand to my nipple and presses it roughly between his fingers. "This. Is. Amazing."

The words are almost incoherent. Even I can barely hear them over the sound of our bodies and the white noise bounding through my ears. But I do hear the voice from somewhere past the pines.

"Is that you, Landry?" A male's voice projects from the area on the other side of the tree line where the golf course is.

"Ah," I gasp, covering my breasts with my arm. Graham pushes it away with a chuckle, not breaking stride.

"Don't," he whispers against my ear, picking up his pace. "Is that you, Paul?"

"Yeah. How are ya?"

He wraps an arm around my front and pulls me up so that my back is against his chest. He leans us both forward just enough to perfect the angle.

My nipples harden as the air tickles them and the exhilaration of the man's voice sounds again. I can't see him, but he sounds close and I wonder if he can see me. Graham doesn't seem to care, just continues to drive himself into my body and bring me closer to the peak.

"I'm good," Graham says, his voice so controlled you'd never know what he was doing. "How are you?"

I don't hear the response. My body bounces on Graham's cock, his hands roaming my body, demanding contact. I wrap my arms up and around his neck and arch my back, needing the release that is so close I can taste it.

His lips find the crook of my neck and he kisses me, nibbling the soft skin behind my ear. That does it.

"Graham," I mutter, cradling my breasts with one arm. "I can't stop this..."

"Let go, baby," he whispers. He drives into me, hitting the spot I love like he's done this a million times. I hear his voice calling goodbye to his neighbor while my world spins wildly out of control.

"Shit!" I cry, biting my lip to keep from calling out too loud. My body tenses around his cock, squeezing it as I feel my body shake. My knees go weak, threatening to collapse. Graham's arm winds around my waist and holds me up, his fingertips searing into my skin. "*Oh. My. God.*"

Trembling as the orgasm hits me in full force, I feel his lips against my neck. "Damn it, Mallory," he groans. "Fuck!" He shudders against my back, his cock pulsing as he finds his mark. There's no way to see his face and I hate that I can't watch him, see what I do to him.

As I struggle to catch my breath, I feel a single, light kiss press against the skin right behind my ear. "You good?" he whispers.

"Yes," I breathe, getting my wits about me. The air seems colder now, my body so much more exposed.

Without even seeing my expression, he seems to know what I need. "Let's get you inside and cleaned up."

He scoops up our clothes, takes my hand, and leads me in the back door.

TWENTY
MALLORY

FROM THE VANTAGE POINT OF the sofa, I watch Graham work in the kitchen. He moves so fluidly, completely at home as he makes us a drink.

On one hand, I feel like I know him so well. But when I think about it, I really know nothing at all. The fact I want to know more leaves me a little uneasy.

He looks over his shoulder, the muscles in his neck flexing as he pours a drink. The soft grey pants he's changed into sit right below his navel and he's shirtless and shoeless.

"What?" he grins, coming towards me with a wine glass and a tumbler.

"Do you cook?"

"That's random," he chuckles.

"No, it's not. You were in the kitchen. Kitchens are where food is made. You are sexy. Men in kitchens are sexy."

"Really? I had no idea."

"Trust me," I laugh. "So, do you?"

He hands me the glass and keeps the tumbler. Staying standing, he looks at me like I'm a touch crazy.

"Sometimes. I don't cook much. Too much goes to waste. I do have a cedar plank I use to make salmon sometimes. It's really good."

"I don't like fish."

"You don't like fish?"

"I think it's because I'm a Pisces," I wince.

"That makes no sense," he chuckles. "I also make crepes. Do you have any strange aversions to eggs or gluten?"

"Nope," I say. "I love all things butter, eggs, and gluten. It's a part of my balance thing. I eat all the terrible things and then do yoga."

"I thought you went to yoga for stress?"

I look at him blankly. "I do."

He laughs, shaking his head, then taking a sip of his drink. "What about you? Do you cook?"

"I try," I admit. "I like to bake. You know, with—"

"Butter, eggs, and gluten," we say in unison before laughing.

Our voices meld together in the air between us. It's a delicious feeling, warm and cozy and even better than I ever imagined it would be.

Pulling my legs up and under me, I watch him in the light of the fireplace.

"I bet your kitchen is a wreck," he says. "I've seen your desk and there are no liquids. I can only imagine you in a kitchen."

"Yeah, it gets a little wild. Want to cook with me sometime?"

"No. No, I do not. I would never survive that with how messy you are," he jokes.

I'm staring. I know it. I know he knows it when he pulls his brows together and tosses me a questioning glance.

"I was just thinking I love looking at you like this."

"In sleep pants?" he laughs. "Wow. I now officially have a complex about how I look in a suit."

"You rock a suit like no one else," I smile. "But this is so different. You look all cozy and casual. It shows that maybe there are more sides to you than the demanding CEO," I wink.

He sits next to me, fresh from the shower we took together.

Sinking into the leather, he lays one arm along the back of the sofa. "I think you know there is more to me than that."

"I do. But I feel like you keep so much of yourself closed off and your nose to the grindstone. Why?"

His features wash in a look that tells me he was expecting this question or one similar. It also tells me two other things: he's prepared to answer it but he doesn't want to.

He doesn't right away. Taking a sip from his tumbler, he watches me over the rim. I expect he's giving me a chance to change the subject, to get antsy by the look in his eye, but I don't. It's time. Things between us keep building, and I don't know to what end.

"I don't trust a lot of people," he says finally. His tone is smooth, but I hear the grit behind it from the force he's using to make himself talk about a subject he doesn't want to broach. "It's hard for me to really open up beyond my family."

"But you have friends, right? And, you know, probably girlfriends sometimes."

He grins, letting his hand fall to my thigh in some kind of comforting motion. I try not to blush. "I have more acquaintances than I do friends, I suppose. I mainly spend my time with one of my brothers or alone. I prefer it that way." He pauses, smirking. "And, yes, I have girlfriends sometimes. But those relationships are very particular."

I gulp, imagining red rooms and contracts. "What do you mean by that?"

"Just . . ." He looks at the ceiling. "I don't spend time with a woman with the expectation, or desire, if I'm honest, that it will become something routine."

Each word is said crisply without eye contact. Every syllable stings my heart. With each rip against the fabric of my most precious organ, it's obvious: I was hoping for more.

Maybe I didn't realize it until now, but it's impossible to ignore the feeling in my stomach. The grinding, tumultuous movement in my soul.

My spirits fall, the wine glass shaking in my hand so I steady it with the other. I smile at him. I don't want him to see me looking dejected.

"That being said, I really like spending time with you, Mallory. You really make this difficult for me."

"Since we are being honest and all," I say, looking at the darkness through the window and thinking, briefly, how it feels like my heart, "that makes things really difficult for me too."

Before he lifts his hand off my leg, he squeezes it. The spot he'd taken right above my knee feels utterly vacant as soon as his palm is gone.

"Mallory, if I have—"

"No," I cut him off. "You have never indicated you wanted anything more from me than professional performance from seven fifty-nine to five o'clock. The rest of this was just a bonus. I don't expect anything from you."

I say the words and I mean them, but they still hurt like a motherfucker. My butt scoots away from him just a bit and his eyebrows shoot to the ceiling, but he doesn't comment.

"You say I make things difficult, but I don't want that, Graham. I'd never want to interfere with your work, with your family."

"Mallory—"

"No. We aren't at work, so I can put my foot down and make you hear me out."

"Oh, like that matters," he mumbles.

I shrug. "If this gets too difficult or hard or weird, I want to stop it before it gets out of control. I like this, but—"

"You don't like this more than I do," he whispers. "I just keep things in boxes for a reason. Right now, they're a mess and I can't handle messes."

"I hate this for you," I say honestly. "You must be so lonely."

"Being alone is better than being in a relationship and making sacrifices you don't want to make. Or having pressure put on you to choose between the other person and what drives you."

"Who did that to you, Graham?"

The lines in his face move, and I see his surprise that I came out and just asked. Frankly, I'm surprised I came out and just asked too, but I want to know.

He sighs and gets up and heads back in the kitchen. His shoulders are stiff as he fills his tumbler again, keeping his back to me as he quickly downs a good portion of the liquid.

A ripple of panic bubbles up and I'm not sure what to do. My purse is in his car, with my phone, so I can't even call Joy to come and get me, but I feel like I should leave. That I've overstepped my boundary by asking.

My mouth opens to issue an apology and an offer to just go when he turns back around. This time, I see that he's made up his mind.

My wine glass rattles as I place it on a coaster on the table in front of the sofa. My breathing gets ragged as he gets closer. I'm unsure what he's going to do or say.

"When I was in college," he says, sitting on the edge of the sofa, "I wanted to go to law school. I thought it was the best way to help my dad's company, which was the only thing I ever wanted. Growing up, Barrett would go to the movies on the weekends or to a friend's house, and I would go with Dad to the office and just soak it up. I loved the excitement, the power I felt sitting at the spare table and listening to his conversations."

He takes a deep breath, refusing to look at me.

"I had everything laid out in front of me. I knew from eighth grade what I wanted to do and how I was going to get there. We had career day in middle school. We had to pick four professionals to go talk to. The other kids were picking the deejay and television guy and whatever. I picked the attorney four times," he laughs, his voice a touch shaky.

With a trembling hand, I let my palm rest against his knee. The corner of his mouth quivers, but doesn't quite turn up.

"My freshman year of college, I met this guy. We had similar interests and started hanging out. We got an apartment together our sophomore year. It was the first time in my life I'd really kind of loosened up some, you know? It was fun," he shrugs. "Second half of my junior year, I had a philosophy class. The first day, this woman walks in. She was a grad student filling in as a teaching assistant."

"You don't have to talk about this if you don't want to," I say softly. The somberness on his face hurts my heart. "Let's talk about something else."

"No." He clears his throat and looks at me, the greens of his eyes clear. "Her name was Vanessa. I fell in love with her that first day."

His admission is a shock to my heart, my hand slipping off his knee.

He continues on, despite registering my reaction.

"I made a few passes and within three weeks, we were together. We'd meet after class at her apartment across town or we'd spend the weekend at mine. We'd talk philosophy and politics, staying up all night debating free will and morality. It was the first time in my life I met someone that I thought really understood me. Appreciated my, well, my brothers would say geekiness."

He forces a swallow, pain written all over his face. Gazing off in the distance, like he's replaying the time in his mind, I sit back and struggle to contain my own emotions—emotions I can't pinpoint, but am acutely aware exist close to the surface.

"We weren't supposed to be fucking around. We knew she could lose her position and maybe even her scholarship, but she was adamant, as was I, that we wanted to be together. So we continued. The entire semester. Each day got deeper, like stepping off a ledge with every tick of a clock. She wanted all my attention, got jealous when I would go home to see my family or my mom would call or Dad would want me to help with a situation at Landry. It just became so much bigger than I could handle. I constantly felt like I had to choose between her and my other obligations. And, no matter what I chose, someone was pissed off. I didn't want to let anyone down."

His eyes darken, his hands locking together in front of him.

"Then one night, it was late and we'd been drinking more than we should've. It was pouring down rain and her apartment was closer, so we decided to just head there for the night. We'd never stayed there on a weekend," he says, his jaw pulsing. "In the morning, her husband walks in."

"No!" I gasp, my hand finding his thigh again.

"I had no idea, Mallory. None."

My mouth hangs open as I both try to process what he said and the look on his face. I've never seen Graham angry before, but this is so severe, I'm almost scared.

"Word got out," he says, spitting the words, "and she was exposed. Apparently I wasn't the only one she was with. Her husband who worked out of town all week, hence why we never went to her house on the weekends, hung her out to dry with the department."

"She deserved that!"

"Maybe," he says. "So all this is going down and she's still calling me, telling me she wants to be with me. She loves me. I was her soul mate. She wants to marry me, have my babies. That shit, you know?" he hisses. "I was so messed up over this girl that I was going to give her a chance to explain. I just wanted so badly for it to be real." His jaw clenches, the muscle in his face pulsing. "Imagine my shock when I went to her house and realized . . . she was gone."

"Graham," I gush, wishing he'd look at me. "I'm so sorry." I want to pull him into my arms. I have to hold myself back from reaching for him.

"I nearly flunked out the next semester. I couldn't find her. I thought she was dead or something. It was the worst period of my entire life. My parents thought the world had fallen apart. They were wanting me to go to therapy, threatening to pull me out of school altogether. I just couldn't function. I was a complete puss."

"What were you supposed to feel? Look what she did to you!" I say, hating this woman for putting this look on his face. "That shit is hard, Graham. Especially when you're going through it the first time and it's that dramatic."

"She nearly ruined my life. That's just putting it mildly. She fucked up my school situation, my relationships with my family. Everything was ripped out from under me in a few months' time while she vanished, not bothering to give me the courtesy of letting me know she was alive until a few months later with a letter and no return address."

He smiles sadly. "I would rather be alone than be in that situation again." He reaches across the sofa and tucks a stray strand of hair behind my ear. "I look at you and think what a good girl you are. When I'm with you, I just want to stay there forever. When I'm not with you, I want to be."

Tears tickle my eyes because I know there's more coming. The epic life-ruiner, "but," that is on the tip of his tongue.

"But I can't be, Mallory." He lifts my chin so I have to look at him. His face is so handsome, so tender, that I nearly can't breathe. "Since then, I've made a plan on how to deal with things before they creep up. I have contingencies for contingencies so I'm not in a place to make a decision based off emotions." He smiles softly. "I don't know how to manage whatever this is between us. There's no blueprint for this, and every experience I have with it tells me to end it now. But I can't," he whispers.

Words are lost to me as I lose myself in his eyes. There's so much to the depths—pain, sadness, hope. My heart is torn in my chest because I don't know what to do.

The confusion over how to respond, what words to piece together, leaves me speechless.

He tugs at his hair, his head buried in his hands. "I hate feeling this way."

"Don't," I say, grabbing his wrist. "You were honest with me. You just told me something you didn't have to and something that was obviously not easy to say."

"I've never talked about it out loud like that." He wraps my hand in his and brings it to his lips. He doesn't kiss it, but just holds it there. "But I wanted you to know what you were dealing with."

"Dealing with?" I say, scooting closer to him. "You're a man that's had his heart broken. I've had mine broken too. I get it. It hurts."

He drops my hand and smiles more beautifully than I've ever seen from him before. "I hope you find love someday. I hope you find some guy that thinks of you the way I do." His grin falters. "I hope he can give you what you need back."

I look away, unable to see the look on his face and deal with the emotions swirling on mine. Just knowing that he thinks of me the way I think of him, yet can't, won't, go forward, breaks my already shattered heart.

"I think I should go home now," I say, needing space.

"I'll get your jacket." He takes my hand and pulls me to my feet. As I turn to walk away, he hauls me in his arms and holds me close. His heart strums steadily in his chest, the smell of his cologne dancing over my senses. When he pulls back, I know things won't quite be the same between us. "You ready?"

"Let's go."

TWENTY-ONE
MALLORY

THE LEMON SLICE DROPS INTO the tea, creating a ripple on the surface. I wonder how far down the undulation goes. If it goes as deep as what I feel from tonight.

"Come in," I shout when I hear the knock at the door. I wait for Joy's face to come around the corner, and when it does, I feel a little relief.

"I came with brownies," she says. A white box from the grocery store is plopped on the coffee table. "What happened to you? You look like shit."

"Gee, thanks," I sigh. "I'm fine."

Her brows raise. "I don't think that's true."

I give her a look of warning as I take a hesitant sip of my tea. I didn't mean to alert her to my demise when she called as soon as I walked in the door. I guess it was somewhat obvious.

"Want to tell me what's wrong?" she asks.

"No."

"Mallory..."

I take a deep breath. "Graham and I had dinner tonight."

She squeals, curling up in the secondhand chair next to the sofa.

If she's concerned about what the material might do to her name-brand shirt, she doesn't mention it. For once.

"Then we ran back to his house to grab some files. We fucked. Then he basically told me, as carefully and sweetly as possible, that we would never be anything."

"Okay then," she gulps, slowly uncrossing her legs. "Um, that doesn't sound sweet. 'Thank you for fucking me. Now go home?'"

"No, not like that." I recount more closely the events of the evening. "You know, I didn't really think there would be anything between us. I mean, I didn't set out for that to happen. He was just a walking check-off list of all the things I'd want in a man and he wanted me . . . on his desk, in his office, in front of his neighbor."

She fans herself. "I'm so turned on by that."

"Stop," I say, shaking my head. "I don't even know why I'm so . . . saddened by his admission. I had no reason to think anything else."

"But it's natural that you hoped, Mal. Or at least entertained the idea. Wouldn't anyone? He's leading you on, screwing you—"

"He really didn't lead me on," I admit. "He never said anything other than an occasional direction to remove my clothes, which I so happily did." I sigh, taking another sip.

She taps her pink, perfectly manicured finger against her lips. I hate the way she looks at me, like I'm some kind of project or a lesser woman because I'm struggling in every department of my life.

"You know what? Forget it," I tell her. "I'll figure it out."

"Nope. Not that easy," she says. "You have to decide what's best for you."

"Yeah. But I don't know what's best for me."

She catches my gaze. "Yes, you do."

My head falls back, my eyes shut. She's right and I hate it. I do know what's best for me. That's the little niggle in my gut, the reminder to listen to logic and not my heart and certainly not my vagina.

"Put your two weeks in," she suggests softly. "File it with Human Resources and not him so he can't just . . ."

"Just do what he does and veto what he doesn't like?" I offer.

"Yes. That. File your notice and come work with me. I have some pull, you know," she winks. "Or go to LA with Sienna. Mal, you're single. Young. Gorgeous. There's no reason you have to stay here. Do something that your soul tells you to."

I laugh. "Whoa, wait. When did you get deep?"

"What?" she blushes.

"*Do something your soul tells you to?* Really, Joy?"

"It was on a card at the pharmacy," she shrugs. "I liked it."

Taking a deep breath, I set my tea on the table. "I don't know what my soul tells me to do. I just want things to be . . . okay."

I can't tell Joy the rest of the truth, that I hope Graham is okay too. My heart breaks for him. I worry that he's hurt or sad, and I wish I could show him how great he is and how capable he is of more than just being a CEO. Although he listens to me sometimes, I know he wouldn't listen to that.

She opens the box of brownies and hands me one. It's gooey and soft and the icing almost runs off the end. After getting herself one, she holds it in the air. I clink mine against it.

"Sucks being an adult, doesn't it?" she asks, her mouth sticking together with chocolate.

"Yeah. It certainly does."

We sit for a while, Joy eating brownies and me watching her. I'm not hungry. And even though chocolate bingeing is how girls deal with things, it doesn't seem appealing. I don't need emotional support. I need answers. Solutions. The fact that I realize this is empowering.

Joy leaves, promising to check on me tomorrow. I lock the door and wind up at my computer. The email from the university is still in my inbox.

With a slight hesitation, I click on it again. The form is at the bottom to apply for enrollment. It sits there, luring me in with the promise of excitement and possibility.

I could be done in a couple of years. Most of my generals are done and transferable, and I know I qualify for student loans.

I remember Graham's words, that I have potential. Is he right? I know I could do it if I had him to ask questions, but I may not have him at all. In any capacity.

A fleeting feeling falls over my soul. My spirits fall, my excitement dampening, as I know what I'm going to have to do. There's only one answer that's logical when it comes to Graham. At least I can see it now. "Fuck it," I say, filling out the interest form and clicking "Submit" before I can stop myself.

***

Graham

FORD'S FACE LIGHTS UP AS he recounts a story of giving a child a soccer ball somewhere on the other side of the planet. His tale is interesting, but watching him light up like I've never seen him before is the best part of it all.

"He would come up to us every time we saw him and say, 'Thank you,'" he says, leaning back in his chair. "It was really gratifying."

"Well, look who it is . . ."

We look up to see Barrett walk in the kitchen of the Farm, Huxley on his heels. He pulls Ford into a quick hug and then smacks me on the back. "What's happening in here?"

"We were discussing the security company," I say. "There's more to do with this than there was your fucking campaign."

"Just think," Barrett jokes, "you would be bored out of your mind without us."

"Or sane," I mutter.

"Hi, Graham. Hey, Ford!" Huxley, the well-mannered kid that he is, waits his turn to talk. He dashes to Ford's side.

Lincoln has always been Huxley's favorite, but after spending a few days fishing with Ford while his mom and Barrett did political things in Atlanta, I hate to tell Linc that he has competition.

"Want to go see if the fish are biting?" Huxley asks.

"Hey, Hux. Ford is working with Graham today," Barrett says, ruffling his hair.

"True," Ford calls, shoving his chair back, "but fishing is way more fun than talking to Graham. Let's go see what we can get into, buddy." As they walk out, Ford leans in to Barrett and whispers just loud enough for me to hear, "Your turn to deal with him. Graham has a stick up his ass today."

"Fuck off," I chuckle. But he's not all wrong.

I had to leave the office today because I couldn't stand the proximity. Not because I wanted to be away from her. Because I wanted to be inside her. I wanted to scoop her up and listen to her laugh and hear her yoga stories and watch her face bunch up as she thinks of a response to something I've said.

Everything about this is impossible. I watched her pull away from the office last night after dropping her off. Her taillights dimmed as she vanished around the corner, and it took everything I had to not jump in my car and follow her.

Purely selfish. That's what I am. There's nothing I can give her, nothing I'm *willing* to give her, more than what we've been doing. That's not fair to her in any way. Yet, I want to keep her in my office so I can breathe her in, feel her closeness. I want to sneak away for a few hours with her wrapped around me and just enjoy being with her. But if I do, everything will fall apart.

"What's up, G?" Barrett sits in the chair previously occupied by Ford. He twists his head as he considers just how right Ford may have been with his interpretation of my demeanor. "You are pissed off."

"Nah," I say, drumming a pen against the table. "I'm fine."

"Talk to me. What's happening? Something with Ford?"

When I don't respond, he snickers. "Oh, I see."

"You don't see shit."

"Oh, I think I do, little brother." We stare at each other across the table, him laughing, me glaring. "Just to be clear, I may be in Atlanta most of the time now, but I still talk. Specifically, to Linc. So I know things."

"If Lincoln is giving you information, and you're taking it, you aren't nearly as smart as I give you credit for."

"Let's see how credible my sources are. I get one guess, all right?"

"Barrett," I warn.

"It is . . . Mallory?"

I shrug.

"I've seen her. She's hot." I shrug again.

"Ford also chipped in that she was really smart, and believe it or not, Dad likes her."

I shrug for a third time, but this time with a warning shot. Barrett laughs.

"Ford also said if you weren't eyeing her—"

"Enough," I shoot, sitting up and clasping my hands together on the table.

"I was only kidding. Ford didn't say that last part, but I knew if I said he did, I'd get a true reaction out of you."

"You are such a fucking politician," I say, relieved that Ford wasn't seriously looking at Mallory. As the relief lifts off me, I slump back again. "Barrett," I wince. "I'm in trouble."

He leans back in his chair, kicking his feet up on the table, looking all smug.

"Mom will kill you for that," Lincoln blasts, coming in the room. "Trust me. I got smacked yesterday for something pretty similar."

We all laugh as Lincoln grabs a seat next to Barrett. As we settle down, I realize they're both looking at me like I'm a suspect in some investigation. Suddenly, I feel very outnumbered.

"So, what are we talking about?" Lincoln asks, blowing a huge pink bubble and letting it smack against his face.

"Your happiness is annoying," I say.

"That's what good pussy will do for ya, G. Try it."

"We were just talking about that," Barrett notes, smiling smugly at me.

"So he has been tapping that," Lincoln exclaims. "Ford said—"

"Shut up, Lincoln."

"Graham was just about to ask me for advice," Barrett tells our brother.

"No, I wasn't."

"Good thing I stopped by then. I feel like this is my area of expertise," Lincoln says. "Women are my thing. I mean, look at it. I'm the one that's engaged and a little Landry on the way. Bring it, G."

"I don't need your advice."

"So we'll give it to you without you asking," Barrett quips. "Does that make you feel better about it?"

I groan, putting my head on the table.

"You go first," Lincoln tells our brother. "We'll save the best for last."

"Lincoln, you're still on a thin fucking line over this wedding bullshit."

"I can't help it you don't have balls," Lincoln sighs. "When I see what I want, I go for it."

I'm not sure what happens, but I hear a scuffle and the two of them start laughing. When I look up, they're looking at me. "Okay, G. What are the problems with Mallory?"

They're both looking at me, their gazes affixed on my face. There's no way out. I'm as stuck in this situation as I am in the one with Mallory, only with this one, I see a way out. It's going to be painful and potentially humiliating, but there is a way.

Sucking in a breath, I say, "The problem with Mallory is there isn't one." Neither of them respond immediately and that annoys me. "Are we done here?"

"Nope," Lincoln says. "So, just let me get this straight, she does like you? Right? Not saying you aren't all—"

"Knock it off, Linc," Barrett laughs. "What's stopping you, Graham?"

"It just won't work."

"I told you I have tips to fix that," Lincoln winks. "They also make these pills..."

I sigh. "Look, guys, I appreciate your desire to help. I do. But I don't need help. I just need... to figure it out."

Barrett leans against the table, his watch clinking against the wood. "When you meet the right one, it's never easy. There were a number of women I was with and it was *so* fucking easy," he says. "They did what I said. They had the right last name or were on the right track to add to my persona for public office."

"Or they wore black fishnets," Lincoln grins.

"And that," Barrett says, pointing at Lincoln, "is how you know they aren't the right one."

"True." Lincoln takes off his hat and twists it around backwards. "What Barrett is saying is true. With Dani, it wasn't easy. Hell, it's still not. She tells me when I'm wrong and sets me straight. And then we had the whole baseball thing. Shit is complicated. The key is—"

"Wanting to figure it out instead of just replacing them," Barrett says, smiling at Lincoln. "It's when you'd rather take all these problems, all this headache, and fight for it because when you imagine another woman's perfume on your skin or someone else's smile looking back at you..."

"You can't." Lincoln smiles at me. "Someone told me once that maybe I couldn't have the job and the girl. Maybe you can't have this delusion that it 'just won't work' and whatever that fucking means, which is stupid, by the way, and the girl. You're gonna walk away with one of them, G—your dumbass excuses or Mallory Sims. You pick."

The door opens and Ford and Huxley walk back in. I've never felt more relieved to see a kid in my life.

"This isn't over," Lincoln warns.

"Did you have fun?" Barrett asks Hux. "Yeah."

"Are you cheating on me?" Lincoln asks, grabbing Hux by the arm and giving him a quick hug. "How are you, buddy?"

"Good. Hey, I heard you were having a baby. I was thinking. If you want to name your kid after me, I'm okay with that."

"I'll pass that along to the boss," Lincoln laughs.

"All right, guys, I need to get back to the office. Ford, I'll get that final insurance paper faxed back before the end of the week. As soon as that's in place, I think we're good to go."

"Thanks."

"Now go get some puuuu. . . . Puppies," Lincoln chokes, looking at Hux. "Puppies. Go buy yourself a new puppy, Graham."

We all laugh, Huxley looking confused, as I walk out of the Farm.

TWENTY-TWO
GRAHAM

MALLORY'S SEAT IS VACANT WHEN I enter our suite at Landry Holdings. Her phone and keys are in a clump on her desk, wrappers from some kind of candy in a heap by her keyboard.

I can't resist. Picking them up and tossing them in the garbage, I head to my office. Door left open.

I try to focus on the contract in front of me, but every time I hear a sound, I look up to see if it's Mallory. It's some Pavlovian dog bullshit and I hate I'm to this point with her.

Mulling over my brothers' words on the way over here, I know they're right. This is going to end one way or the other. It always does. It's the natural progression of things.

Mallory deserves more than this. She should have the world, someone she can love and mean it. She needs a relationship in which she can fall in love like Alison or Danielle and be safe in it. Besides, I couldn't watch her decide she loves me, then realize she doesn't. *I wouldn't survive that.*

I've avoided her today. She's avoided me too. Getting to the end of this might be easier, and less of my decision, than I thought. That should afford me some relief. Instead, it just winds up my anxiety even worse.

She comes in the suite. Cellophane crinkles through the air and I laugh. *She's such a fucking mess.*

"Hey," she says, poking her head around the door. "I'm going to take off, okay?"

"Is it five already?" I ask, looking at the clock.

"It's five-thirty, actually. I stayed over to finish up something for your father."

"Really? I didn't know anything about that."

"It's no big deal," she says, waving me off. "But I do need to get going."

"Do you have plans?"

"I have yoga." She steps inside my office and I almost choke. Skin-tight pants are stretched over her curves while a white shirt hugs her top. "Are you okay?"

"Fine," I say, wheezing. Clearing my throat, I imagine her at dinner with Keenan. "Could I ask a favor of you?"

"Sure. I wanted to talk to you anyway," she says, pulling her eyes away from mine.

My stomach fills with dread. Heavy, foul, infuriating trepidation. "What about? You can come in, if you'd like."

She considers it for a good bit before taking the steps to the chair across from me. "After today, Ford's company will be good to go for the most part. I'm just waiting for you to sign the insurance paper and then I'll get it faxed back."

I scoot a sheet of paper across the desk. "I signed it. It's done. I'll fax it though. It has to get there by six or the offer is void and we'll have to start from scratch again."

"I'll send it," she says.

"It has to be there before you leave. If not, we won't be guaranteed that rate and we need that rate to hit budget."

"Don't you trust me?" she grins, taking the paper. I look at her warily, but she's right. I do trust her.

"That being said," she says, clearing her throat, "I'd like you to replace me. As soon as possible, preferably."

There's no sunshine in her face, no ease that I'm used to seeing and that winds the dread even tighter.

"Things between us are too complicated for me to keep coming in here every day. I mean, you . . . I . . . we . . ." She looks at me through her thick lashes, begging me to help.

"I understand." The air moves between us, as heavy as the dismay I feel, and I want to reach for her, but that's the problem in and of itself. "I don't want you to go. Can I say that?"

"You can. And I don't want to go, for the record," she sighs. "It's too hard to come here, and I'm not even making a pun this time," she smiles weakly. "I never should've crossed the line with you because we work together so well. But I did."

I think back to all the times we crossed the line and realize the most serious ones weren't the times I was inside her body. They were the times I was inside her mind. When she was burrowing herself inside my heart. That's what got us to this point. It's why this conversation feels like I'm being suffocated. If it were only a physical thing between us, I'd manage. It's not. It's becoming so much deeper than that.

"I did too," I admit.

She nods. "I know a girl, actually, that might be a good fit. I can get her resume, if you'd like."

But she won't be you.

This is for the best. I know it, even though I can't help but hear the scream inside my brain, yelling at me to talk her out of it.

"Are you sure? I don't want you getting yourself in a situation because you leave your job. I can transfer you. You suggested that before, remember?"

"Yeah. But I really think I just need a clean break from you, Graham. You're kind of like crack and I need to go cold turkey."

I grin at her analogy, but there's no happiness in my smile. "I'll write you a shining recommendation," I promise. "I could even help you find another job. You'd be an asset to anyone that would be smart enough to hire you."

"Thank you," she whispers.

I force a swallow. "So, my favor?"

"Sure. Shoot."

I can hear nothing but white noise as I fill my lungs with air. "Lincoln is getting married this weekend. It's at the Farm." I watch her eyes widen, anticipation written all over her pretty face. "Would you do me the honor of being my date?"

"Graham..." she says warily.

"You're going to leave here soon, and let's be honest, I probably won't see you again." My jaw clenches as I say it, but I press forward. "You'll go live some other life, and I wish you the best with it. But since we're stuck together for a little while longer, let's make the best of it. What could it hurt?"

I know the answer. It's only going to make it hurt worse in the end, but I'm willing, for the second time in my life, to take the hedonistic approach. "Are you sure?" she asks. "It's your family, and a wedding at that, and I..."

"What?"

She shrugs.

"And you'd be my date and I'd be honored to have you on my arm." When she doesn't agree, I lean forward. "Don't make me go alone. My brothers won't let me live it down."

Slowly, inch by inch, her face gets a glow of that sunshine I miss. "When you put it like that, I suppose I could help you out."

"There's one more part." There isn't. That was it. Just the wedding. But seeing how easily she agreed, now I'm going to press my luck. "There's a golf outing with my brothers the day before. We're all going. It'll be a nightmare, but it's what Lincoln wanted to do. The girls of my family are going to the clubhouse and having a shower for Danielle. I thought maybe you'd like to go on my behalf."

"What? On your behalf? That makes no sense, Graham."

"Yeah," I say, thinking on my feet. "My mother will be there, both my sisters. Alison and Danielle and a couple of her friends. I thought it would be nice if you went. I know it would mean a lot to Lincoln too." That last bit is a stretch. Lincoln won't care. He's only worried about Danielle and making her happy. *Bingo!*

"Dani isn't from here," I say, laying it on thick. "She doesn't have a lot of friends here and I know Lincoln really wants us all to come out and support her."

"I don't even know her," she points out.

"Yeah, but she's heard us all talking about you." I gulp and prepare to wind a little more truth to this. "It would mean a lot to me."

She sucks in a breath, warring over her decision.

"Please?"

"Fine," she exhales. "I'll do it."

"Great! I'll—"

"Not so fast," she says, waving a finger at me. "I'll go on one condition."

"What's that?"

"You go to yoga with me tonight."

"Mallory," I groan. "Be reasonable."

"I think this is very reasonable. I'm considering accompanying you to a wedding and a bridal shower for someone I don't even know. That's a lot I'm giving you, Graham. You can certainly give me an hour of yoga."

"I don't yoga."

"You'll yoga just fine." She stands, nestling her hand in the crook of her hip. She knows what she's doing because she smirks. "You'll need to be at the studio by six." Like the decision has been decided, she takes the insurance papers and bounces to the door. "Oh, and Graham?"

She looks coyly at me.

"Yes?" I ask.

"Don't be late."

***

Mallory

I HAVE NO IDEA WHY I do this to myself. Laughing out loud, I correct my inner monologue. I *do* know why I do this to myself. At least this time. I want to see Graham Landry relaxed. He's been going so full-tilt with all the things on his plate that I want to give him a few minutes away from the office. Just a piece of time where there's nothing to do but *be*. Factoring in that I might see some muscle, and if I'm lucky, some sweat, doesn't hurt either.

Stretching out for the last thirty minutes, I feel nice and limber. Everything is tingly, but that probably has nothing to do with the moves I've been holding and more to do with the headlights suddenly shining in the front window of the studio.

I'm aware I'm an addict and I measure my drugs in Grahams. Just like anyone that has an insatiable craving for something, I want to horde the remaining moments I have with him because once it's over, it's over. It has to be. I can't take a gratuitous huff of his stick from time to time. My breath catches as he walks in the studio. Dressed in a pair of black workout pants that, as opposed to most men, fit him semi-snugly. Like his suit pants, only not. Only, quite possibly, better. A sleeveless black shirt covers his torso, his arms on display for my gratification.

He glances around, biting his bottom lip. "So this is a yoga studio?"

"It is." I pop up on my bare feet. "Ever think you'd be in one?"

"Nope." He gives me a mega-watt grin, tossing a grey duffle bag on the floor. "Shoes off?"

"Please."

I watch as he casts off his shoes and socks and then pads across the floor and to the mat I have laid out for him next to mine. "I hope you're happy," he says, looking uncomfortable. "I left a stack of papers unsigned to be here."

"You must really want me to go to that wedding," I tease.

"Something like that," he mumbles, turning in a full circle. "There are mirrors everywhere. This studio could be used for another purpose, if you follow me."

I smack his arm, making him laugh. "Focus, Graham."

"Okay, okay. What first?"

"Just sit and stretch out. Get loose."

He sits and looks at me.

"Don't act so excited," I say, sitting next to him. "You'll wear out your energy before we get started."

"I'll try to rein it in."

He mimics my movements. For someone in such great shape, he's as stiff as a board. It's almost comical, but I don't comment on it. I just enjoy having him near me outside the office. Besides, he's clearly out of his comfort zone enough without my prodding.

"This is yoga?" he asks, stretching one arm overhead. "This is stupid."

I hop to my feet and get behind him. "No," I say, taking his sinewy arm in my hand. "*This* is yoga." I turn his palm and pull his arm farther out and up.

"Fuck," he grimaces. "Easy there, tiger."

"See? You yoga just fine." I take his other arm and manipulate it the other way. "How does that feel?"

"Wonderful."

It feels wonderful to me too to have him in my hands. To be able to touch him and have a reason. "Let's Downward Facing Dog."

"I hope that's a pseudonym for doggy style."

"No," I laugh, taking a big step away from him before I rip off my clothes and bend over in front of him. "This." I pose in an inverted V and look at him. "Do this."

"Nah," he grins, sitting back. "I'll just watch you. The view is phenomenal."

I fall to my knees. "The deal was you do yoga. Not watch me do yoga."

"I'm here. I yoga'd."

"No, you stretched. Kind of." I flash him a look. "Your body is so stiff."

"I thought you liked me stiff ?"

We grin at one another, but the longer we hold it, the heavier everything suddenly feels. A chasm has been dug between us, a crater we can't overcome. Things aren't as easy as they used to be.

"I'm sorry, Mallory," he says, sitting upright. His arms over his bent knees, he looks at me.

"It's okay." I pop up in a plank and focus on my breathing. "We both know what it is . . ." I drop onto the floor, facing away from him. "And what it's not."

"I wish I could be something different."

"No. Don't, Graham. You're brilliant how you are."

He moves to the front of me so I can't look anywhere but at him. "Can I tell you something?"

"Sure. Unless it's something like you don't want me to go to the wedding because Joy has already committed to letting me borrow a dress. That's no easy feat, my friend."

"I didn't consider you didn't have a dress."

"Oh, I do," I lie. "I just wanted hers."

"I could get you one," he offers.

"And I could not wear it."

He chuckles. Taking a deep breath, he slowly looks at me. "I just, I want you to know the real reason things between us will never be anything."

My throat burns as I force a swallow past the boulder-sized lump. "I think we already discussed that."

"I only gave you a part of it. The easy part to admit."

"Graham, there was nothing easy about that conversation for you."

"True. But I don't want you walking away from this thinking this is your fault or you did something wrong or there's something wrong with you that would prevent us from being together."

I frown, my heart breaking. "Do we have to do this?"

"It's important to me," he whispers. "If you decided you had feelings for me, then decided you didn't, I think . . . I think that would be very difficult for me to deal with."

I know this has something to do with Vanessa, the bitch I'd like to kick in the face for screwing up this man. Even so, I don't know how to respond. My heart sings, yet breaks, at his admission and all I can do is watch him wrestle with his emotions.

"I dislike very much when things aren't planned for," he says softly. "I like numbers. Schedules. Dates. Then you walked in my office and sort of took everything I want and threw it all in the air with your water bottle and papers."

"I'm not asking you—"

"No," he says, reaching for my hand. "I know you're not. You're not asking anything of me. But I'm struggling here because . . ."

Standing, I walk behind him and take his shoulders in my hands. I work them back and forth, the quietness of the studio comforting us both. "Promise me you'll start doing something for you," I say finally. "Maybe you don't yoga, but you could get a massage. From a man," I add with a gulp. "I could get you a standing appointment every month. I know you would go if it was on your calendar."

Chuckling, he tilts his head and looks at me through his thick, dark lashes.

"And you need to keep some protein bars in your desk. You go too long in between meals," I add. "I can have Hillary's House start bringing you breakfast—"

"Mallory," he breathes, but doesn't continue.

"Just . . . take care of yourself, Graham."

He doesn't say anything, but he doesn't have to. I'm glad for it because if he did, I might cry.

TWENTY-THREE
GRAHAM

"*PROMISE ME YOU'LL START DOING something for you.*"

It's that line, that one little sentence, that's fucked with me all night. It's why I burned my salmon, why I knocked over a new bottle of Blanton's, my favorite bourbon. It's why I left the shower running for a good ten minutes before I realized I never got in.

I think about the small things she does for me. The way she goes out of her way to take care of things, the way she worries about me. As much as I love being with her physically, the way she feels against me, this part of her is what hits me in a way I haven't felt before. It's what I can't shake, what I fear will leave a hole when she leaves.

When she leaves.

"Shit," I groan, pressing my hands against the glass door to the patio. I'm all tied up, a complete fucking wreck, and I really don't even have the energy to try to straighten it out.

Shoving off the glass and turning towards my briefcase on the kitchen table, I pull out a few files I need to work on. I glance at them and realize—I don't care. Not like I should. Something is off and it's not Landry Security or Lincoln's contracts. It's something else.

I slam the files on the table and they hit it with a smack. Something rolls out of my briefcase and drops to the floor. A wide grin tickles my lips. Laughing, I scoop it up and hold it in the air. A roller bottle with a label for "Stress Relief " catches the light. "Mallory," I whisper. "Damn you."

I could call up a woman and try to distract myself. I could . . . *try to replace her.* My brothers' words rip through my mind, leaving a trail of awareness behind.

I can't replace her. I don't want to. Hell, I couldn't.

There's no way to switch her out for another woman. It would take two, three, maybe even four to amount to all the things she's becoming to me.

Before I can contemplate that too much, my phone rings. I don't even look at it. I just answer it, my brain too fogged up by my realization to think straight.

"Hello?" I ask, preoccupied.

"Graham?"

The phone wobbles in my hand and I almost drop it to the floor. Surely I'm wrong. I must be so twisted over Mallory and stressed out that I'm imagining things. That has to be it.

"Graham?" she asks again. Her voice is clear this time and exactly how I remember it.

I force a swallow, my emotions strung all over the place. I've waited to hear her voice for years, wondering what I would say to her. Now that she's on the line, I have no idea what to say at all.

"Vanessa?" I ask.

"It's me," she says breathily. "I wasn't sure if you'd remember my voice."

Images of her lying in my arms, of her smile, and then of her husband's face standing at the end of her bed flip through my mind. My stomach knots.

"Why are you calling me?"

"Lincoln's wedding is all over the entertainment channels and magazines. He looks so much like you did back then." She pauses. "How are you, Graham?"

"Vanessa, I . . ." I scrub my hands down my face, searching desperately for some calm in the center of this storm. "So you see my brother on television and you think, 'Oh, I'll call up the guy I fucked over years ago'?"

She's taken aback by my tone, and frankly, so am I. Whatever I thought I'd say before isn't what I'm feeling right now.

"Where's your husband?"

"We split up a while ago," she admits. "I should never have married him in the first place."

"No, you shouldn't have," I say. "You probably fucked him up too."

"What?"

The anger I've felt towards this woman boils to an all-time high. "Did you have no conscience at all? You were married, Vanessa. Married. Do you have any idea what that even means?"

"Graham . . ."

"Then you fuck with me, both literally and figuratively, because it wasn't good enough for you to get my cock. You had to go worm your way into my life, cause problems for me with my family." The more I say it out loud, the clearer it becomes.

"I loved you!"

"You didn't love anyone but yourself. I doubt you even understand what love means." As the words tumble from my lips, I laugh. "I didn't understand what love meant until recently."

A long pause settles over us, my outburst giving us both time to think. I remember all the ways I felt about Vanessa and all the ways I feel now towards Mallory. They're completely different. Black and white. But one wasn't love and the other . . . might be on its way there.

"I was thinking I might be in Savannah in a few weeks. I thought maybe we could meet up. Say hello."

"No." It's a simple answer, a one-word shut down.

"You don't even want to think about it?"

"Vanessa, I wish you the best. I can honestly say that with no reservations. I hope you have a terrific life and get everything you want. But none of that has anything to do with me."

"I'm not asking to date you again or—"

"Good. Because we didn't date then and we aren't about to do anything now. We aren't friends," I say over top of her objections, "we aren't acquaintances. We aren't anything."

"You can't say that."

"I just did. Goodbye, Vanessa."

I end the call and place my phone on the table. I imagine Vanessa's perfume on my skin and her smile looking back at me. I can't.

Picking up Mallory's roller ball, I roll it onto my forearm and breathe in the scent of lavender. I'm sure it's less to do with the oil itself and more to do with the woman that gave it to me, but as soon as fragrance hits my nose, my frustration starts to melt away.

***

Mallory

"THERE THEY ARE!" DIGGING THROUGH the back of the towel closet in the bathroom, I spy the container of batteries I've been looking for. "Why are they in here?"

Shrugging, I pull them out and take them to the kitchen to their rightful spot: the junk drawer.

The house smells like cinnamon and sugar, the sweet scent of snickerdoodle cookies. I woke up happy this morning, even though I went to bed a little down in the dumps. Leaving Graham after our yoga exercise was a moment I'll always remember. Not because it was super sexy, because it wasn't. It's also not because he said anything sweet or profound, because he didn't.

When his hand touched mine, it wasn't with any ulterior motive. When his lips kissed my cheek, it wasn't foreplay. When his eyes met mine, he wasn't seeing my face or my body. He saw . . . me.

In those few seconds, a warmth rushed through me. Something

was exchanged between us in that moment, something realer than we've experienced. As he saw me, so did I.

The way he looked at me, with respect and admiration and maybe even something else that I'm too afraid to consider, shook me. The longer his gaze lingered on me, the more I felt like the woman I've been searching for. And as our conversation turned to our plans for the future and he began insisting I go back to school, for business, no less, and he asked how he could help facilitate that, I felt like the world was at my feet. It was the feeling I used to have. The one I lost so long ago.

That's what I took with me to bed and that's what I woke up with.

A feeling that maybe I'm going to be okay.

And I get to see him today. That doesn't hurt.

Popping the cookies out of the oven, I make sure the picture frame I purchased off her registry this morning is wrapped. The tape didn't want to stick, but it looks pretty.

The mossy green dress I wore to my first day at Landry is laid on my bed. I slip it on and add a pair of heather heels and a simple gold necklace. When I look in the mirror, I do something I don't normally do: I genuinely smile.

For the first time in a long time, I know the girl looking back at me. I see her strength, her confidence, and while they might be cracked, they're there. They were gone for so long.

"You've got this. You're going to be okay," I whisper in the mirror before grabbing the gift, my keys, and heading to the Savannah Room.

TWENTY-FOUR
MALLORY

THE SAVANNAH ROOM IS A beautiful estate in the city. There are grounds to walk and enjoy nature, as well as a golf course and tennis courts. In the center of the gardens is a network of old, brick buildings that have been maintained since before the Civil War. The main part is used for large gatherings, political events, weddings, and rallies. There are smaller conference rooms along the periphery.

Glancing at Graham's text, I veer my car to the side towards the golf course. A valet greets me, says nothing about the state of the interior of my car, and whisks it away. I'm left standing in front of the clubhouse.

A gentle breeze blows across grasses, carrying with it a feeling of warmth. Of new beginnings. Tucking the gift in my arm, I climb the stairs and hear the sounds of talking and laughter right away.

The door is opened as a man exits and I duck inside. My heart is strumming in my chest as I look for Camilla or Sienna. I don't know anyone else. I'm not sure why I'm here. It's stupid. It's silly. It's—

"There you are!" I hear Sienna's voice above everyone else. Soon after, she makes her way through the small crowd in a lilac shift dress that hits her mid-thigh, almost making her look like royalty. "I'm so glad you're here."

"Me too." I must not be convincing because Sienna laughs.

"I'm sorry. I am happy to be here. I'm just a bit nervous."

"Don't be," she scoffs, her eyes bright. "Everyone is great. I can say that and mean it. How many girls can say that about their sisters-in-law?"

"None," I laugh as she leads me across the room. I deposit my gift on a large table near the window overflowing with packages. "Everyone, this is Mallory Sims. I went to school with her."

"I remember you," Mrs. Landry says, pulling me in for a quick hug. "How are you?"

"I'm fine. Thank you for asking. You?"

"I'm fine, sweetheart." She senses my apprehension and helps wash it away with a kind smile. "Mallory, this is my friend Paulina, followed by Alison, Barrett's girlfriend, Macie, Danielle's friend from Boston, and the woman of the hour, Danielle Ashley."

Everyone says hello, giving me small waves and welcomes. They're a beautiful group of women, perfectly coiffed, yet so warm and inviting. They all go back to their conversations as Camilla joins me.

"Overwhelmed?" she laughs.

"No, strangely," I admit. "It's not as bad as I thought it would be."

"Come on." She leads me towards Danielle, who is wearing a short, white dress. Her dark hair is in curls and a stark contrast to the fabric. She looks at us with a giddiness I can only imagine. "Dani, this is my friend, Mallory. I know Mom did an introduction, but I wanted to make sure I did it personally."

Danielle pulls me in for a one-arm hug. "It's so nice to meet you. I've heard so much about you."

"You have?"

"Yes," she giggles. "Lincoln said he met you the other day." She leans forward conspiratorially. "He also said Graham is a little smitten with you."

My cheeks turn the color of the roses on the table. "I don't know about that."

She shrugs. "That's the word on the street. I also might've overheard a conversation between the two of them the other night. Linc had Graham on speakerphone while he worked out, so it's not like I was eavesdropping," she winks. "But Graham seemed defensive when it came to you."

"I heard that too," Alison says, smiling as she comes up on my other side. Her golden dress shines, making her look even more radiant than she already is. "I'm Alison, by the way."

"It's so nice to meet you," I say, shaking her proffered hand.

"You too." She stands next to Danielle. "Are you from here?"

"Yes, although I haven't lived here in a while. It kind of feels like I'm new here, to be honest."

"Welcome to the club," Danielle laughs. "I need to find a good bakery here. Know of one?"

"I do," I tell her. "There's a place near my house called Corner's. Best cinnamon rolls you could ever want."

Danielle sighs. "Girl, you just found yourself a new friend. When I get back from my honeymoon, I'm going to get your number and we are going to the bakery!"

Alison laughs, putting her hand on her belly. "If I'm home, don't the two of you even think about leaving me out. I can get nuts over a good cinnamon roll."

My heart swells as I listen to these women make plans for the three of us. The bakery turns into a full-blown lunch that turns into a day at the spa. Before I know what's happening, a date is set, reservations are made, and the deal is done.

I think I'm grinning like a teenage girl being included at the cool lunch table. That is, until the door opens and some of the best-looking men I've seen in my entire life walk in. *Together.*

They come in like a stampede, a burst of movement and noise, laughter and shouts, that makes all of us back up to make room.

Their shirts are wet, water dripping off their hair.

"It's raining," Lincoln says, shaking his head. Droplets fly off of him like a dog after a bath, making Camilla shriek.

"Stop it," she says, swatting him.

Over the top of the pack, in the back, I find Graham. He's watching me with a tentative smile. When I return it, his spreads across his face.

The guys filter out, some to their girlfriends or wives, some to the catering table. Graham comes straight for me.

"You're here," he says, like he thought I wouldn't be.

"You're wet."

"That I am," he chuckles. "We got to the third hole and it just cut loose out of nowhere. I had to ride in the cart back with Lincoln, hence the reason we are wetter than everyone else. He hit every puddle from there to here."

Laughing, I notice he's right. He's almost completely soaked whereas most of the others aren't quite so wet.

"How are things in here?" he asks.

"Things in here are great," Danielle says, sliding up beside him. "I told her I've heard a lot about her."

"That was nice of you," Graham says, looking at her out of the corner of his eye.

"We made plans for two weekends from now. So mark that on your calendar, all right?" Danielle asks.

Alison comes up behind me. She must be mouthing something to Graham because I see him watching her over my head. He shakes his head. "You two are as bad as my brothers," he groans before turning towards me. "You would think a bright woman like you would've stayed away from those two."

Our conversation is interrupted by Mrs. Landry. "Ladies—and gentlemen, I suppose—it's time to open gifts."

Everyone begins to shuffle towards the front, but Graham pulls me to the back and around a corner. There's a nook there with a shelf that runs along the top of the room. We can hear the other guests down the hall, but there's no one around.

"Is everything okay?" I ask, my breathing picking up.

His gaze is heated as he stands in front of me. "It's more than okay." Our lips taunt one another, one of us leaning toward the other and then stopping before the other one begins. It's a dance, a step forward, a step back, pure torture that is this close to falling over the edge. "Mallory, I . . ."

I drop my chin.

"When I walked in here and saw you in the mix with my family . . ."

Lifting my eyes to his, I see them shine. Something is different with him. I can't put my finger on it, but it seems like some of the burden he carries is gone.

His green polo shirt makes his eyes look brighter, his hair darker, his smile whiter. More beautiful and handsome than usual.

I tell myself not to. I try to resist. But my hand finds his cheek, and as soon as I touch him, he rewards me with a smile.

"Will you stay with me after the wedding?" he asks quietly.

"But—"

"I know what you're going to say. You're going to remind me of our conversation at the house and probably reiterate all the things I said to you. But stay with me, Mallory. Please."

I can say no. It's on the tip of my tongue. But instead of just giving in to him, going along with the look in his eye because I have no other choice, I realize . . . I do have a choice.

Studying his features, I let myself pause. Gazing in his eyes, feeling the energy rippling between us, I know my answer and it's because it's what I want—not because it's what he wants.

"Yes, Graham," I say. "I'll stay with you."

His lips find mine in a kiss that has nothing to do with sex, nothing to do with being in an alcove away from his family. And that says more than any words ever could.

TWENTY-FIVE
MALLORY

"THANK YOU," I SAY, HANDING a man in a tux my keys. He looks at my car and crinkles his face. "It's just a few takeout bags. Don't pretend yours doesn't look like that."

"Whatever you say," he grumbles, climbing into the driver's seat.

If today was any other day, I would rip him a new one for implying I'm less than a vision of cleanliness. Maybe I am. That's not the point. The point is only assholes point it out.

"Hi, Mal!" I look up to see Sienna and Camilla coming towards me. In matching yellow bridesmaid's dresses, their hair swept up in fancy chignons, they look beautiful. "That dress on you is gorgeous. Graham's going to die," Sienna gushes.

"It's Joy's," I say brightly. "It's pretty, isn't it?"

"I love how it tucks right at your waist. And that pink is definitely your color," Cam smiles. "Did you just get here?"

I nod, looking around the Farm. Soft, twinkling yellow lights lead down the path towards the back of the house. Fabric in shades of yellows and pinks is draped over the walkway, creating an inviting, stylish ambiance. Guests bustle around, some with champagne flutes in their hands, all dressed to the absolute nines.

It's breathtakingly beautiful. Simple and elegant at the same time.

Very Landry.

"We need to be going inside," Camilla says. "We have a few pictures to take before the wedding starts."

"I still can't believe Lincoln is getting married," Sienna laughs. "I never thought he'd be first. As a matter of fact, I thought he'd be last."

"Me either," Camilla agrees.

"You're staying for the reception, right?" Sienna asks me.

"Um, I think so. I'm at Graham's mercy."

"That sucks."

"Why?" I laugh.

"Because he never stays long at things. He stays until the moment he can leave," Camilla answers. "He's not a people person."

I yelp as a hand presses against the small of my back. When I look back, my eyes lock with Graham's. It's a mixture of all-out fire and the sweetest warmth I can imagine.

"Hey," he whispers, his palm pressing into me a little more. "You look absolutely beautiful."

"Thank you."

"We're out of here," Sienna scoffs playfully. "I think we're getting pictures in just a few minutes, G. Don't be late. Mom is already an emotional mess."

"I won't," he says to her, his eyes still on me. "Thank you for coming."

"Of course," I say, finding my voice.

"I hate I couldn't pick you up and bring you here myself. But, being Best Man and all, I had duties to fulfill."

He offers me the crook of his arm and I take it. It's impossible to miss the twinkle in his eye as we make our way towards the archway next to an open-air structure. It's loaded with flowers—a happy, carefree, elegant visual as soft music plays from hidden speakers.

"After the ceremony, the reception is in there." He points to an open-air structure that nearly glows from the candles lit inside. "I'll meet you there."

"Sounds good."

Our steps slow as Graham's father rounds the corner, spying us, and makes a beeline our way. I start to remove my hand from Graham's arm, not sure if it is appropriate, but his hand clamps down on mine, making it impossible to move.

"I didn't know you were joining us today," Mr. Landry says. "It's nice to see you, Mallory."

"It's nice to be here, Mr. Landry."

"You can call me Harris."

"I'll try," I laugh. "You're technically my boss."

"Graham is your boss. I'm just an old man that makes sure his son doesn't get out of line." He looks at Graham and smiles proudly. "I have a feeling he's doing just fine."

My heart fills, even more so when Graham squeezes my hand. Mr. Landry looks at me again. "I wanted to thank you again for helping sort out that contract this week. I'm not sure it would've gone through without you, Mallory."

"What are you talking about?" Graham asks, his brows pulling together.

"Lincoln's contract for the foundation he and Danielle are starting had a few hiccups. I mentioned it in passing when I was in the office for Ford's meeting, and she jumped right in and helped get some details straightened out."

Mr. Landry smiles proudly at me. He's handsome, an older version of Graham, with a deep voice and an easy charisma. I can only imagine what he was like in his youth.

"I didn't know this," Graham looks down at me, a look of intrigue on his face. "When did you do that?"

"That's why I stayed late the other day," I remind him. "Remember?"

Mr. Landry clasps Graham's shoulder as he heads towards the house. "Pictures in a few minutes, son."

"I'll be there," Graham says, still looking at me. He turns his body to face mine, a little smile trying to break across his face. "Why didn't you mention Lincoln's contracts to me?"

"You were busy," I explain. "You had all of Ford's things on your desk and Lincoln's contracts were something I could handle quickly without your involvement. There were no decisions to be made, just a shuffling of information." When he smiles, I return it as my heart flutters in my chest. "I was just trying to take a few things off your plate, Graham. I hope that's okay."

He bends down and presses the simplest kiss against my lips. I see it coming, but it's quick enough that there's no time to prepare. When he pulls away, I'm breathless.

"Thank you," he whispers almost reverently.

"For what?" I say, my voice sounding shakier than I'd like. "For doing my job?"

He just smiles. "For so many things."

"That sounds like a cop-out," I laugh.

"It is, in a way. I . . ."

"Graham!" We turn to see Sienna standing on the back porch. "Mom is freaking out. We never, ever wait on you. She's certain the world is falling apart today."

Graham chuckles and indicates for her that he needs one second. His gaze returns to me as he forces a swallow. "I don't want to be here long tonight. I'll make my speech, watch them cut the cake or whatever, but we're leaving as soon as the opportunity presents itself."

"Your sisters warned me you do this," I laugh.

"I probably do," he sighs. "But tonight . . . it's different."

"Okay."

He walks towards his sister. There's something about his posture that strikes me. It's not his usual purposeful walk, like he had somewhere to be ten minutes ago. Today, his hands are in his pockets, his posture easy. As he reaches the steps, he hesitates, looking back at me. When he catches me watching him, his face breaks out in a huge smile. I return it, feeling my heart nearly burst in my chest. He simply shakes his head before disappearing inside.

THE SMELL OF FRESH FLOWERS drifts through the air. A fairly small group of people, maybe thirty or forty, sit in white chairs with yellow tulle tied in a bow on the backs. The pastor reads from his script while everyone watches Danielle and Lincoln.

They're beautiful, magazine-like, as they hold hands and face one another in front of their friends and family. I'm not sure Lincoln is listening to the words being spoken. He's just gazing at his bride like she's the only person here. It's fun to watch, and I understand why the woman beside me elbowed her husband in the side and told him to take notes.

My gaze, however, is affixed to the man right behind the groom. The one slightly taller, slightly darker, much broodier. The one out of the group of brothers that seems slightly frustrated by having all of this attention on him, the only one that didn't mug for pictures before the wedding started. Barrett teased him that he was too uptight, but I have a feeling it was because he would have had to look somewhere other than at me. Because that's all he has done—looked at me like he's never seen me before. Sometimes it's like we're sharing an inside joke, but other times it's like he's completely perplexed at me sitting here amidst his family.

All the time, however, he's looking like he wants to jump off the step someone built for this occasion and whisk me away.

"Lincoln?" The pastor nudges the groom and he laughs.

"Sorry, Pastor Frank."

"That's fine," he says to a bubble of laughter from everyone. "It's time for your vows."

Lincoln turns and takes the ring from Graham and hovers it over Danielle's finger.

"I, Lincoln Harrison Landry, take you, Ryan Danielle Ashley, to be my wife. I promise to keep coffee creamer in the fridge, chocolate donuts on the counter, and ice water by the bed." He winks at Danielle, who blushes. "I promise to listen when you're mad, hug you when you're sad, and put your needs and desires before mine, even when you ruin my favorite shirts."

He clears his throat and looks at the sky. Graham steps forward and puts a hand on his shoulder. It's then we see a single tear trickle down Lincoln's cheek.

I dab at my eyes, watching Danielle's Maid of Honor hand her a tissue and Lincoln get himself together.

"I love you, Dani. I love you more than I ever thought I could love anyone," he says, his tone heavy with emotion. "You make me a better version of me, even though I didn't think that was possible."

Everyone laughs as Lincoln shrugs, his swagger back. "I promise to make this season the best one of our lives."

He leans in to kiss Danielle, but the pastor puts his hand on Lincoln's chest. "Not yet, Lincoln."

Everyone laughs again as Danielle gets Lincoln's ring and begins to place it on his finger.

"I, Ryan Danielle Ashley, take you, Lincoln Harrison Landry, to be my husband. I promise to not only love you, but cherish you forever because I want you to know each and every day how much I adore you. I promise to support you in everything you do and be your partner in all your endeavors. I'll keep fake cheese in the pantry," she says, her voice cracking, "and do the cooking so you don't burn the house down. I . . ." Tears run down her face too quickly for her to finish her sentence.

As I soak up mine, I feel Graham looking at me. Flipping my sight to him, his brows are pulled together.

When our eyes meet, his features soften as his eyes widen and he takes a step back, like he's seen an apparition.

"You okay?" I mouth, feeling my heartbeat pick up.

He nods, a slow smile spreading across his face. Our little moment is halted by a burst of cheers and applause from the crowd.

"I now give you Mr. and Mrs. Lincoln Landry!" the pastor announces. "You may *now* kiss the bride."

This is usually my favorite part of a wedding. The first few moments of the union, the kiss that seals the deal. But today, all I can do is return Graham's grin.

TWENTY-SIX
GRAHAM

MY ENTIRE FAMILY SITS AT a huge rectangular table eating, drinking, and laughing. Some of our friends sit at smaller tables around us or under the tents put up to extend the space.

The stone columns are wound with clear lights, the fireplace that my siblings and I have sat around and told stories on more nights than I can count growing up is lit, giving the area a very intimate touch. Flowers dot the centers of each table, along with remnants of dinner and wine. Lots of wine.

"Come here," Mallory says from beside me. She reaches up and loosens my tie. She's done this before and it's one of my favorite quirks of hers. "There. Is that better?"

"Yes." I smile at her, the softness of her features made even more beautiful in the soft light of the candle in the center of our table. It occurs to me that I didn't know it was bothering me to begin with. "It is, actually."

Her grin widens. "You had that look in your eye."

"Which one is that?"

"The one that looks like you're ready to stand up and leave. I figured if you were more comfortable, maybe you would stick around." She leans in closer. "I think your family would appreciate that."

I'm sure they would, but I'm antsy. My foot is tapping on the floor, my fingers itching to grab my fork, pick up my glass, smooth my tie. I can't sit still. I want to get out of here, take Mallory home, and talk to her. The event planner comes up behind me and taps me on the shoulder, letting me know it's time to make my speech. I grab Mallory's hand and give it a gentle squeeze beneath the table and then stand. Within a few seconds, everyone is quiet and watching me.

"May I have your attention for a few minutes?" I ask the gathering of our loved ones. "As the Best Man, I'd like to say a few words. First of all, I'd like to thank you all, on behalf of my entire family, for coming tonight. This was put together in a complete rush, but we all have come to expect that from Lincoln, haven't we?"

Everyone laughs as Lincoln voices his objection.

"Even so, it was put together beautifully and I know I speak on behalf of everyone, Danielle, when I say we're honored to welcome you into our family."

She raises a glass as Lincoln nestles her under his arm to shouts of celebration.

"Growing up, I got stuck with Linc a lot. Barrett was older and Ford and Linc were oil and water for a bit. That left me to pick him up from practice or drop him off at the field. Because that's where he always was—playing ball.

"To see him give that up for someone is pretty incredible. It speaks volumes about how he feels about you, Danielle. Thank you for making him happy and straightening him out. And for taking responsibility for his antics now that you're his wife."

Everyone laughs again, but I'm distracted by Mallory's hand on the back of my leg. When I look, my breath is almost whisked away. In the sparkling lights, surrounded by everyone I love, having her look up at me with the sweetest smile on her face hits me in a place I can't comprehend. It's a stillness, a satisfied feeling washing over me that

I've never felt before. "Congrats, Lincoln and Danielle. Everyone, raise your glass to the bride and groom," I say, taking my seat as the guests toast the newlyweds.

Immediately, I'm grasping under the table for her hand. Once her palm is lying in mine, I find that stillness again.

"You did great," she whispers in my ear.

Before I can respond, Ford rises from his seat in between our sisters. "I may not be the Best Man, *technically*, but I'd still like to say a few words."

"Oh, God," Linc jokes. "I didn't pick you, Ford. You don't get a speech."

"Yes, you do, Ford," Danielle laughs. "Don't listen to him."

"See? You're already losing your manhood, Linc," Barrett points out to everyone's amusement. Lincoln just shakes his head, but the grin on his face gives him away.

"So, Graham was right. Lincoln and I would fight to the death over a video game or who got the last piece of Mom's apple pie," Ford laughs. "But God help the poor soul that messed with one of us."

"Like Nate Caster. Remember that?" Lincoln bursts out laughing.

"Yeah," Ford chuckles.

"You boys swore you didn't do that!" Mom interjects, her mouth falling open. We all laugh as the truth hits her. "You little rascals. I don't care if you're married or not. We're going to talk about this!" She tries to sound authoritative, but can't quite keep the amusement out of her tone.

Once we've all quieted down, Ford continues. "That's how we roll, Dani. We're a family in every sense of the word. We'd do anything for each other. I hope you're ready for that." He turns his sight on Lincoln again, his face sobering. "Lincoln, my brother, it's an honor to be here tonight to see you start this next phase of your life. I can't tell you how proud I am of you. For going after what you want and not letting her walk away. To Dani and Lincoln."

With a gentle nod and a lump obvious in his throat, he sits down as we all raise our glasses again. Camilla pats his arm as his eyes drop to the floor.

"Is Ford okay?" Mallory whispers in my ear.

"He'll be fine." I turn to see the concerned look on her face. "He let a girl go once, before he went overseas. I'm not sure he's ever gotten over her."

She starts to respond, but stops when everyone starts laughing. Barrett is rising out of his seat now, a huge grin on his face.

"My turn," he laughs. "I've done a few things in my life that have made me proud. Things I think have made my parents happy."

"This isn't about you!" Lincoln shouts. "Keep the focus over here."

"Give me a second," Barrett sighs as the wedding planner stands near the fireplace, looking helpless.

"Don't worry," I call to her. "I'll make sure you get a great tip."

"Thanks," she says weakly.

The chaos that is the Landry's is in full effect, everyone talking amongst themselves. A few servers come around with more wine as others cart in a tall wedding cake.

"As I was saying," Barrett says, quieting everyone, "I think we've *all* made our parents proud. When I won the election last year, or when Ford enlisted in the military. Graham, the golden boy that he is, makes them proud every day."

Mallory squeezes my hand as I shoot Barrett a look.

"But none of those things make them any prouder than they are right now with Linc choosing a bright, respectable, beautiful woman to be his wife," Barrett says. "Danielle, you are a wonderful addition to our family. You make our brother happy in ways nothing else ever has."

"Lincoln," Barrett continues, "we give you a lot of shit. We tease you and make fun of you and generally try to make your life hell," he winks. "But I want you to know, watching you over these past few months, I've learned more from you than I have from almost anyone. Except Dad. And maybe Graham," he laughs. "You've shown me what it means to go for what you want, how to have courage to jump with both feet and not look back. I'm honored to be your brother and Dani's now too. Congratulations."

Barrett tosses a wink at Lincoln who just smirks.

"Huxley?" Barrett says, looking around. "Will you come here for a minute?"

Hux appears next to Barrett wearing a miniature tux just like ours.

"Hey," Barrett says.

"Hi."

"Have you had fun today?"

"Yes."

Barrett smiles at the boy. "Have you been listening to what my brothers have been saying tonight? I mean, I know I tell you not to listen to them usually . . ."

Huxley laughs. "Yes. I've been listening."

"Good." Barrett ruffles Huxley's hair. "I've been thinking. You know I'd do anything for you and your mother, right?"

"Yes."

Mallory gasps beside me, her hand falling to my thigh. I don't want her to move it, so I place my hand on top of hers as we watch my older brother put into play the plan we made earlier this week.

I watch her out of the corner of my eye. Her eyes fill with tears, a sweet smile on her beautiful lips. The lights hanging behind her head make her look like she's glowing, and for a split second, I can see her and I in place of Barrett and Alison. I can imagine what Barrett is feeling, the nerves I gave him hell for having. The fear she'll say no. The hope that he can spend the rest of the life with the woman he can't replace.

Just like I'm positive I can't replace Mallory.

"I'd really like to make you and your mother official members of the Landry family," Barrett says.

"Oh my God," Alison breathes, her eyes glistening with unshed tears.

Barrett pays her no attention, focused solely on Huxley. "In order to do that, I would have to marry your mother. Do you think it would be okay if I did that? If I married your mom? I need your permission before I ask her."

Huxley leaps into Barrett's arms, burying his head in his chest. They have a muffled conversation that no one can hear but the two of them.

Something comes over the room, a feeling so heavy that we all feel it. As I look from one face to the next, most dabbing at their eyes, I finally land on Mallory. She's watching the display in front of her, one hand on her chest.

I look at this girl, the one that literally fell into my arms, and wonder if I could possibly put her there for good? It's a crazy possibility, one I'm not sure is even feasible. *For good* would indicate there's love there, and while I'm not sure if I'm ready to say that about her and I'm not sure she feels that way about me at all, in the middle of my family of all things, I'm considering it.

Barrett sets Huxley back on his feet and turns to Alison. He gets down on one knee to gasps from every female in the room.

"Alison, there's not a chance I'm ever going to let you go. Whatever decisions I have to make in my life, wherever I end up, I want to do them with you and Huxley by my side."

He extends a small, black box to her and pulls the lid open. She gasps, tears streaming down her cheeks, as she looks at the diamond catching the lights from above.

"Will you and Huxley be mine forever?" Barrett whispers.

She doesn't answer. Instead, she lunges into his arms to the excited cheers from the family.

"Say yes, Mom!" Huxley shouts, bouncing on the balls of his feet.

Alison pulls back. "Yes!" she shouts.

"Let's party!" Lincoln shouts as the music is turned up and everyone clamors to their feet.

"Come on," I say, rising and tugging Mallory's hand. With a

hurried step, I lead her into the night. The air is crisp, the stars shining brightly overhead.

My heart is thundering away, my thoughts going a million miles per second. Pulling in as much fresh air as I can muster, I try to calm the insanity ricocheting through me.

Twirling Mallory around, I draw her into my arms. She hesitates for half a beat before melting into me.

Her head tucked under my chin, I wrap her up and hold her tight. I feel her hands under my suit jacket, pulling me as close to her as she can.

Neither of us speaks. Neither of us moves. We just stand under the starry sky in each other's arms.

"That was incredible," she says finally, her breath warm against my shirt. "Your family is amazing, Graham."

"Yeah, they are."

She plants a kiss to the center of my chest and then pulls back, looking at me. "We can't leave."

"And why not?"

"It's a wedding. And your brother got engaged," she whispers, her eyes shining. "Let's stay for a while."

I want to say no, to tell her the plan is we go home. But I can't say no to that look in her eye. "Okay," I give in. "We'll stay. But you have to dance with me."

We head back into the tent, the scent of chocolate donuts flowing from inside, her hand in mine.

"And I don't want to catch you dancing with Ford."

She giggles. "You better behave then."

TWENTY-SEVEN
MALLORY

"NO, NOT ONE MORE!" I giggle as Sienna tugs at my hand. "My feet hurt."

"Your feet can't hurt!" Danielle exclaims. "It's my wedding reception."

"We've been at this for hours," I say, the wine sending me a little off balance.

"You're a lightweight," Macie laughs. "Come to Boston with Danielle this summer. We'll show you how it's done. Right, Danielle?"

"Let's take her to Shenanigans! Do they still have that jukebox in the corner? The one with all the old school stuff we love?"

Macie's eyes light up. "They do! Will and I were there a couple of months ago with Crew and Jules. I think I spent a week's check on it."

Alison grabs me by the arm and twirls me around, wine sloshing from her glass, as a new song begins to play. When we realize it's a slow one, a chorus of "Ah's" can be heard.

The dance floor begins to empty. The music softens, the beats turning smooth and easy, and I see Graham coming my way. His hands in his pockets, his tie now undone, his jacket missing, he looks like I've always hoped to see him look.

Relaxed. Carefree. Happy.

I throw my arms around his shoulders as he pulls me into him, holding me tight against his body. He smells delightfully like sandalwood and soap as I lay my head near his heart.

"Have you had fun tonight?" he asks softly.

"You know what? I have," I admit. "It's been a lot of fun actually."

He kisses the top of my head and I squeeze him. Maybe it's not the best thing in the world to let myself get so close to him, but it feels right. It makes me happy. So I choose to do it and have faith that if things go the way they're planned, or if they don't work out, I'll survive.

We move in a circle, entwined in each other's arms. We've danced many other dances tonight, but as Boyz II Men croon at the late hour, our bodies loosened by wine and whiskey, this one is different. Our guards are down and all I can do is smile against his chest.

"Well, well, well," Lincoln says as he and Danielle sidle up next to us. "Look what we have here."

"Go away, Linc," Graham laughs.

"That's no way for the Best Man to talk to the groom," Lincoln jokes.

Danielle gives him a stern look. "You are a troublemaker."

"Which is why you love me, babe." He smacks a kiss to her lips. "Well, G. I'm married off, Barrett is engaged. Since Ford doesn't have a girl, that means you're next."

"Lincoln Landry!" Danielle chastises him. "Don't put Graham on the spot like that."

"Danielle Landry," Lincoln starts then stops. "God, I love the sound of that."

"You're a beautiful bride," I tell Dani. "Congratulations again."

She grins at me. "Thank you."

Lincoln whisks her away in some spinning dip move that makes everyone laugh and move out of the way. Graham's chest rumbles as he, too, can't deny his amusement.

"You know," he says, "I've always thought Lincoln to be the most immature out of us all."

"You might be right."

"I hate to admit it, but I think I might be wrong."

When I pull away and look up at his face, he's still watching his brother. His brows are pulled tight.

"Lincoln is really no different than me," Graham notes.

"I beg to differ. He's silly. Goofy. You're Mr. Control Freak. Serious."

"True." Graham looks down at me again and spins me in a circle. "But look at him." He uses his chin to motion towards the groom. "He's the happiest guy here. He's the one out of all of us that risked everything in his life to get the one thing he wanted."

I think about that. I've heard Lincoln's story and how he had to pick between the sport he loved and the girl he loved more. It's a classic fairytale, a romance for the ages.

"Did he need a boost of confidence? Sure," Graham says. "But he pulled the trigger. He made a very mature decision."

"So what are you saying?" I ask.

"I'm saying that ridiculous brother of mine was capable, when the time came, to figure out what he wanted in life. He did it faster than any of the rest of us, no matter what public office we were in, what job title we had, or medals were around our neck." He chuckles. "I can't believe I'm giving kudos to Lincoln for something serious."

I stand on my tiptoes and kiss him lightly. "Don't worry. I won't tell."

"Won't tell what?" Camilla and her father dance their way to us. "I love gossip."

"They don't call you Swink for nothing," Graham says, shaking his head.

"Mind your own business, Camilla." Mr. Landry tosses me a wink. "May I cut in?"

Graham's grip cinches down on me.

"I'm your father, Graham," Mr. Landry laughs. "Here. Dance with your sister."

Camilla takes her brother's hand, against his silent objection, and guides him away from their father and I. Mr. Landry takes my hand in his and gently places his other respectfully on my hip.

His forehead is lined in a way that showcases years of worry, hard work, and late nights. But it's the lines around his eyes and mouth that paint a different picture. They tell the story of love and laughter, of ballgames and Monopoly. They speak of tea parties and car washes and early morning breakfasts.

"I want you to know," he says in a voice an octave lower than Graham's, "that I never get involved in my children's private lives."

I don't know what to say to that, so I don't say anything. I just let him move me along to the music.

"Graham has always been a peculiar child. When he was born, he didn't cry. The nurses had to tickle his feet to force him to cry to dry his lungs."

"Really?"

"Uh-huh." He smiles down at me. "He's always been an old soul, one of those kids that seems to be wise beyond their years. He didn't want to play ball with Lincoln or go chasing girls with Barrett. He wanted to go to the office with me. I remember one Christmas, he asked for a calculator," he chuckles.

"In the last few weeks, I've seen such a change in him," Mr. Landry continues. "I always wondered what would happen if he *really* fell in love. Would he pull away from the business? Would he channel some of the passion that drives him into something else? I see that some with Barrett. Now that he has Alison and Huxley, I don't expect him to be in politics very long. Same for Lincoln. I think we can all see the changes Danielle has made in him."

"Certainly," I agree.

"My curiosity has been satiated when it comes to Graham. I now know what happens to Graham when he falls in love."

"Mr. Landry," I stammer, my anxiety beginning to soar. "I'm not sure what he's told you, but I don't think he's in love with me."

His chuckle is loud and hearty as he shakes his head. "Maybe not. I surely can't speak for my son. But I can tell you that I know a thing or two about my boys, and Graham is well on his way, sweetheart."

My cheeks flush and I look away. I'm not sure he's right, but I can't stop the little bud of hope that blossoms in my belly.

"Graham's work over these past few weeks has only gotten better. It's funny, in a way, to see him a bit strewn about. But it makes his mother and me happy to see him living outside of his office for once. And that, Mallory, is because of you."

"I don't know what to say."

"You don't have to say anything. I just want to ask that you give my boy some patience. Lord knows he's probably in over his head," he chuckles. "But if I know one of my sons, I know Graham. And I know Graham will come around."

The music ends and a faster number replaces it. Graham is to my side in a second flat.

"Here you go," his father says, taking my hand and placing it through his son's elbow. He leans in and whispers something to Graham. I don't know what he says, only that it makes Graham smile. They nod, a silent exchange of some unnamed emotion, and Mr. Landry disappears into the sea of people.

Graham looks at me, his eyes shimmering. "You ready to go?"

"Absolutely."

TWENTY-EIGHT
MALLORY

THE HOUSE IS DARK WHEN we enter. All the wine I consumed has made me sleepy and I lean against Graham as we enter the house. He takes my jacket off and grabs a blanket off the sofa before guiding me back outside onto the patio.

I doze off, warm from the alcohol and the fire Graham started in the fireplace. He awakens me, having changed into a pair of black sleep pants and a long-sleeved, black shirt.

"Hey, sleeping beauty," he whispers, sitting down beside me. I struggle to open my eyes as I sit up. "Come here."

He moves me so I'm leaning against him, tucked protectively under his arm. My hair splays across his shirt, my legs tucked up under the blanket. Nothing is said and not a muscle is moved besides the rising and falling of our chests. It's completely still outside. There are no barking dogs or police sirens. Just Graham and I and a crackling fire.

"If I could just stay here, like this, for the rest of my life, I would." His statement wakes me up. I think I mishear him, but when I look up at his face, he's watching me. "I love having you here."

"I love being here," I say, snuggling into him more. "I really just love being with you."

I wait for the regret, but the wine must have dulled my reactions, because I feel none. I also don't feel drunk, just buzzed, and I'm not sure if that means I'm safe to speak or I'm so out of it I need to play dead. "What would it take," he says, clearing his throat, "for you to give me a chance?"

"A chance like in a raffle?" I ask, trying to stop the roaring of the blood past my ears.

He laughs quietly. "No, Mallory. A chance as in maybe helping me trying to figure out how to love."

Drunk, buzzed, or sober, I'm wide awake. I'm afraid to move because that might shatter this alternate reality I've woken up in.

"How to love yoga?" I offer.

Moving me so I lie across his lap, he sighs. "I'm blaming this on Lincoln."

The confidence in Graham's posture that I've never seen him without is gone. His features are stern, his face pulled tight. There's a glimmer in his eyes, but I can't tell if it's from the flames of the fire or something . . . else. "I have some issues," he begins. "I know that. I can be exacting and difficult and a little overbearing at times."

"A little?"

"A little," he says, giving me a look. "I thought I was happy before you came into my life. Everything was in its place, everyone in their roles, and I liked it. It was comfortable and predictable. Then you walk in and take all that and toss it on the floor."

He runs his fingers through my hair, brushing it away from my face. "It drove me crazy at first. I had an anxiety attack for the first week," he laughs. "But then something changed."

Sliding my hand so it touches his chest beneath his shirt, I try to encourage him to go on.

"I guess it was partly Lincoln and a speech he and Barrett gave me at the Farm that I can keep my crutches or keep you. They told me I'd know when I'd fallen in love because I couldn't replace her. I wouldn't want to." He shifts me on his lap so I'm sitting up more. "Imagining you not coming in to work every day makes me not want to go either, and that job is all I've ever wanted. Then seeing you with my family . . . I get what my brothers were saying, Mallory."

"Oh, Graham," I say, feeling his heartbeat quicken under my hand.

"I've never been in love before. I'm not sure how it works. If we get to that point, and I mess it all up . . ."

"You've been in love before." The words sting as I reference Vanessa, the one woman I would risk getting arrested to punch in the face.

"I haven't," he says, looking me in the eye. "I might have thought that at one time, but I'm one hundred percent sure that wasn't love. A young infatuation, maybe. But love? No."

My heart leaps in my chest and I struggle to sit up. My head is a bit wonky from the alcohol, but I press on.

"What are you saying, Graham?" I ask.

"I'm saying . . . I'm saying I'd like to risk my mental stability and grip on life to have you in it. But I'm warning you—"

I leap forward, pressing my lips to his. He winds me up in his arms, kissing me for all he's worth. When we pull back, we're smiling and breathless.

"Was that a yes?" he asks. "You didn't even hear the disclaimer."

"This isn't a contract," I laugh. "There are no execution dates or amendments or fine print."

"That's what I mean. I don't know how this works."

"It works like this: we take each other for what we are. We know each other well enough to know our weaknesses and annoying behaviors."

"Like the trash in your car?"

"No," I state. "Like the fact your stapler has to sit three inches from your desk phone. That's annoying."

"That's practical!"

"Well, I'll overlook that and you overlook the misplaced scrap pieces of life on my floorboard."

He rolls his eyes, but laughs. "Fine. But we'll never take your car anywhere."

"Compromise, Graham. It's a key to relationships."

"I don't do that well."

"I'll teach you," I say happily.

"I'm going to need a learning curve," he admits. "I need you to have patience with me."

"And I need you to give me room to grow," I volley back. "I've been making progress on me and I don't want to lose that."

He kisses me sweetly. "I don't want you to lose that." He stands, offering me his hand. "Come on."

"Where are we going?"

"Inside."

"Why?"

He smirks. "I want to celebrate with my . . . girlfriend?"

"That's so high school," I laugh.

Shaking his hand, he motions for me to take it.

"How do you plan on celebrating?" I ask, pressing my lips together. He wiggles his brows.

"I think we managed to do that," I say, wiggling my eyebrows back at him, "out here last time, didn't we?"

"Last time was different."

"Why?"

He grins. "Last time you weren't mine."

Swooning, I take his hand and let him lead me into the house.

THE SENSATION OF LIGHT WAKES me up. It's odd because my room has one small window that faces west, so there's not a lot of sunlight in there. Especially in the morning.

Stretching, my arms brush over sheets that aren't mine. They're softer, silkier . . . nicer. My eyes flip open and land on a large painting of a city in the dark. It's a black canvas with dots of white and pink and blue. You can make out the streets and mountain ranges. It's gorgeous. It's also not mine.

I roll over and face the bedside table. Graham's watch and day planner sit there next to a blue lamp with a cream-colored shade.

Flopping back against the mound of pillows in his four-poster bed, I can't help but giggle as everything from last night floods back. His declaration. His sweet smile. His delectable tongue.

Shivering, I burrow under the covers as I hear something in the hallway. It takes a few seconds for him to appear.

Wearing a pair of grey boxer briefs and nothing else, he carries a wooden tray and a big smile. "Morning," he says. "I made you breakfast."

Scents of bacon and pancakes drift through the air, blending with the smell of Graham. It's a divine, heady combination.

I sit up and realize I'm naked. The air hits my nipples, causing them to form stiff peaks. Graham's eyes go to them immediately.

"Don't think about it," I warn. "You have to feed me first."

He grins, climbing in bed with me. "I don't know what I love more. Seeing you in my bed in the morning or just seeing you naked."

I swipe a slice of bacon off the tray and stick it in my mouth. "Perfect. Not too crispy, not too limp."

"There's nothing about me that's limp."

"True that." I wipe the bacon around the plate, picking up the excess syrup. "This is the best way to eat it right here."

I dangle it over my mouth in a very un-ladylike fashion.

"This explains so much," he notes.

"Like what?"

"Like why there was syrup on the console of your car and why it smelled like bacon."

"Sue me." I open my mouth and begin to drop the bacon into it when a drizzle of the maple goodness misses my tongue and slides down my breast.

Graham is on me in a second, the bacon falling on the bed. I shriek, reaching for it, but he pins my hands above my head. His eyes burn with unbridled lust. "If I tell you to keep your hands here, will you listen?"

"What do you think?" I tease, kicking the blankets off my body. I lie on his sheets, completely exposed. His free hand, the one not holding my hands against the headboard, cups me between the legs.

"I think you can't be trusted."

His mouth lowers ever-so-slowly until it hovers just over my syrup-covered nipple. I arch my back, desperate for contact, but he just pulls back. Looking at me through his lashes, he grins. His tongue darts out, barely flicking the top of my pebbled bud.

I moan, struggling to work my hands free. He keeps them still against my effort.

The top of his tongue lays flat at the top of my chest and rolls slowly down the sensitive skin of my breast. The trail behind it is chilled, a stark contrast to the heat of his mouth.

My head falls deeper into the pillows, his free hand gripping my vagina harder. One finger slips inside me and I release a moan.

My hands are released and I reach for him, but he pulls back. He turns back to me, a strip of bacon in the air, dripping with sticky goodness from the breakfast plate.

Holding it over my body, the sweet liquid falls to my skin, trickling wild lines from my thighs to my neck.

Graham looks at me with untamed, yet reverent eyes. I'm desperate for his touch. He lies along my legs, holding himself up over my abdomen. A smirk graces those delicious lips.

"I think I'll have my breakfast like this," he growls. "Lie back. Eyes open. I want you to watch me lick this off of you."

His tongue dips into the pool of liquid in my belly button and I nearly jump from the contact. He growls and I know to stay still. I want to stay still. I don't want this to end.

He works his way around my stomach, following the ropes of syrup as they crisscross my body. His tongue is hot, his fingers tucking under me and squeezing my ass. I try to shimmy, to make his fingers find my opening, but he knows my game and doesn't budge.

Looking me in the eye, he starts a torturously slow path from my stomach up my breastbone. Then, in a flash of a movement, he sucks my left nipple.

"Gah!" I exclaim, feeling a burst of pleasure shoot through me. My fingers run through his hair, encouraging him to suck harder, take in more. He sucks the sweetness from my skin and looks at me, licking his lips.

Pressing on my clit, he laughs. "This is going to be a good fucking day."

"I hope so," I laugh. "Now start the fucking me part."

"Oh no," he says, leaning back and stripping off his briefs. "Not today."

"What do you mean 'not today'?" I ask, alarmed.

"Today, I'm enjoying you. Savoring you. Relishing the fact that I have an entire day of you all to myself."

"That," I say, reaching up and pulling his face to mine, "you most certainly do."

TWENTY-NINE
MALLORY

HUMMING A TUNE, I ENTER the last data from a report Graham gave me into our system. A few simple clicks and a flourish as I hit enter and it's complete. And so is the work day, for all intents and purposes.

We haven't discussed what happens in thirty minutes, when five o'clock rolls around. I don't have yoga class tonight, but I also don't want to assume he wants me to come over. This is new to us, especially to him, and I know he'll need to ease into this. Hell, so do I.

I think we were both surprised at how easily today went. We were so much better at setting our chemistry aside to get the job done than we were before this past weekend. Maybe it's because we know where we stand and that we will have that time, time to say and do all the things that are running through our minds, when the day ends.

Tidying up, I put together a few notes for Graham and stick them on the corner of my desk. Since I have a few minutes to spare and Graham isn't back from a meeting with Gulica Insurance and Ford in the conference room, I pull out a file for Lincoln's charity and get to work on it.

I'm putting some numbers into a spreadsheet when the office

door opens. I smile and turn, expecting to see Graham, when my grin falters. A woman is standing in the doorway. Long, jet-black hair hangs to her waist and bright pink lipstick paints her mouth. She eyes me suspiciously, and while I have no idea who she is, I instantly don't like her. At all.

"Can I help you?" I ask politely, turning to face her head-on.

"I'm looking for Mr. Landry."

"Graham?"

"This is his office, isn't it?"

I stifle a smart-ass comeback. "Yes, it is. What can I do for you?"

She gives me a cocky grin as she takes me in. There's no denying she sees me as some sort of competition. "You can let Graham know I'm here."

"Well," I say, as sweet as sugar, "he isn't here right now. Would you like to leave him a message?"

"No. When will he return?"

The door opens again and Raza walks in with her cheery smile. Once the door is closed behind her, the smile fades.

"I'm not sure when he will be back," I say, flashing Raza a look to stay quiet. "I'd be happy to take a message for you."

"I'm sure you would."

"Look," I say, standing. "I'm not sure what it is you want, but—"

"I'm sorry," she interjects. "What was your name?"

Pointing at the name plate sitting front and center on my desk, I grin. "Mallory Sims. And who might I have the pleasure of having in my office this afternoon?"

"I'm Vanessa Shields." As my blood runs cold, her smug grin stretches wider. "I see you've heard of me."

"Yes, I have. Aren't you the lady that overflowed the toilet in the restroom last week?"

Her eyes narrow. "No. That was not me."

"Oh. Sorry for the mix-up." I look at Raza. "What can I do for you?"

"I had a question about a charge to Ford's account. Graham also said you could take a look at this note from Camilla and let me know how to proceed, but it can wait."

I can almost see steam rising from Vanessa's ears.

"Let me take care of this," I say, nodding towards Vanessa, "and then we can discuss."

"I'm not leaving until I see him," Vanessa states.

"What do you want him for?"

She takes a deep breath and looks towards Graham's office. "I told him I was coming to town. We talked about having dinner. I'm free tonight and wanted to see if he has plans."

Her words punch me in the stomach. I feel like the wind has been knocked out of me. As hard as I try not to show the cracks in my veneer, she sees them.

"Yeah, honey," she says. "I'm the love of Graham's life. Get used to it."

I toss the pen in my hand on my desk and start around the corner of it. My eyes locked on this bitch standing in front of me, I see red. "What you are is a manipulative, filthy whore."

"Excuse me?"

"You heard me. I didn't stutter."

"You don't even know me."

"You're right and you don't know how lucky that makes you."

She moves her head side to side in a bitchy, snotty bob. "Was that a veiled threat?"

"If I want to threaten you, I'll do it in the open. Because that's what women do. We keep things on the up-and-up, say it like it is." I glance at Raza and then back to Vanessa again. "You know, little things, like . . . if we're married."

Her face pales.

"What you did to Graham is repulsive. You're nothing more than a deceitful, disgusting excuse for a woman."

"How dare you!"

"*How dare you*," I spit. "How dare you walk in his office and pretend like you have some right to talk to him."

"He'll be the judge of that."

"No, *I'll* be the judge of that." I march to my desk phone and hit the button for security. "George? This is Mallory. I need someone in my suite, please."

"I'm not leaving here until I talk to him. Get my drift?"

"You'll be leaving here when George gets here," I laugh. "And I'll ensure you never get through those doors again. Get my drift?"

George's partner, Marty, bursts through the door. "Ms. Sims, is there a problem?"

"Can you escort her out of here, please?"

"I just talked to Mr. Landry last week. He's expecting me," Vanessa says.

Her words cut me to the core, even though I don't think I believe them. Why would Graham talk to her and not tell me, especially after our conversation last night? It can't be true. I won't believe it.

Marty looks at me and raises his brows. I stand taller. "Please see her out."

He angles himself towards Vanessa and asks her to leave. She argues with him for a moment before glaring at me. "You're fucking him, aren't you?"

I grin. "No, Vanessa. You fucked him. He makes love to me."

I'm not sure that's true, but it's enough to get to her. She starts thrashing around, yelling obscenities. Marty subdues her, guiding her out, but not before she tosses an envelope at Raza.

Once she's gone, the air still filled with her crazy energy, Raza and I stare at each other.

"What was that about?" she asks.

"Honestly?" I say, trying to block out all of Vanessa's accusations and settle down. "I'm not sure."

Raza picks up the envelope and places it on my desk. "I'll come back tomorrow."

"Good idea," I mutter, trying to catch my breath as the adrenaline starts to wear off.

I watch her go, and a few short seconds later, Graham

streaks by the glass. My heart flutters as I watch him race to the door, coming to my side. I don't know how he heard about Vanessa so fast, but by the tempo of his steps, I know he must have.

"Did you send the fax to Gulica on Friday?" he barks before the door is even shut behind him.

Startled at the question, one I wasn't expecting and catching me off-guard, I stutter, "Yes, of course. I sent it before I left."

"They didn't get it." He marches to my desk and stands in front of it, fury radiating off him. "You know what that means? It means Landry Security is now on hold."

My eyes go wide, my heart stills in my chest as he looks at me with a mixture of anger and pity. My head spins as my mind is yanked from one thing to another so quickly, I feel sick to my stomach. "You're kidding me."

"Does it look like I'm kidding? Everything we've worked on for months now is in jeopardy because we don't have insurance. We can't move forward on anything, and when we do get things in line, our premiums won't be locked in. They'll likely be three times higher than they would've last week. Damn it!"

"Graham, I'm sorry," I rush, jumping to my feet. "Let me find the confirmation sheet from the fax."

He slams a paper in front of me, shaking my pencil holder. "Here it is. It clearly says 'line busy/no answer'. Did you bother checking it?"

"I thought I did," I whisper. I have no idea how I missed that because it's obvious. "I must've picked it up and just filed it."

"You just cost Ford's company weeks, Mallory. *Weeks.* Their offer was predicated on a date—which was Friday. I made that very clear. Now we have to go back through the process of getting it inspected and approved."

"Graham, I'm sorry."

He takes a step away from me. "I should've done it myself."

Tears lick my eyes, red-hot bubbles of liquid pooling at the corners. My hand shakes as I try to steady myself. "What can I do? There must be something we can do?"

"I'll take care of it. You can go ahead and go." He looks at me as he starts to walk away. "I'll be working late."

"Graham, I . . ." I look down at the envelope from Vanessa and don't know what to do. "You had someone here to see you."

He looks at me with a gaze of pity. "We'll talk about it tomorrow."

"But I need to talk to you—"

"I have enough to deal with today, Mallory. Whatever you're dying to talk about will have to wait." He turns on his heel and disappears in his office.

With tears streaming down my cheeks, pieces of my heart in limbo, I grab my bag. As I'm going out the door, Ford is coming in.

"Hey, Mall . . . ory," he says, then stepping back out of my way as I rush past.

***

Graham

"FUCK!" MY VOICE BOOMS OVER the sound of the door shutting. Reaching up, I tear away at the knot in my tie and instantly think of Mallory and the way she does it for me. That only angers me more.

My eyes pull shut and I try to regulate my breathing. I suddenly know what *seeing red* means. Everything is pulsing so quickly through me that I'm dizzy.

I don't fail. I don't make mistakes of this caliber, ones that cost thousands of dollars and weeks of time. But I trusted her to do it. I thought she understood the importance.

"Hey." I whirl around and see Ford standing in the doorway. He watches me warily. "What the hell just happened?"

"About what?"

"About what?" he repeats. "About Mallory running out of here practically bawling."

The look on his face tells me much more than any adjectives he uses to describe her. I've never seen him look at *me* this way, like he's second-guessing me.

"She was probably crying because I pointed out her fuck-up."

"I didn't say she was *crying*, Graham. I said she was *bawling*."

Choking back a lump in my throat, I look at my brother. "I just told her I'd take care of it."

He shakes his head. "I have a feeling you said a little more than that." As he walks deeper into my office, he shoves his hands in his pockets. "No one is more upset about this than I am. It's my company, my bottom line at the end of the day. But there are worse problems to have."

"I don't fail," I say through clenched teeth. Despite my narrowed eyes, my hands shake as I place them on my desk. Her face floats through my mind, the shock written all over her features.

"No, you don't and you didn't this time. But you are about to."

I hang my head.

"I've been around the world," he reminds me. "I've seen real problems, real issues, and it makes things like this seem pretty inconsequential in comparison."

He gives me a second to respond, but I don't. The anger that was spilling over a few seconds ago wanes, the flames of fury doused with a dose of reality marked by Ford's words.

"So what? We will pay a little more for insurance and we'll start awhile later. That's all fixable," he says. "As long as our family is happy and healthy, everything is fixable."

I raise my eyes to meet his and regret it as soon as I do. For maybe the first time ever, one of my brothers is putting me in my place. He could forego all the words and just look at me like that and his point would be well made.

"What you just did," he says, "may be a whole lot harder to fix."

As the smoke begins to clear, I see the situation with a clarity that makes me sick. "I . . . I don't know what to do."

"You better fucking get a plan together, G."

"If I were her, I wouldn't talk to me."

"If I were her, I'd tell you to go straight to hell," he points out. "But I have a feeling she may be more forgiving than me."

When I don't move, he steps closer. "Graham, if you don't reach out to her now—not tonight, not tomorrow, *now*—you just might end up in the same boat as me."

"What boat is that?"

"A boat with more pride than sense. It's a lonely fucking place, brother."

I whip out my phone and press her name. It rings three times before I'm sure I was put to voicemail. Glancing at Ford, he winces.

I call her again and am sent to voicemail on ring number two.

"I'm out of my element here," I say out loud on the verge of panic. "What do I do?"

He stands stoically in front of me. "You have to talk to her." "But she won't talk to me."

"So, go to her."

It sounds like simple logic, an answer that should've been obvious. "I don't know where she went."

Scurrying by my brother, I sit at her desk. Pulling open her drawer, I rifle through her things until I find her calendar. "She doesn't have yoga tonight."

"She's probably at home," Ford offers. "Did you think of that?"

"I . . ." I fight the calamity in my brain. "I don't know where she lives." His jaw drops and I groan. "We just started doing this thing. I've never been there."

"That's an issue for another day."

My body tenses as the door opens and Raza walks in. She's all smiles, hips swinging, until she sees the look on our faces. "I'm sorry. I thought this would be a better time."

"Better than what?" Ford asks as I continue to rifle through

Mallory's drawer. It's a mess, but instead of irritating me, I find it sort of comforting. "There was a woman in here earlier. I came in to ask about a couple of things, and she and Mallory were in a heated conversation." Ford and I exchange a glance as I stand. "Who was she?" I ask.

Raza shrugs. "I don't know. Mallory called security."

My blood chills as a host of images flow through my mind at what might have happened for Mallory to call for help. "Was there a physical altercation?"

"Oh, no. Nothing like that. The woman was just demanding to see you and Mallory refused. She didn't like that much."

"Who could it have been?" Ford asks from beside me. I shake my head.

"No clue. What was said, Raza?"

Her cheeks flush. "The woman said she was the love of your life. And she didn't like Mallory's response."

"Oh, fuck." My gaze flips to Ford's. "Vanessa."

"That crazy bitch," my brother hisses.

"Yes!" Raza cries. "That was her. Vanessa. She seemed a little crazy, to be honest. Mallory let her know, in no uncertain terms, what she thought of her and that she would never contact you through Landry as long as she worked here."

"She was jealous," Ford smirks.

"No," Raza disagrees. "I didn't get that at all." She looks at me with a simple smile. "I felt like she was protecting you more than anything."

My breath is stolen, my heart crushing inside my body. "My God."

Ford and Raza exchange a few words before she leaves, none of which I'm privy to. All I can do is think of Mallory and the words I said and the pain she must be feeling.

If I were alone, I'd scream out in rage. If I were home, I'd slam my fists in a punching bag. If I were running, I'd go so hard that my legs would give out just so I could override the shame I'm feeling now.

"I'm going to—" I begin before my gaze rests on the corner of her desk. A white envelope bearing my name in red ink sits like a loose grenade. Swiping it up, I stick it inside my jacket pocket and look at Ford. "Her resume is in the lower left-hand corner of my desk. Text me her address."

"Where are you going?" Ford asks as I dash towards the door.

"To find her. To make this right."

An eruption starts in the pit of my stomach and creeps through my body. The fire courses through my abdomen, then my chest, and creeps up my face as reality, the truth of everything, slams into me with no mercy.

I dial her again but it goes straight to voicemail. "Fuck!"

THIRTY
MALLORY

"I'M GOING TO BE FINE," I lie as Joy pulls me into a hug. "I just want to be alone for a while."

"I don't know if this is a good idea," Joy admits, letting me go. "Should you really be alone right now? I could just go fold towels or wash the front windows or something."

"You? Wash windows?" I laugh through my tears. "That I want to see."

"Well, I'd probably just sit there and read a magazine, but it sounded good," she shrugs. "Besides, you're crying."

I wipe my face with the end of my shirt. "It's not a sad cry." I look at her and shrug. "Not completely, anyway. I'm so mad at him."

"You have every right to be." She picks at a pink fingernail. "You don't think he lied to you though, right? He wasn't talking to Vanessa."

"I don't think so. I think he would've mentioned that to me."

"Sure he would've."

I blow out a breath. "You know what I'm mad about? That he wouldn't listen to me. He just looked at me like I was a piece of shit because I made a mistake. Like nothing else mattered in that moment except for what he was feeling."

"That makes sense and it's not unreasonable."

"If this would've been a few weeks ago, I would be completely heartbroken. I'd feel like a failure. But now . . ." I shrug again. "Now I'm pissed off."

"That a girl!" Joy laughs, almost making me smile. "Are you sure you want me to leave? There are no classes tonight. You're going to be alone."

"That's the plan. I just need to think, and I think best here."

She nods, looks at me like she thinks I might jump off a bridge, and picks up her bag. "Call me if you need me."

"I will." I sit and wait for the front door to close.

Tears stream down my face, soaking the girl power t-shirt I tossed on haphazardly in the parking lot. It's wrinkled and had been in my backseat for who knows how long, but I wasn't planning on coming here after work today. I wasn't planning on any of this.

Facing the mirrors on the far wall, I start my stretches. Silently begging for the peace I usually feel here to come, I go through the motions. One pose leads fluidly into the next, followed by the third. Then fourth. By the fifth, I'm not finding any serenity.

The silence is loud, every buzz from the refrigerator in the back sounding like a swarm of bees. The drip in the bathroom sink is relentless. Sounds I've never heard before, never noticed, build on the fear that's knotting my stomach in the worst way.

Maybe I shouldn't be alone.

Crawling across the floor, I dig my phone out of my bag and turn it on. There are missed calls from Graham. I know that before they show. But I don't expect him to call in right as I press the call button for Joy.

"Mallory?" His voice is a rush—ragged and pained and uneasy. It hits me hard in the feels. So hard, in fact, that I fall onto my back and just hold the phone to my ear. "Mallory? Are you there? Please, talk to me."

"I have nothing to say to you."

"Shit," he groans. "I'm sorry."

"Not good enough," I sniffle.

"Where are you? Let me explain."

I sit up, watching myself in the full-length mirror. "I don't feel like listening to you explain right now, Graham. You hurt my feelings."

He groans. "Please . . ."

"You know what? I wanted to explain and apologize to you earlier and you didn't have the decency to listen to me."

He sounds like the wind just got knocked out of him.

"I made a mistake," I continue, fueled by the strength I see in the mirrors. "People do that. We aren't all perfect like you."

"I'm not perfect," he groans.

"Guess what? I know that. I know you're just as far from perfection as I am."

"You're wrong," he says quietly. "I'm much farther away than you are."

My heart pulls at the sadness in his voice. I just have to remember that he made me sad today too. It's easy to recall that when Vanessa's face shoots across my mind.

"I forgot to mention something." I glare at my own reflection. "Actually, I didn't forget. You didn't give me the chance."

"Vanessa . . ."

"Yeah. She was in to see you."

"I knew nothing about that. I swear on my life, Mallory, I knew nothing about that."

"She said you talked a few days ago. I'm assuming since you didn't mention it that she's full of shit."

He doesn't respond right away and I think I gasp.

"Well, I think I stand corrected," I say bitterly.

"No, Mallory," he rushes. "Just listen to me."

"Why should I?" I say, standing. My heart is racing too hard to stay sitting. I need to walk off some of this energy. "Because you were so kind to me today? Because you treated me with such respect? Because you gave me the opportunity to explain, so I should afford you the same?"

He starts to talk, but I just laugh. "You know what? Fuck you, Graham."

And I end the call.

***

Graham

I TAKE MY EYES OFF the road enough to double check the address on the building in front of me with the one on Ford's text. They match.

My SUV slides to the curb of the pale yellow complex with black shutters hosting more paint chips than a hardware store. I barely get it in park and the ignition off before I'm out the door.

"That's a fire lane!" someone shouts behind me.

The front doors are security-less and I let myself in. The lighting in the foyer is barely decent. Tapping repeatedly on the "up" button, I pace a circle.

I can barely breathe. If I don't find her and talk to her and make her see how wrong I know I was, I'm going to lose control in an epic, newsworthy way.

"Hey, buddy." I spin around to see a man in an eighties band rock shirt leaning against a pillar. A cigarette hangs out of his cracked lips. "If you need to go upstairs, take the stairs unless you want to still be waiting in the morning."

"Where are they?"

He motions down a hall and I give him a little wave as I race down the tile. My shoes slapping against the floor, I pop open the door and race up the stairs to the second floor.

I go over a million things to say, a thousand ways of apologizing as I knock over a table with a flowerless vase and don't stop to pick it up.

The carpeting lining the hallway is reminiscent of a cheap hotel with stains that make me nauseous. I find her number and knock as loudly as I can get away with.

"Mallory?" I call. When no one answers, I pound again. "Mallory!"

Reality hits that she might be inside and I can't actually force her to come to the door. Trying the handle, I find it locked. I jiggle it more quickly before my fist hits the wood veneer again, harder this time. "Mallory! Open up! Please! I'm sorry."

The door across the hall swings open, the smell of stale cigarettes flowing towards me. I cough, fanning my face, shooting the guilty party a nasty look.

"Keep it down out here!" A woman snarls, a pair of oversized glasses on her face. "Some of us are tryin' to sleep."

"Do you know if Mallory is home?"

"Who's Mallory?" she asks.

"Never mind."

I lean against the wall, my cheek pressed against the door. My eyes squeeze shut as I imagine her on the other side, listening to me. "I'm so sorry, baby," I say. "No, sorry isn't the half of it. Please open the door and talk to me. *Please.*"

"She ain't there!" the woman grimaces behind me. "Get on out of here or I'll call the poice."

"If you're in there, I beg you, open this door."

I give her a long moment to answer, but nothing happens. Giving the door one final glance, I head back down the hall to the stairwell. I try her number again. "Pick up," I mutter as I climb into my SUV, ignoring shouts from the fire lane monitor. "Come on, Mallory. Come on, baby."

I can't lose her. Not now. Not before I ever really had a chance to have her.

As reality hits and I realize there's a chance she won't want to see me again, I know what Lincoln and Barrett were talking about: you know when you love someone when it's not easy and you'd happily take the frustration before you'd consider not having them.

If she throws this in my face every day, if she teases me or makes me pay for this for longer than I care to imagine, I'll do it. I'll sign on that dotted line with a flourish because not having her is not an option. "This is Mallory Sims . . ." Her voicemail begins and I have half a notion to listen to it, just to hear her voice.

Tearing out of the parking lot, my tires squeal as I hit the highway.

THIRTY-ONE
MALLORY

MY LEGS ARE TOGETHER, MY head nearly touching my knees, when I hear the front door open. Lifting my chin, my breathing hiccups.

He's standing in the doorway, his suit jacket in his hand, his tie askew and halfway unknotted. The silky black strands I love to touch are sticking wildly up in all directions. But it's his face, the tautness of his lips, the hesitation in his eyes, that I see most clearly.

Our gazes connect in the glass in front of me as he ambles slowly across the room. All I can hear is my heartbeat thrashing in my chest as anticipation of this moment bears down on me.

He removes his shoes and socks near mine, adds his jacket to the pile, and then joins me on the floor.

He settles in beside me, mirroring my position. He grabs his calves through his dress pants and stretches. I feel him looking at me, his gaze asking me a million questions. I just look at my red-painted toes that I had done for Lincoln's wedding.

After a few minutes, the tension gets to be too much and I roll away from him and onto my stomach. I press up with my hands like a cobra. He follows suit.

Out of the corner of my eye, I see his tie dragging the ground, the sleeves of his shirt unbuttoned and rolled to his elbows. His forearms flex, the vein in the side of his neck pulsing. Everything about this image is as un-Graham-like as it could be.

"I expected you to rip my ass when I walked in. Aren't you going to say anything to me?" he says, dropping to the ground as I do.

"No." I roll away from him again, sitting in a butterfly style.

"Good. I'd prefer you listen, too."

"I didn't say I was going to listen to you either."

He chuckles, which only angers me. Glaring at him straight away, I suck in a breath. Mistake. I can smell his cologne and the energy rolling off him, and I have to exhale it as quickly as I took it in. I won't just brush this under the rug, no matter how I feel about him.

"Mallory, I'm sorry."

That's all it takes for the tears to haunt my eyes again, blurring the outline of his chiseled face. His own eyes are filled with so much emotion that I have to look away.

"You've said that already," I reply.

"So I have." There's a note of insecurity in his voice that I've never heard before, a hint of hesitation that seeps in the words. He blows out a long, strangled breath. "I shouldn't have acted like I did today. It was childish and I'm completely mortified that I did it. To you of all people."

"You should be," I say, swallowing the lump in my throat. "What you did today was bullshit, Graham. Complete bullshit. Be mad at me. Point out my fuckup. Fire me, for heaven's sake. But talk to me like I'm an errant child worthy of no respect? Nope."

"Mallory..."

"I'm not done." I turn to face him, the words flowing. "As your employee, I won't stand for you to talk to me like that. As your ... whatever I am to you—"

"Mallory—"

"Stop interrupting me," I demand. His lips close, his eyes going wide. "I don't know what I am to you. I don't know how to define it.

But I will tell you one thing: there is no role I'll play in your life, or anyone else's, where I will overlook this."

My chin lifts and I look him in the eye. "I spent too many years being silent about what I wanted. I went with the flow, didn't rock the boat. Sure, it made for smoother waters for a while but that was at the expense of my happiness and confidence. I know you were angry today and you verbalized that in a way that you wouldn't normally. But that doesn't mean I'm going to sit back and not say a word. No one is going to talk to me or take me for granted like that again."

"No one talks to me like this either," he chuckles.

"I do."

"Which is why I love you."

The words are out in a flash and we both recoil just a bit as they land on our ears. I still, my eyes going wide, matching his.

"I was angry today," he says softly. "I own that. I'm not going to lie to you and tell you I wasn't or that you misunderstood the situation because we both know you didn't. I didn't stop and think and separate everything out. I just flew off the handle."

"Yes. You did." My shoulders sag even as I fight them to stay strong.

Just thinking about it hurts—my pride, my feelings, my heart.

The light in his eyes dims. "What you don't know is that today was a day of firsts for me." He takes a deep breath. "The first day I woke up and stared at a woman before getting out of bed, wishing she would never leave. The first day I failed at something as the head of Landry Holdings. The first day I felt the complete and utter fear of losing someone."

"You felt that way with Vanessa," I remind him. He grins as I spit her name like the piece of poison she is.

"No, I didn't," he emphasizes. "With her, I felt confused. Fooled. Betrayed when she left. I didn't feel anything like I felt today. Not close. When you left and I realized what I had done, I felt crushed, Mallory. Absolutely slaughtered."

That softens my fury and I give him a tipoff by the grin threatening to break out across my lips. His eyes go to my mouth, almost pulling it up by sheer will.

"Vanessa did call me a few days ago. Before Lincoln's wedding," he says, his words measured. "I intended on telling you after the wedding. You were threatening to quit and I was so focused on figuring things out with you first. I knew if I told you before, it would be an added thing to deal with."

"But you didn't tell me," I point out, my tone heavy with annoyance.

"Because I forgot."

"Sure you did. I'm so sure it just slipped your mind because that's a normal reaction."

He scoots closer, but doesn't touch me. I feel my body wanting to reach for him, needing the comfort I've come to find in his arms.

"I did. It's the God's honest truth. Think about it: you've been at my house since the night of Linc's wedding. Having you in my home, seeing you in my kitchen, in my bed, having you to talk to, to kiss—Vanessa was the last thing on my mind."

That whittles down my anger a little more. "What did the letter say?" I'm afraid of the answer and hate that he has some kind of connection with this woman in any way.

He leaps to his feet and digs in the pocket of his jacket. He's nearly frantic, his hands flying through the pockets until he lands on the one in the inside lining. "I don't know what it says," he says. "By the way, Raza told me what you said to her."

"I don't care if it was out of line—"

"Baby," he says, turning around and giving me a sexy smile, "that made my day."

"Really?"

"I'm always the one going to battle for everyone else. You could've had her wait or called me in to deal with it, but instead, you did it. You went to battle for me." He crouches next to me, his eyes now glistening again. "Here."

In his hand is the envelope from my desk. He shakes it in the air. It rustles like an unwarranted tax paper or court summons.

"I don't want that," I grimace.

"I don't know what it says and I don't care. If you do, here, have at it." When I don't take it, he stands and walks to the garbage. Eyes on me, he rips it down the middle and deposits it in the can. "Satisfied?" he asks.

"Kind of," I shrug, trying not to grin.

He's back in front of me in a flash. He takes my hands in his, rubbing his thumbs over my palms. "I'm warning you—I'm not leaving here without you. I told you once that I wouldn't pretend we didn't happen."

"You were talking about fucking me," I laugh.

"That statement has been amended to mean *more*." He stands and tugs me up too. "I want to take your favorite things about me—my passion and intellect, as you say—and apply them to you every day. If you give me a chance, I promise to make you feel like the most treasured woman in the world."

"You make a lot of promises," I tease.

He wraps his arms around me and pulls me towards him. His lips hovering over mine, he whispers, "Only the ones I intend on keeping."

"Forgive me," he breathes. "If I ever act like that again, you can leave and I'll help you pack your bags. But that won't happen. You have my word."

"Pack my bags?" I say, lacing my fingers through his hair. "That sounds a little much, don't you think?"

"I was at your apartment today." He pulls away. "I'm going to have a hard time letting you go back there."

"I am," I insist. "That's a deal breaker. We're taking this slow. While I love Danielle's gung-ho attitude with the marriage and a baby, that's not me."

His breath is hot against my lips as he brushes them against each other. "Will you forgive me?" he asks.

I look him in the eye and see something swirling in the depths of the greens and blues. I'm not sure what it is or what to call it, I just know it's a look new to me.

As we sit on the floor and he takes my hands and holds them on his lap, I study his face. The lines are taut, a look of concern etched across his forehead. His hands are warm as they encompass mine, squeezing them gently as I choose how to respond.

"When I'm with you," I begin, my voice cloudy, "I feel like I can conquer the world."

"You can," he whispers. "I can't wait to see you achieve all the things I know you can. And I'm ready to help you in any way I can to make sure you have the means and energy to do it. I want to support you in every way, Mallory."

My cheeks blush. "You make me feel like I could run Landry Holdings if I wanted to. Your whole family trusts me with things that are so meaningful to them. I can't describe how that makes me feel." I look to the floor, searching for words. "When I wake up in the morning, I smile. Do you know how odd that is for me?"

"Not a morning person?" he winks.

"No," I chuckle. "But knowing I get to spend time with you makes me excited for the day. I feel like . . ." The words I'm about to say crash in my throat and I nearly choke on the emotion they bring.

His hand cups the side of my face. "Like what, Mallory?"

"Like I can do anything. Like I used to feel a long time ago."

He draws me into him, holding me tight. Twisting me so I sit on his lap, he embraces me in the middle of the studio. "You matter more to me than I thought possible," he breathes. "I didn't realize it until I watched you walk out today and it hit me: all the things my brothers said were true. This thing between us isn't easy, yet I can't imagine not doing it. Spending time figuring it out doesn't feel like a potential waste of time. It feels like the only option because I can't replace you with something else. I don't want to," he adds vigorously.

I pull back and look at him as his phone chirps in his pocket. "You can get that if you need to," I say, needing a little breather anyway.

He takes out the device, looks at it, and holds it in the air between us. "It's Vanessa. How would you like me to handle this?"

"With a restraining order?" I volunteer, hoping the escalation in my blood pressure doesn't cause me to black out.

With a deliberate hand, Graham answers the call. "Hello?" He listens for a few seconds before speaking again. "If you think, for a second, that I'm going to listen to you after the way you treated Mallory today, you are crazier than I thought."

He looks at me, his features softening. "We are nothing more than two people that share an awful memory." He reaches for my hand and I place my palm in his, waiting with bated breath to see how this goes. "We never loved each other, Vanessa," Graham says. "I've only been in love once. Once you know what that feels like for real, you know if you've felt it before. I haven't. Not with you."

My smile causes my cheeks to ache as I wrap my arms around his middle. My chest lies against his side, his arm pulling me in closer, as he begins speaking again.

"Try it and see what happens," he says, his voice cold. "But if you bother me, Mallory, or anyone in my family, you won't like the consequences."

He stiffens against me. "Consider yourself on notice: you are not welcome on any Landry property. If I see or hear from you again, hell will break loose."

His phone slides across the floor and lands against his jacket. I stand still, holding him, afraid to speak. I don't know what she said, but I do know she got to him and that's hard to do.

"I've wasted so much of my life because of her," Graham mutters. "Not anymore."

He lays me back against the mats, his body rolling with some unnamed emotion. My heart races as he lies on top of me, holding his weight off with both hands. "No one can just walk in here, right?" Lifting my shirt and the hem of my sports bra, he exposes my breasts.

"You're going to worry about that now after you had me with your neighbor listening?"

He grins, melting my heart. "I told you, that was then, when you were just a beautiful woman I was enjoying. This is now."

"This is now," I whisper. I'm not sure what all that means, but I know hearing the words fall from his lips, pregnant with so much promise, feels like the best thing in the world.

Closing my eyes, I enjoy his kisses. I relish the way Graham makes me feel. Beautiful and wanted—sure. But it's more than that. So much more.

EPILOGUE

Six months later

Mallory

"YOU'RE LATE." I LOOK UP from the stove to see Graham entering the kitchen with a big smile on his face. Although he was supposed to be home two hours ago and lunch is now cold, I can't even pretend to be mad at him.

He tosses his keys on the counter. They completely miss the basket he used to be so anal about hitting. "We decided to go a full eighteen holes." Glancing around the kitchen, he takes in the cracker crumbs on the floor, egg shells sitting in a pile of dropped egg whites on the counter, and more dirty mixing bowls than one person should have while making a meatloaf.

His brows furrow for a split second and he stutter-steps before coming up behind me. Wrapping one of his strong arms around my waist and urging me backwards into him, he kisses my neck. "The kitchen smells good, but not as great as you."

Kisses are dotted against my ear, down my neck, and across my shoulder. I'm on the cusp of telling him we'll wait to mash the potatoes and taking a quick trip to the bedroom when the door opens again.

"Never fails," Ford mutters, entering the kitchen from the garage. "I can't go anywhere with my brothers now without some major PDA."

"Jealous?" Graham laughs.

Ford doesn't answer. Instead, he takes a baby carrot, dips it in a glob of ranch dressing, and pops it into his mouth. He crunches it much louder than necessary. "What's for lunch? Dinner?" he tosses out, looking at his watch. "I don't know what you call it this time of day."

"Linner?" I volunteer. "I made meatloaf, mashed potatoes, green beans, and a vanilla cake with vanilla icing."

"It looks like what you made is a mess," Ford teases. "I'll just sit over here and wait for Graham to realize it."

Graham kisses me loudly on the cheek, earning a groan from Ford. "Really, G?" Ford gasps. "I think you're stepping in a hunk of raw hamburger right now. That doesn't needle your inner control freak?"

"I've learned to let go a little," Graham grins. "Or maybe I'd just rather fight with her in a different room."

Ford shakes his head, his hair now grown out a little. It's more blond than his brothers and glows in the late afternoon sunlight. "You've all turned into pussies."

Graham swats my behind. "I have no problem with that." He moseys across the kitchen and takes a seat next to his brother. "Did you get registered for school today?" he asks me.

"I did!" I can't keep the squeal out of my voice. "I'll take a few classes this summer and should be set to get into the business school this fall." Resting the spoon in my hand on a piece of paper towel, I nearly bounce up and down. "I'm so excited, you guys. I have to take another math class, though. Someone will have to help me."

"I can tutor you in exchange for a few sexual favors," Graham winks.

"I was hoping you'd say that."

Graham laughs as Ford shakes his head. "The only bad thing about this is having to get a new Executive Assistant."

"I'll find you one," I remind him. "She has to be smart and organized and not cute."

"Send all the cute ones my way," Ford snickers. "I'm getting to the point where I need help."

"Good problem to have," I note, turning back to the stove.

Graham gets up and swats me on the behind as he passes. "I'm going to grab a shower. Be out in ten."

Watching him take his shirt off as he leaves the room, I can't take my eyes off him. My heart is so full, nearly bursting at the seams with how much I feel for this man.

Over the past few weeks, I've learned more about myself and relationships than I did in years with Eric. I now know, without a doubt, what it means to be loved. Graham loves me. He doesn't tell me every day, but he shows me. Unequivocally.

He still has days where he wants to work late and not have dinner with me. I have moments where I feel like he should be home with me and not at the office. Instead of those situations blowing up into huge arguments, we try to talk it out. We try to remember what's important to the other person and make that a priority. It's a learning curve—sometimes we get it right, sometimes not. But Graham always says you know it's the right relationship when it's not always easy. Then he laughs. I don't get it, but I do always get a kiss, so it works.

I grab my ice water before joining Ford at the table. "Did he beat you again?"

"Yes. You've managed to calm him down enough that he's nearly as good as Lincoln on the golf course. Thanks for that."

I shrug. "You're welcome."

He smiles at me with the kindness I've come to expect from him. Ford Gregory Landry has the biggest heart of any of the Landry's. He's also the fiercest, which I can appreciate . . . especially when it was him that took the phone away from me when Vanessa called in the morning after she dropped off the envelope. It was also Ford that took the visit from the police officer about said conversation. Lucky for him, the officer was a former Marine too and believed Ford's side of the story and arrested Vanessa a week later for trespassing when she tried to get in my office again. He and I have gotten close.

In a past life, I think we were brother and sister. He's rebuffed my attempts at setting him up, but I'm still working on it. Ford deserves to be happy and I don't think he ever will find happiness until he has a family. He was just cut from that cloth. I see it in his eyes when he looks at Barrett and Alison, Lincoln and Dani, and even me and Graham although we have a lot of work to do.

"Can I tell you a secret?" Ford asks, smiling like a rascal.

"You can, but I don't promise not to repeat it."

Chuckling, he picks up his water bottle. "Out of all my brothers' girls, you are my favorite."

"Ah, Ford. You say that to all the girls."

"Sometimes," he laughs. "But I mean it this time. Especially because I need a favor."

"Typical," I sigh. "What do you want?"

"Can I borrow your yoga studio for a day one weekend? I want to do a self-defense course and I don't have a location. Our building is too officey. I need mats and space."

"Um, you kind of own the yoga studio," I laugh. "It's a Landry business. I just run it."

"Come on now," he teases. "You know Graham bought that for you."

"Don't say that. It makes me feel weird."

"Why?"

"I don't know," I laugh. "It just does."

The lines around his eyes crinkle. "So I can use it? We can get together one day this week and find a day?"

"Yes, Ford. You can use it."

"Good."

"Now, on to the return favor..."

"Oh, shit. Here we go," he groans.

"You didn't think it was that easy, did you?"

Graham's feet slap against the tile as he makes his way in the kitchen. "You aren't asking her for a favor, are you? She always gets you good in the trade."

"He did," I say cheerfully. "Now I'm figuring out what I want as a payback."

"I had no idea you were such a predator," Ford sighs.

"She's worse than Barrett," Graham laughs, sitting down beside me. "So, let's hear it. What are you going to do to poor Fordie Boy?"

I tap my finger against my lips, pretending to give it thought. Truth be told, I already know what I want. I was going to do it anyway. At least now, he'll have to participate willingly. Or semi-willingly, knowing him. "In return for use of the studio, I am going to set you up with no less than two blind dates," I say.

"The hell you are!" he laughs.

"I am," I insist. "And you will go happily."

"To a place with forks," Graham chips in.

"Yes. To a place with forks. I'll ensure the ladies are sweet and pretty and kind and would do you justice."

He groans, rubbing his hands down his face. "I don't know, Mal. I'm not really feeling it right now."

"When is the last time you had a date?" I sigh. "A real one. Not one of those things where you pick someone up for a quickie."

"I don't do that!"

"You do," I say, wagging my finger towards him. "Should I bring up the girl with the word KARMA tattooed on a certain body part?"

"Hey, how did you know about that?"

"Linc," Graham and I say together.

We all laugh, the ease of the family now extending to me. I've never felt anything like this. So accepted and incorporated into everything they do. They respect me, maybe even love me, and I adore them right back. All of them.

"Your last date was the girl you broke up with before you went over-seas, right?" Graham asks.

Ford's face falls. He stands and goes to a cabinet in search of a glass.

Graham and I exchange a look and he waves me off.

"It's time to move on," Graham presses. "I know it's not what you want to hear, but someone needs to fucking say it."

"Lincoln said it yesterday," Ford sighs, his back to us.

"Well, as much as it hurts to admit, Linc was right."

Ford glances at me, his eyes meeting mine. "She has to like comedies and running. I don't trust a woman that won't eat a hamburger, and if she takes longer than a half hour to get ready, I'm out."

"Deal."

He doesn't look sure about it, but seems to accept the idea. "We can start looking next year."

"Damn you," I laugh, moving to Graham's lap. "Why are you so hardheaded?"

"I'm not," Ford says. "Dating isn't something that really interests me right now."

"Because of her?" Graham says, squeezing my thigh in another warning. Ford nods, a small, barely noticeable movement of his head, and Graham exhales. "Okay. We'll drop it," Graham says.

Ford stands and heads towards the garage door. "I'm going to check on Trigger. Your neighbor, Paul, was walking his dog on the golf course and volunteered to take Trigger too."

I nearly choke on my water at the thought of Paul walking his dog.

Graham pats me on the back.

"We'll wait to eat with you," Graham tells him as we both ignore the curious look Ford tosses our way. The door swings shut behind him as I regain my composure.

"I'm sure he won't ask me why you just shot water out of your nose at the mention of Paul's name." Graham rolls his eyes. "Should I tell him the truth or just say it was awkward timing?"

"Don't tell him you fucked me while he was twenty yards away!" I giggle. "That makes me seem like some kind of exhibitionist."

"I think you just might be. You liked it an awful lot that night."

I cuddle into my man, breathing in the scent of his cologne. "When do I not like it with you?"

Looking at him, I watch his face light up. He kisses my nose, then bumps me off his lap.

"Hey," I protest.

"I can't take it anymore." He grabs a white towel out of a drawer and begins cleaning up the kitchen.

Drawing one leg under me, I watch my man in action. He wipes up my spills, brushes off the counters, sweeps up the messy floor. The amazing thing is, he does it without a word. I also know he won't mention it later.

Graham lets me be me. He's never asked me to change who I am despite all my idiosyncrasies that I know drive him nuts.

He certainly touches my body in every imaginable and even unimaginable way . . . but he also caresses those harder to reach areas like my mind. My heart. My soul.

Every day I spend with him, I feel more like the person I was meant to be. It's like he holds my hand, guiding me but without pressure. Offering support but not instructions. Giving me space to figure things out while giving me a soft spot to land when things go awry.

Graham has changed how I view a lot of things. He took my preconceived notions of life and love and switched them all around.

He catches me watching him and makes a disgusted face as he picks up an egg shell. Even as his features are all squished together in mock-horror, I see something there I've not seen in anyone else. Not when they're looking at me. It's in his beautiful eyes that I learned the difference between Graham's love and everyone else's. Love isn't the words you use to say it, but the actions you take to prove it's true. Graham proves he loves me every day—faults and all.

"Are you going to get up and help me?" he teases, stretching his arms to the side to indicate the enormity of the mess.

I think about it for a half a second. Grinning, I sit back in my chair. "Nah, I'll just watch you. The view from here is too damned good."

The End

Want more of the Landry family? Ford's book, Swear, is up next. Turn the page for Chapter One.

MORE FROM ADRIANA LOCKE

Chapter One

Ford

Blind dates would work out so much better if you were actually blind. And deaf. And maybe a hundred miles away.

My head pounds with the remnants of Blind Date, and final date, Number Three's ridiculous giggle last night.

Each candidate hand-selected by my brother Graham's secretary-turned-girlfriend-turned-pain-in-my-ass seemed decent at first. All were pretty, fairly intelligent, and each of them were memorable ... just for the wrong reasons. It is possible that maybe, just maybe, I just hold them to an impossible standard set by a woman a long time ago. Either way, it is what it is.

"Mr. Landry?" My secretary's voice chirps through the Bluetooth. "Are you there?"

I take the exit for the freeway and sigh, coming back to reality. "Yeah. I'm sorry, Hoda. I got distracted. What were you saying?"

"I was saying that Graham stopped in a little while ago. He said your cell must be dead because you aren't answering. He asked me to have you call him as soon as possible."

"It's a ploy," I tease. "He's just seeing if you're scared of him."

She laughs. "I'm pretty sure he already knows that, Sir."

"He's a big baby. The whole asshole thing he has going on is just a front." Graham's name blinks across the dash. "And now he's calling me."

"Please answer it."

Chuckling, I hover my finger over the call button. "I'll be back in the office in a few. Talk to you then."

I click over and don't get a chance to greet him. He just talks.

"Hey, Ford, I was looking over the numbers and—"

"I hear you've been terrorizing my employees again. Can you knock it off? I'm not fucking mine. She might quit."

"I'm not fucking mine either. I fired her and then moved her in with me. Remember?"

"Gee, that's right. She—"

"Hi, Ford," Mallory singsongs into the phone, clearly loving catching me off-guard.

"A little warning would've been nice, Graham."

The Georgia sun is hot and high in the sky, blazing through the windshield of my truck. I've been out of the office in meetings with potential clients all morning. I'm desperate to get back to my to-do list, a glass of tea, and some uninterrupted hours of work.

Landry Security is my baby and we're just getting off the ground. After a couple of tours of duty in the military, something I never expected to be a career, this is my first foray into something all my own. Something I'm in charge of, my brainchild. Although Graham, the CEO of our family's business, Landry Holdings, was instrumental in putting it together, it's now all mine. And I love it.

"Before you guys go talking shop, how'd the date go last night?" Mallory asks. "Neither of you called me, so I was hoping that meant it went well."

"She spent fifteen minutes giving me a dissertation on nail polish, Mal. A quarter of an hour discussing the way the light bounces off reds differently than pinks. And although she volunteered to wrap her legs around my face and let me do my own little experimentation, the conversation was mind-numbing."

"But," Graham interjects, "did you do the experimenting?"

"Damn right I did."

"Just stop it, both of you," Mallory sighs. "Let's focus on what matters: you didn't hit it off?"

"No, we didn't hit it off. I mean, I hit it and got off, but ..."

"I'm starting to wonder whether you really want to find someone or not," Mallory groans.

I can't help but laugh. "I told you from the beginning I don't. I only went along with this blind date BS because you made it a requirement to borrow your yoga studio to train my security guys. Otherwise, I'd be—"

"Hooking up with women with 'KARMA' tattooed across the top of their butt cracks," she deadpans.

Graham's laugh booms through the truck speakers, making me wince.

"I'm never telling Lincoln anything again. Our brother has no loyalty," I say, trying not to laugh too. "And for the record, there were butterflies along with the lettering."

"Oh, that makes it better," Mallory says, sarcasm thick in her tone.

Graham's laugh breaks through our banter again. "Sometimes I listen to you two and wonder if you're the siblings and I'm the outsider."

"Oh, no, G. You brought her into this family. That honor is all yours."

"Damn right it's an honor," Mallory teases.

I unscrew a water bottle with one hand and bring it to my lips, keeping my eyes on the road as my brother and his girlfriend banter back and forth.

Moments like this remind me of how different things are from what I expected when I was discharged and moved back to Savannah.

My brothers, all three of them, are settling down. Graham has Mallory. Our oldest brother, Barrett, the newly minted Governor of Georgia, has Alison, and Lincoln, the youngest, walked away from a major league contract to marry Danielle.

At least my baby twin sisters, Camilla and Sienna, are as confused about their lives as me.

Mallory clears her throat. "So ... how do you feel about one more blind date?"

"I feel like that's the most ridiculous question I've ever heard. My debt is paid. Move along."

"But I saved the best for last," she promises as I swerve through traffic and let loose a slew of profanities.

"Hey! Where are you?" my brother asks.

I check the overhead signs and relay the information. "Why?"

"Great! This is perfect. Can you do me a favor?"

"Depends on what it is."

Sliding my truck between two semi's, I get rewarded with a loud honk from the one behind me. I give him a little wave. He doesn't know I've driven heavy machinery in the middle of gunfire in a war zone. Twice. I do the honorable thing and ignore him flipping me the bird.

"I need you to swing by a place not far from you," Graham says. "I'll text you the address."

"I'm going there for what?"

"To check it out," he says blankly. "I told them we'd swing by and give them a security plan and estimate."

"By 'we' you mean me."

"Semantics."

The text comes across the screen and I see I'm not far at all from where he needs me to go. Still, I need to get back to the office and have little interest in picking up a small job on the side.

"I don't really have time for this," I sigh. "What kind of thing is it? We talking personal security? Business? What?"

He takes a deep breath that worries me. Something about the way he does it causes the hair on the back of my neck to rise, but before I can call him out on it, he replies. "I'm not sure. I just had a quick conversation about it and am doing it as a personal favor to a close friend."

"I suppose I could send Mike." I start to mentally go through the schedule and remember where he's working today and if he can make it to this side of town before the end of the day.

"This is a personal favor, Ford. I need you to go. Not Mike."

I can't tell him no. Graham does everything for our family and keeps the businesses running like the well-oiled machines they are. There's nothing I could ask of him that he would deny. Even though I have no interest in this little mission, I have to do it, and he knows I will.

"Fine," I groan. "Just check it out and provide some kind of plan?"

"Yeah. Just go and see what you think. I have confidence you'll work it out when you get there."

"You owe me, asshole."

We say our goodbyes as I take the exit I need. Before the country song on the radio is over, I'm pulling up in front of the location.

"He's got to be kidding me."

I parallel park my truck across from a row of storefronts. Glancing at my phone, I read the address on Graham's text again. Then I look back at the numbers just below the mint green awning with the word "Halcyon" spelled out in bright pink letters. The numbers match.

I can't believe what I'm seeing. Why in the world would Graham send me here? He knows my business plan and the types of customers I want to attract. This is not it. This is almost disrespectful.

With a groan, I grab my phone and call my brother back and mince no words.

"Are you fucking joking?" I ask. "You sent me to some little shop called Halcyon?"

He tries not to laugh. "I take it you made it."

"Graham, for fuck's sake! I'm trying to run a reputable business here and you send me to provide security for a little ... whatever this is. A department store? No, it's not even that."

"It's a boutique," Graham supplies.

"Well, you can call that *boutique* and tell them Landry Security is booked. I'm not providing some rent-a-cop service."

"You are going inside and doing a visit because the contract has been signed," he says carefully.

"I haven't signed shit."

"No, but I have."

I almost come out of my seat. "You can't do that!"

"I already did."

"Graham, what the hell?" I say, my blood starting to boil. "Why would you do this? You can't do this. I'm the CEO of Landry Security."

He sighs, his irritation as thick as mine. "And I'm the CEO of Landry Holdings, which owns Landry Security. So, in a way, I'm your boss."

"Apologize to Mallory for me."

"Why?"

"And Mom. Tell her I'm sorry."

"What the hell are you talking about?"

"I'm going to kick your ass."

He laughs. I don't.

"There's already been a deposit paid. Just do the review and then if you really don't want to do it, I'll figure it out. But I need you to do this for me."

I glance at the building again. There is black paper hung so you can't see in, but white Christmas lights outline the windows from the inside. Next to the door, there's a sign with "CLOSED" written in red.

"Graham, this is such a waste of my time."

"Maybe. Possibly. Probably," he chuckles. "But I've committed and I need you to follow through."

"You need committed," I mutter.

"Just do it for heaven's sake."

"Fine," I growl, opening the door of my truck and stepping out on the street. Locking up behind me, I stride through the two lanes of traffic to the sidewalk in front of Halcyon.

The bakery next door has its door propped open and the smell of cinnamon rolls takes away some, but not all, of my irritation.

"I'm here," I let him know. "And when I'm done, I'm coming for you."

"I'll be waiting."

"You should run. It's gonna hurt, brother."

"I'll try to prepare myself."

Rolling my eyes, I end the call and slip the phone back into my pocket. My palm pressed on the bright white door, I give it a gentle shove.

Read Swear here.

ACKNOWLEDGMENTS

THANK YOU TO THE CREATOR, first and foremost, for giving me the tools to do what I love to do.

To my family, Mr. Locke, the Littles, Mama, and Peggy and Rob: You are all the bomb. Your enthusiasm never wanes and I can't tell you what that means to me.

To my team, Kari (Kari March Designs), Lisa (Adept Edits), Kylie (Give Me Books): Another one bites the dust! Thank you for working with me yet again. I appreciate you all more than I can describe.

My PA, Tiffany, has brought so much light and time to my day. Thank you for hopping on this crazy train and lending the skilled hand you do.

It's simply amazing that some of my betas will even speak to me at this point. Jen C, Susan, Jen F, Ashley, Candace, Joy, and Carleen: You read this thing more times than any person should. In the midst of your lives, you fit in my project, my insanity, and incoherent PM's all times of the day and night. You didn't give up on me. You didn't back away when things got hard. You never failed to encourage me and hold my hand. You ladies are incredible. Thank you.

Michele, Robin, and MaryLee: Thank you for making room in your day for Switch. I know it was rough and a little hard to get through, but I appreciate your feedback and attention to detail. I can always count on you.

To my admins, Jen C, Jade, Tiffany, and Stephanie: You four keep the wheels turning (and laughs coming!). Thank you for your time monitoring my groups and keeping things running like a well-oiled machine.

To Ebbie, the organized soul that keeps our FitBit Challenge running in the Books by Adriana Locke group: Your kindness and spirit inspire me every day. Thank you for taking over this project and doing it so cheerfully. You make a difference in so many lives, including mine.

To Mandi: I could ramble here, but what could I say that would make sense to anyone but you? ;) Every day, it's you. You know what I mean. Love you, Pres.

To Lisa, Jade, and Alexis: Life . . . Ish girls are the bomb! You administrate one of my favorite places, send the best stickers, and are some of my favorite (unfiltered) people. Thank you for always being girls I can count on.

Candi, my Locke Librarian, digs in and records all the "Locke history". Thank you, my friend, for reading once for fun and twice for details. Your notes bail me out more than I care to admit.

To bloggers: I can't thank you enough for not just reading, but for reading and spreading the word about what you love. Thank you, too, for choosing to pick up my stories. I know you have choices; I appreciate that you consider my work.

Books by Adriana Locke and All Locked Up: You are my people. Thank you for your support, love, enthusiasm, and energy. I love you.

ABOUT THE AUTHOR

USA Today Bestselling author, Adriana Locke, writes contemporary romances about the two things she knows best—big families and small towns. Her stories are about ordinary people finding extraordinary love with the perfect combination of heart, heat, and humor.

She loves connecting with readers, fall weather, football, reading alpha heroes, everything pumpkin, and pretending to garden.

Hailing from a tiny town in the Midwest, Adriana spends her free time with her high school sweetheart (who she married over twenty years ago) and their four sons (who truly are her best work).

Her kitchen may be a perpetual disaster, and if all else fails, there is always pizza.

www.adrianalocke.com